TILL THE END OF TIME

motion picture title of

THEY DREAM OF HOME

by Niven Busch

Five marines of different ages, interests and backgrounds are suddenly faced with the problems of picking up the patterns of their civilian lives. The one link common to each is the experience of living and fighting together in the foxholes and jungles of the South Pacific.

How these men make their adjustment to civilian life, and how the bond of their mutual experiences overseas enriches and strengthens their postwar destinies, is the theme of this absorbing novel. From this fine book, RKO has fashioned a stirring film starring Dorothy McGuire, Guy Madison and Robert Mitchum.

Says James M. Cain, author of *The Postman Always Rings Twice:*

"With this sardonic, yet overwhelmingly sympathetic tale of five GI Joes, and what happened to them when they got home, Niven Busch takes his place as ͏ few genuinely important ͏ not only for his racy, pur͏ literary gift, but for the ͏ servation and consistent ͏ ing he brings to bear ͏ social theme he has chosͅ

They Dream of Home

NIVEN BUSCH

They
Dream
of Home

GROSSET & DUNLAP
Publishers
New York

By Arrangement with D. Appleton-Century Company

PRINTED IN THE UNITED STATES OF AMERICA

TO
MY FATHER
BRITON BUSCH

O young man O young comrades
It is too late now to live in those houses
Your fathers built—

CHAPTER 1

THE TRAIN WAS LATE. CROWDED WITH SERVICE MEN, excursionists and defense workers, it had dallied all night, chuffing and backing on sidings, flagged down for freights, or else proceeding with a cramped, methodical dignity, slowly and cautiously, as if unwilling to take advantage of the cleared track. All night it had traveled through the summery fields of California, and now, at last, the open country lay behind and the city just ahead. Like a runner who, though hopelessly out of the race, nevertheless wishes to finish with some show of style, the train picked up speed; it swayed from side to side, leaping restlessly across trestles, blowing peremptorily for crossings.

From the windows the passengers got their first proof that the journey was almost at an end. Sometimes the track ran parallel to six-lane boulevards closely packed with traffic; sometimes it dashed across industrial acreage where factories and mills shoved raw outlines at the morning sky. Clusters of houses were slowly linked together, their straggle no longer accidental, forged now into the real beginning of the city.

Now the streets were closer together, the clicking

of the ties faster, and the pound and roar of the engine and the scream of its whistle ever quickened in rhythm: the city seemed to be reaching out, to be spreading the network of its houses and boulevards to capture the train and throttle its insulting clatter. And as if for protection against this very scheme, the tracks multiplied mysteriously with each second that passed, so that the train was now surrounded on each side by six or seven pairs of glistening steel rails. An overpass, black with coal and Diesel smoke, reared ahead: the train slid under it—and in that second suffered a great loss in energy and stature. It slowed to a crawl; its yelling voice was still, its exuberant gambols now reduced to a decorous trembling hardly strong enough to shake the tiny rainbows of sunshine in the dining-car tumblers. The train was in the station yards; it passed a crossing where a feeble bell was tinkling, and from somewhere a gray concrete ribbon sprang out of the ground and slid along beside the wheels —the station platform. With an elegant little shudder, like a woman sneezing, the train stood still. The trip was over.

Immediately in all the cars a great bustle ensued; in the coaches and chair cars the passengers seized their belongings and crowded into the aisles, shoving and elbowing each other, and stepping on one another's feet—a useless procedure, since the doors were still locked and it was impossible to get off. In the compartment cars the narrow aisles leading from each vestibule were so crowded that the porters had great difficulty in carrying out the luggage. "Lots of time, folks," they begged, their voices smooth with placation and sweat shining on their weary, creased black faces as they flattened themselves, bags and all, against the steel wall.

"Ain't quite in yet, gentlemen," they said. "Be two, three minutes more. Just let me set this bag down hyer."

The bumping of bodies and valises on the door of the drawing-room roused Cliff Harper from his dream of homecoming. He had been away at war; this was his first glimpse of Los Angeles in nearly two years. He turned from the window, a look of wild excitement on his face. He was a gangling, big-jointed young man in the uniform of a private of Marines, first class.

"Hey, you guys," he said. "We're in."

The announcement drew little reaction from his two companions. One, a Marine corporal, was asleep on his drawing-room divan. He was a young Jew with a broken nose and a mop of wiry red hair worn long for a Marine and pulled down partially over his forehead; his mouth was open, and his breathing, though regular, was manifestly alcoholic.

The other occupant of the compartment was a Master Gunnery Sergeant—a pot-bellied, powerful man in the middle fifties. He wore the World War I, China, and Haiti ribbons and nine of more recent origin including five battle stars. The light from the window, falling across his face, cast deep, skeleton-like circles around his eyes, under his heavy brows.

Each of his companions wore the Silver Star, but the sergeant had the Navy Cross.

"Take it easy," he said. "They haven't opened up the doors yet. Anyhow, it's women, children, and civilians first. You guys sit tight before you get trampled in the rush."

As he spoke there was a knock on the compartment door and a corpsman put his head in.

"Could you fellows give me a hand with him?" he asked.

He looked anxiously from Cliff to the sergeant. The sleeping corporal, hearing a new voice, opened his eyes,

3

looked at the corpsman, and went back to sleep again.

Neither Cliff nor the sergeant made the least response. They seemed to be awaiting further information.

"We'll have to take him out through the window," the corpsman said. "I hate to ask you fellows, but I'll need some help."

The sergeant cleared his throat. He seemed to push his eyebrows, thick as little snouts, toward the corpsman.

"What do you mean, you hate to ask us?"

"I just figured you'd be getting off the train, Sergeant," the corpsman said. "I figured you'd be in a hurry."

"You figured wrong," the sergeant said.

Out of principle he disliked and was, if possible, rude to all men connected with the medical branch of the Corps—he could not have told why.

"We'll help," he said. "One inside, two outside. That how you want it?"

"That would be fine," the corpsman said. He was an intelligent-looking young fellow with an aquiline face and an indoor pallor. As he started to withdraw, the sergeant said, "How is he, goddam it?"

"Why, he's fine," the corpsman said. "Just fine and dandy."

"Don't tell me he's fine. He's a sick boy, that's what he is. He's goddam sick and don't make no mistake about it."

"I know he's sick," the corpsman snapped, his eyes hardening. "I thought you meant how is he feeling this morning."

Evidently he was getting tired of the sergeant's precise tone.

"Well, how's he feeling?"

"I just told you, he's feeling as well as can be expected. He's had a very comfortable night."

4

"I'll bet," the sergeant said. He took no further notice of the corpsman, who, after a moment, compressed his lips, withdrew his head, and closed the door.

Matt Klein, the red-headed corporal, was now sitting up. With one grimy hand he pushed his hair back from his forehead. He blinked at the sunlight, hastily turning his eyes from it; swinging his feet to the floor he sat in the position of Rodin's "Thinker." He ran his tongue over his lips, opening and closing them with a loud clacking sound.

"What'd he want, Gunny?" he enquired of the sergeant.

The sergeant, once more staring straight ahead, made no reply; Matt shifted his gaze to Cliff, who said, "Wants us to help get Perry off. Says we got to take him through the window."

The red-headed corporal nodded several times. His large face, on which the freckles stood like blotches, had an air of owlish calculation. He shook his head sharply, then clutched it in pain.

"Christ, how I hate grappa," he said. "Worst drink in the world."

Gunny, the sergeant, turned his brooding gaze on him at that. The sergeant's face, weather-beaten to the color of a saddle, was creased in deep, vertical lines.

"Listen who's talking," he remarked with melancholy scorn. "Listen to the Mayor of San Francisco. Brother, if you hate it that bad, whyn't you leave some of it around for other people?"

"Don't kid me," the corporal said. Again he worked to get the sense of taste back into his mouth.

"Maybe some of the folks up in Frisco enjoy it. Maybe they could of had a good time with it."

"Lay off me, Sarge," Corporal Klein said wearily.

5

"Some other time—okay. But right now, just lay off me. I can't take it." He leaned over and spat into the cuspidor.

The sergeant chuckled. "Oh, you killer-diller," he remarked. "Can't take it, huh? The Mayor of Grappa, he can't take it."

"Think we'll have to take the window out, Gunny?" Cliff asked after a pause.

The sergeant shook his head. "Sash is plenty wide enough to pass a stretcher through. Seen it done lots of times. Matt," he said to the corporal, "think you feel strong enough to help that corpsman? Okay, go in there and tell him so. Cliff and me will be out on the platform, and we'll take him as you ease him out. Here we go...."

Reaching into the rack over his head he pulled down three sea-bags, piled so that by jerking out the under one all three dropped almost simultaneously into his arms. He shoved one at each of his companions, then opened the door. Passengers were streaming from the train now, carrying their luggage or collecting it from the piles which the porters made near the steps of each car: with intent faces they were hurrying along, bound for the tunnels which led to the waiting-room and street.

Cliff and the sergeant, hardly noticed in the throng, moved along outside the car; here, at a window where the corpsman was visible (leaning close against the glass, his pale aquiline face pointed anxiously toward them), they stopped, while the window, not without difficulty, was opened and the screen removed. Now the corpsman leaned out, glancing importantly up and down the platform over the heads of those passengers who, sensing that something unusual was about to be enacted, had collected around Cliff and Gunny. Clearly the corpsman

6

was expecting other arrivals, some reinforcement for the job ahead; he stretched his neck out of the window while the people below him elbowed each other trying to see what had attracted his attention. Far down the platform a lieutenant of the Navy Medical Corps had issued from one of the tunnel entrances of the station and was bearing down on the group—a choleric but competent-looking man, stooped, with rather protuberant eyes and varicose veins in his cheeks from drinking. With him were a corpsman and a couple of civilians, one an immensely tall, saturnine individual in baggy clothes, carrying a camera with a flash-light attachment, the other middle-sized and very dapper, with a hard, waxy Irish face and a tough city manner. Instead of the lieutenant, to whom every one was looking for authority, it was the Irishman who immediately took charge.

"Stand back, *please*," he snapped in a voice like a race-starter's. "There's a wounded man in that compartment—he'll need air." Turning to his tall associate, he demanded, "What do you think, Pop? Can you get it while they pass him out?"

The tall man shook his head and an argument ensued, the tall man backing out into the now awed spectators and focusing his camera on the window. Meanwhile, after a low-voiced conference between the medical lieutenant and the corpsman, the end of a stretcher appeared in the window and was seized by the upstretched hands of those below. An operation which had begun in fumbling and guesswork had somehow become skilful and even merciful: with hardly a tremor or jar, never touching the window-sash, the stretcher was miraculously freed from the train, was being carried—a corpsman at each end of it—toward an ambulance waiting in the parking lot at the end of the platform. Some of the spectators, feeling that the show was over, turned away, but a few lingered, walking beside the smoothly-carried stretcher and accompanied by the three Marines, the lieutenant, the Irishman with the whiplash voice, and the tall dreamer with the camera.

The Irishman trotted up beside Cliff, who was walking with long strides, his arms hanging straight at his sides and his head bent down.

"You Harper?"

"Yes, sir."

"The old guy is Gunnery Sergeant Earl T. Watrous," the Irishman stated, consulting a slip of paper. "And the wounded boogy is P. Kincheloe. Is he a private too?"

"No, sir," Cliff said, "he's a seaman in the Navy."

"Navy! Wasn't he with you guys in action?"

"Yes, sir. He was with us."

The reporter consulted his list.

"Kincheloe, Tabeshaw, Klein," he read. "Where's Klein, Corporal Klein?"

From slightly behind the stretcher a coarse, grating voice said, "Here! I'm Klein. What do you want?"

"Just checking," the Irishman said. "Say, Lieutenant, could we get a picture as they lift him in?"

"You'll have to make it fast," the lieutenant said. "This boy is going to the hospital."

The tall man, somehow cut loose from his morose speculation, already had the picture. Straightening, he ran a few steps, squatted, faced the other way. Bending savagely above his box he made a few harsh and incredibly fast and decisive motions. Now apparently he had another picture, for he got up dreamily. Speaking to the Irishman, the only person present whom he ever seemed to find worth addressing, he said with sleepy truculence, "How about a group?"

8

"That's it," the Irishman rasped. "Can we have a group, Lieutenant, right here back of the car?"

Inside the ambulance, where he lay on his stretcher, nothing could be seen of the wounded man but the outline of his head, stiffly held upon the tiny pillow of the stretcher, the eyes open, glistening with a white and secret shine, the face turned to one side.

Once more the tall man backed off with his box, facing the three Marines now lined up at the rear of the ambulance.

"Only four of them," he said bleakly, raising his head. Apparently it was only when looking in the finder of a camera that his mind would function—but, as his present observation bore witness, it then functioned brilliantly.

"Right," snapped his associate. He whipped his list out of his breast pocket. "Tabeshaw—where's Tabeshaw?"

"Private Tabeshaw with you fellows?" the lieutenant asked.

Sergeant Watrous said, "If you want Private Tabeshaw, gentlemen, you got to send five thousand miles for him."

The Irishman's waxy features tightened. He was afraid he had made a faux pas.

"You mean—something happened to him?"

"I mean he's in the service," Sergeant Watrous said. "Private Tabeshaw is on Naru Island, or he was, the last I saw of him."

"We thought he was discharged with you guys," the Irishman said belligerently.

The sergeant's lower lip sagged. He shook his large, graying head.

"He ain't here," he said.

"His name's on the list, a member of the group that

9

got the decorations," the Irishman said. Clearly it annoyed him when things did not go the way they had been figured in the City Room.

"Well, what the hell," he said. "Take it anyway. You," he said, addressing Matt Klein, "would you swing around, a little more toward me? That's it—you had that decoration covered up."

While the picture was being taken, re-posed and taken again, a newsboy moved close to a man with a brief-case who was standing on the platform—one of those passengers who, lured by the curiosity common to travelers, had stopped to watch.

"What's wrong wit heem?"

The newsboy, of Mexican extraction, had the coarse black hair, bare feet, and tough birdlike voice of his kind.

"With who, sonny?"

"Heem. In there."

He pointed at the harsh dark profile seen so clearly, so terribly, in the sanitary gloom of the ambulance.

"He's sick."

"On the train, he get seek?"

"He's been wounded, sonny," the man with the brief-case said out of the reaches of his mighty knowledge. "He's a veteran, that boy is, home from war. He was wounded in action."

"Holy Cow," the newsboy said. "Is that on the square?"

"Ask him," the man with the brief-case said, pointing to the lieutenant.

"Holy Cow," the newsboy said. "A wounded guy—"

Taking one more jerky glance into the ambulance, he turned away. He ran at a dog-trot down the ridge of smooth blue shadow cast upon the platform by the roof of the express-office.

"I seen a wounded guy," he said, kicking with his bare feet at cigarette butts and papers that lay in his path. "I seen a wounded guy, I seen a wounded guy—I seen a wounded guy, an' he's a nigger."

CHAPTER 2

"THANKS A LOT, FELLOWS."

The Irishman jerked his chin in farewell salutation. He knuckled Matt with his elbow, started to shake hands with the sergeant but changed his mind.

"Watch the *Express*," he said over his shoulder. "Second section ... should be in to-morrow ..."

He turned to scamper down the platform, following the tall man who already had established quite a lead on him.

Cliff blinked. Standing in the sun so long made it hard to see. There was a click behind him; he whirled around. Both corpsmen were in the ambulance; one of them had pulled the step up and was now closing the door. The driver started his motor, the lieutenant got up on the seat beside him, and the ambulance drove out of the turn-around onto the street. The three Marines stood together on the station platform, watching it weave competently through the traffic.

"We can go out to the hospital and see him," Sergeant Watrous said.

"Sure," Matt said. "Wednesdays and Sundays is visiting days. I asked the corpsman. If you get a special card, you can go out any time."

Cliff's eyes—small and rather somber eyes set under protective juttings of strong bone—searched Matt's face. He was committing to memory this information as to the days he could see Perry. He had planned to say good-by to the black boy, but they had taken him away too fast. Still, as Matt said, he could go out and visit him. It wasn't as if old Five-by-Five were really separated, cut off from the Group.

That was one thing that would never happen. They were not going to be cut off, none of them, or even split up in a way that would destroy the Group. This they had decided on the S.S. *Solace*, coming from New Caledonia, and also at Mare Island, where they had gone through further doctoring and resting-up to fit them for civilian life. They had been together too long and they meant to stay that way; having enlisted from one area and hence being discharged to the same area would, at least, make this a good deal easier.

There was no sense roasting yourself, standing in the sun—no rhyme or reason to spend the rest of your life beside an oil smear that an ambulance had left on the clean pavement. Led by Gunny, the three men began to walk slowly along the now deserted platform. Imperceptibly, the Sarge's pace quickened and the others followed his example.

"Don't know what come over me," the Sarge said,

"wastin' time around here while my folks are standin' downstairs waitin' on me. . . ."

"Honest, Sarge?" Cliff said, a stab of anxiety going through him. "Is that where they are? Wouldn't they have come up on the platform?"

"They don't let them up here no more," the Sarge said. "They stand down in the station, back of a rope. We got to go through the tunnel."

"Judas, you're right," Cliff said, remembering. "I bet my folks are down there, too, my dad and mother."

He spoke urgently, yet his progress was not stimulated. A meeting like the one now looming up took a minute to think over.

Corporal Matt Klein also seemed unwilling to hurry.

"Ain't nobody waitin' for me but my uncle," he remarked.

"Ain't you glad to see your uncle?" The question came from the Sarge.

"Nobody's never been glad to see that chincy son-of-a-bitch," Matt said. They were in the tunnel now that ran under the tracks, smelling of urine, disinfectant, and farewells; they walked a little apart, each preoccupied with what lay ahead. It was as though the separate worlds to which they were now moving had stretched partitions into the tunnel, dividing them from one another.

The tunnel swerved up and ended, abutting suddenly on a cleared space, fringed with faces behind a rope. With a curious, throttled cry, a small gray-haired woman ducked under the ropes and threw herself on Gunny; just behind her, beaming a welcome but not quite rash enough to defy the barrier, stood a very neat, flabby man around thirty years old and a handsome young woman wearing a corsage of camellias, who was

13

holding by the hand a stocky child of three or four. Disengaging himself from the woman's embrace, Gunny was immediately engulfed in this waiting group. Cliff turned to look for Matt, but the latter was already at the end of the roped area, walking with his arm around a runty, bandy-legged man in an open-necked sport shirt.

Cliff was alone. There had been no time for good-bys. All in a second his two comrades had been seized, removed by other concerns. He stood still, his sea-bag on his shoulder, looking around him nervously: for the first time he was conscious of the hugeness of the station, the height of its vaulted ceiling echoing with the metallic amplified voices of train despatchers, and the confusion of crowds moving in different directions, saying good-by and hello, buying tickets, feeding children, and gawking in front of the bulletin-boards. He set the sea-bag slowly down, his heart beating fast, his eyes never stopping their search for the persons whose presence would give him an anchor in all this. Not since he had been a boy, coming back from a vacation visit and met by relatives at another station in this same city, had he been so eager for the sight of a familiar face.

Had there been a mistake? Could the telegraph operator have got the time wrong in the wire he had sent? Had his folks been here but decided that he wasn't coming?

Cliff's nerves fluttered. The shaking which had bothered him since his last combat experiences started up again; he could feel it in his hands and wrists. Anxious to steady himself, he gripped his thumbs with the other fingers of each hand. He looked up at the big electric clock on the station wall—and at that instant the long hand of the clock, as if mocking him, gave a grasshopper-leap from one minute-station to the next, a galvanic hop which seemed to say that even time, here at home, was no longer what it had been, that it was an unknown element or, at least, one so speeded up that there was no longer any accounting for it.

Cliff began to sweat. His uncertainty, as on that boyhood occasion of waiting in a station, emphasized his youthfulness. Clearly he was young to be wearing the uniform he had on, let alone his campaign ribbons and decoration. In spite of his height, his lanky, powerful build, and his man's face with the marks of suffering and resolution on it, he looked lost, unfinished somehow, as if he had been conceived in a great mold, embodying a noble and distinctive purpose of his race or sire, and then, half through the processes which would have fulfilled the design, this purpose had been changed or forgotten and he had been dumped out to shift for himself. Leaning his sea-bag against his knee, he fumbled in his blouse, got out a handkerchief, and wiped his face. He was wondering whether to wait where he was or find a telephone and ring his parents' house.

Perhaps they didn't know. Perhaps the telegram had never reached them.

He had just decided that the proper thing to do was to stay where he was, at least for another five minutes or so, when some one touched him on the shoulder. A man—a well-dressed, prosperous stranger, wearing steel-rimmed glasses and a tan linen suit—stood before him, holding out his hand. Only as he shook hands, saying, "Hello, Dad," did Cliff perceive that this stranger was his father.

Meanwhile a middle-aged woman in a blue print dress, with a hat falling off the back of her head, clutched him round the body with one arm, trying with her free hand to grapple his neck and pull it down in order to kiss him.

Her lips were quivering and the cords in her throat working with emotion.

"Cliff, my boy, my son," she said. She began to weep, dabbing nervously at her eyes while people standing near-by looked at her with sympathy.

"Hello, Ma," Cliff said. He looked from his mother to his father in an embarrassed, friendly way, making an effort to get used to them.

"Doggone," he said, smiling at each in turn, hampered by his mother's weight, which was pulling him forward and the contrary pressure of the sea-bag against his legs, pushing him back. "Gosh darn it all. I was commencing to think I'd missed you."

❧ **CHAPTER 3** ❧

THUS, ON A PLEASANT DAY IN JULY IN THE YEAR nineteen hundred and forty-three, a hero came back to his own city. He rode through the streets in the family automobile, a well-washed and sizable but somewhat shabby sedan, sitting in the back seat with his mother while his father drove. His mother had her arm through his and kept on looking at him all the way home.

"You're thinner, Clifford," she said several times.

Since there could be little argument on this point, he

offered none, except to venture at length, "It wasn't so bad, Ma."

This seemed to strike the wrong note. His mother turned away. Tears sprang to her eyes.

"Don't talk about it, Clifford," she said. "I know you don't want to talk about it."

This statement surprised the hero; he was quite ready to discuss any subject whatever; moreover, he did not know to which his mother had reference. Not wishing to offend her, however, he refrained from talking and the rest of the trip was passed chiefly in silence.

Mr. Harper, the hero's father, belonged to the straight-arm school of automobile manipulators. He gripped the wheel near the top with both hands; holding his arms stiffly outstretched he drove at a fast clip, blowing his horn at intersections when the lights were about to change against him. Though his son had been away so long, getting him home rapidly became imperative. No more time must be wasted.

The day suited a hero's return. A breeze was blowing, moving a few lazy clouds across the brilliant sky; flags stood out handsomely from the flagpoles of the city, and the short skirts of the women on the sidewalks blew against their knees. Now and then some lofty window caught a sunbeam at a sharp angle and tossed it out across the lower roofs. On all sides, men in uniform were to be seen, and at the boulevard stops newsboys were selling papers with blurred, three-inch headlines telling of the progress of the war.

Rapidly, as the Harper car wound through the streets, the tall, somber buildings of the business district fell behind; the streets became narrower, the houses residential. The car was passing places now which the hero knew well; they looked different, smaller for the most part, or shabbier, but still undeniably right, full of intimate messages. And then they were on The Street, and Cliff mentally counted the houses from the corner— Doc Gannon's, and the brown house in which the Merced sisters, spinsters, had lived twelve years and which they had sold to a horticulturist, and the Hulburds', and Burdicks', the richest family on the street, and then The House, squarish, secretive, unchanged. The house had a curving walk, a sharply sloping roof, a porch crouching in a large sweep round the parlor windows. It had four rooms downstairs, three upstairs, and a hedge of Cecil Bruner roses on one side of the yard. The paint was a little shabbier, the lot had shrunk a little, but the Cecil Bruner roses were in bloom and the lawn had been mowed and trimmed away from the edge of the walk.

It was all right. It was home.

Mr. Harper put the car in the garage while Cliff and his mother went in the front door. He set down his seabag and loosened the top buttons of his tunic.

"How does it look, Cliff?" his mother said, surprised at his long silence. "Does it look the same to you?"

And he answered, "Fine, Mother. It looks just fine."

"You're not tired from the trip? I don't suppose you're hungry?"

"You've got to stop supposin', Ma," Cliff said, trying to produce a tone he felt his mother expected of him, to conceal the strangeness of all this. "When do we eat?"

Mrs. Harper hesitated. "You're sure you wouldn't rather read upstairs? We've got a colored girl again. I could . . ."

"I'm telling you, Ma, I feel fine."

Upstairs, Cliff made a mistake. He did not notice what his mother wanted him to notice, namely, that his prized possessions had not been removed or disturbed in any way. On the desk was the engineer's drawing-set he had been given when he was fourteen. Over the bed was a high-school pennant, and on the walls were framed snapshots of himself and various friends. His old school-books and certain novels he had read and liked were in the book-case by the bed—*Silas Marner, The Call of The Wild, Hans Brinker or The Silver Skates*. Each of these volumes had appealed to him at widely separated periods in his past, but this had made no difference—they were still here, all lumped together, stolidly awaiting him. Some of the other objects in the room he had to ask about—a carefully rolled and braided strap, for instance, on his dresser. This, his mother told him, was a sling he had been making for his .22 rifle.

Cliff had forgotten about the sling. He had even forgotten about the .22 rifle.

"I didn't have to get the room ready for you, Cliff," his mother said. "It has always been ready. Any day or night you came home, you would have found it this way, just the way you left it."

Cliff was vaguely uncomfortable, and his mother sensed this. She explained to him that he was tired, that he should lie down and take a rest. She kissed him and asked him whether he was glad to be home and when he replied that he was she seemed quite satisfied; she turned down the spread for him and went out of the room, closing the door.

Cliff did not immediately obey her injunction about lying down. He took off his blouse and walked restlessly about the room, trying to get used to it. After a while he took the prized possessions which his mother had left out and put them away in drawers. This helped some, but not enough. The hero lit a cigarette and thought it over, and he got an idea. From his sea-bag he took an oil-silk package which contained five photographs. These were snapshots of each of the Marines who had been with him on the station platform and train and in addition a snapshot of the Indian scout, Bill Tabeshaw, and a group shot taken in boot camp, depicting himself with these four men.

Cliff stuck the pictures on the wall with the thumbtacks which had previously supported the high-school pennant. Then he lay down on the bed to study the results. Thoughts which had gone through his mind over and over in recent weeks came back with added force. Every one of these guys was a great, a wonderful guy.

But being wonderful guys wasn't enough. They would have to stick together. That was the important thing.

His experiences of the past now emphasized this truth so that there no longer seemed the slightest doubt of it. Here he was at home, just where he had wanted to be for months, and he had found he was a stranger here. He was back on the street where he had lived before, in his own room, with his own family—and yet those five guys were the only guys he felt at home with. Even having their pictures on the wall was important. It was a reassurance that they might not have to split up.

If they stuck together they could get through anything, do anything. This he knew beyond a doubt. It had been proved to him a thousand times. Even Bill Tabeshaw, though from another area, might come this way some day. Then the Group would be solid. It would be the way it had been before.

You could do it. Four guys could do it—five, if you counted the Indian. Or maybe four and a half guys, since certain subtractions had been made in Perry Kincheloe.

All right. So you had four and a half guys. What was

the matter with that? In combat you could do plenty with four and a half guys: why couldn't you do at least as much in what they called Civilian Life?

Four and a half guys were four and a half times stronger than any single man in the United States. Besides, they were organized. They'd had training.

It was a very simple proposition, as he saw it, but one that required careful thought. When you were a kid and went to school and wanted to know why you had to study instead of having some fun for yourself they told you that you couldn't be a damn fool all your life. You had to get ready for the Struggle for Existence.

That was it in a nutshell. Well, struggle meant opposition, and if you had opposition you had conflict, and conflict was combat, and combat was war.

When you got there you were saying something. You were talking about a subject you knew something about.

CHAPTER 4

WITH TWO EXCEPTIONS THE MEN OF THE COMBAT group with which Cliff Harper had seen action were all members of Company G, 5th Battalion, 22nd Regiment of the —— Marine Division, Reinforced. The exceptions were Perry Kincheloe, the Negro, and Bill Tabeshaw, the Indian scout.

Properly speaking, Kincheloe had not been a Marine at all but a Seabee Steward's Mate who had come ashore, in an APD boat, carrying supplies. When a coral reef had ripped the bottom out of the boat, Kincheloe had waded ashore and picked up a rifle on the beach; this act, according to the method by which military allocations were then being conducted on that island, automatically attached Steward's Mate Kincheloe to the beach-head.

Before becoming a casualty Kincheloe had been the strongest man in Company G. He was coal-black, intelligent, and very cheerful. George Company had nicknamed him Five-by-Five because that was the way he was built, and Perry was proud of this name. He loved to show off, and at loading parties or any activity requiring muscle he performed amazing feats. In the action in which Cliff had been wounded, for instance, Five-by-Five had carried the front end of Cliff's stretcher unassisted, through the worst kind of jungle, while two men and at times three alternated on the back end.

William Tabeshaw was a Zuni Indian from Stinking Creek, New Mexico. He was slender, wiry, and morose and had a violent temper which had brought him several long stretches in the brig. But though his nature made him resistant to discipline, Tabeshaw compensated for this weakness with a genuine talent: his knowledge of woodcraft. Tabeshaw had been a raider scout; he had not been permanently attached to any platoon but detailed from one to another and even from one company and regiment to another as need for his services arose. Like Kincheloe, he had been added to George Company a few hours before their last patrol.

The order had come through at sixteen hundred of a sopping, dismal September evening. The Marine regiments occupying the southernmost tip of an island, on which they had landed a few weeks previously, had been harassed for days by shells from a six-inch field piece which the Japanese were firing from the tall ridge in the center of the island. Air reconnaissance thought they had the gun spotted on the far slope of a hill called Mae West. It was now up to the colonel to make sure that the gun was really there, and if so, to destroy it. If the gun wasn't there, then there wasn't much the colonel could do about it. But if it was there and was also moved nocturnally, after the well-established habit of its artillerists, then a third task fell to the colonel, namely, to find out where it had been taken.

Hence the order, which was a call for a demolition patrol. A runner from headquarters took it to Lieutenant Cole, a three-months' wonder straight from Quantico, bivouacked now with George and Easy Companies upon a marshy elbow of the Retu River. Lieutenant Cole was suffering malaria and dermatitis. He could not go with the patrol anyway, being in charge of the position; much to his discomfort he got out of his blankets and went down the creek to look for Gunnery Sergeant Earl T. Watrous and told him what had to be done.

Any patrol on that island was apt to fall to Sergeant Watrous. He knew how to handle difficult jobs. Gunnery Sergeant Watrous had been a Marine for over twenty-six years. He had campaigned in China, Haiti, and Nicaragua, and it was known also that he was a grand-father and had a wife and two grown sons back home, one of them a lieutenant in the Navy. There even had been some silly talk, before the First Marine Division left San Diego, that old Gunny was too stiff in the joints and weighted in the butt to climb down landing nets or wield the only Marine arm for which he had any respect

—a Springfield bolt-action rifle, model 1903. Sergeant Watrous had proved such talk absurd: he had put on such a show during the weeks before embarkation that Colonel Brennerhan had no choice but to bring him along.

All features of combat duty annoyed Sergeant Watrous somewhat, but two chiefly: being away from his family, and the bad chow. Only a few times, through the long years of his service, had he been stationed in any one place long enough to set up housekeeping with his wife, Emmy, and—as he still thought of them—the kids. Lacking own sons he made substitute sons out of the men in his company; even as he stood in the sodden jungle, sown with terrors and fast thickening with what might well be his last night on earth, Sergeant Watrous was plagued by a fatherly anxiety.

Technically, a patrol of this kind was supposed to be made up of volunteers, but Sergeant Watrous had a special method of inducing applications. He picked out the men he wanted and told them what they had to do. These were the volunteers. At seventeen hundred the Sergeant assembled them in Lieutenant Cole's tent to be briefed. They went through their own lines at a little after eighteen hundred hours.

On that island, as throughout the Solomons, days and nights are of equal length, the sun rising and setting approximately at six, summer and winter. The rain had lifted a little, and the patrol, though using the utmost precaution, went forward quite rapidly. Following their directive they located the enemy field-piece, killed the sentries guarding it, and destroyed it with dynamite—a task which in spite of its fearful hazards, was accomplished without loss of a man. The patrol was on its way back, when heavy firing broke out in the direction of base and it became evident that enemy vessels screened by the bad weather had moved up within range of the island and were shelling the beach-head and the installations behind it. There seemed a good chance that the patrol might be cut off by an enemy landing party. There was no chance to go back. For the rest of the night the patrol stayed exactly where they were. About a hundred yards from the spot of jungle in which they were lying the enemy had recently bulldozed a road, and over this through the next several hours Japanese units moved up in the rain, supporting the assault which was coördinated with the landing action.

By morning it was evident that both elements of the enemy plan had been at least partially successful.

During the night the patrol had suffered two casualties: Pfc. Hugo Wrenn, 19, of Los Angeles, California, had been killed by a sniper, and Pfc. Clifford Harper had been wounded in the abdomen. By exposing himself momentarily in order to draw fire, Sergeant Watrous had flushed out the sniper and killed him; however, even with this danger removed, the patrol's chances of surviving the day were not particularly good.

That they did survive can be explained only by the fact that their cover was good and that the area in which they were hidden lay considerably north of that in which the main action was taking place. During the day the men used what was left of their water and emergency rations. Some prayed; some overhauled their weapons; nearly all of them slept. The danger of their position did not affect them seriously because all had confidence that Sergeant Watrous would find a way to get them out.

During that day, at Colonel Brennerhan's Headquarters, the patrol was reported missing. It was routine on that island to report thus any patrol which had been absent more than twenty-four hours. Few marines thus reported were ever later reported anything else, and being in this category made the men lying at the foot of the ridge known as Mae West feel a good deal like ghosts. In spite of their confidence in Sergeant Watrous, several members of the patrol said mental good-bys to places and people precious and distant.

It was clear that if any move was to be made it must be made sometime during this night, their second night away from base. Such was the assumption of Sergeant Watrous, who, as soon as the last light had left the sky, issued the necessary orders to the men nearest him. A stretcher was improvised out of a poncho and two sticks and Private Harper placed on it. Then, with the Indian in the lead, the patrol slipped down the ridge.

The going was very rugged. Naturally, it was more rugged for the wounded man than for the rest, and after a couple of hours of it Private Harper requested in a whisper to be left behind. For a while these requests were ignored, but as the night waned more attention was paid to them; there was still at least a mile of jungle to be got through before daylight, and it was now increasingly evident that before this distance could be covered Private Harper would be dead. As long as the stretcher was in motion his wound bled, though the bleeding seemed to terminate at intervals when for one reason or another the stretcher was set down. The patrol's chances of regaining their base still depended on the position of the Jap lines; if there were enemy outposts to be by-passed, the chances were that none of them would make it. If, on the other hand, the Jap lines had been moved as a result of the night's engagement, it would be an easy matter to send corpsmen back for Private Harper. With proper medical attention he might be successfully transported, whereas in his present condition this could not be accomplished.

Leaving a man who had been wounded on patrol was not an easy decision to make, but Sergeant Watrous had made such decisions before. At zero four hundred Sergeant Watrous gave the wounded man a hypodermic of morphine and left with him two units of ration D, the chocolate ration. Around Cliff Harper, in the darkness, the patrol made preparations for resuming their journey. They fussed with their clothes, tightening the pins and laces which held together the water-stained and damp-rotted seams of their utilities; they did everything, in short, which would keep from their minds the fact that they were leaving Private Harper. No word had been passed out that they were leaving him but everybody knew it. There was no rebellion against the decision: the patrol accepted what had happened in the way that they daily accepted the events of battle—little by little, never completely letting the full thought of it into their minds.

Nearly every man of the patrol, as he got ready to go, looked curiously toward the spot in the darkness where the wounded man was lying; he had become suddenly apart from them. They had now been split into two worlds: five men in one world, Clifford Harper in the other.

Calmed by the injection, Cliff had his eyes closed. Billy Tabeshaw led the way, Sergeant Watrous and Privates Kincheloe, Teal (later killed), and Matt Klein following in that order.

CHAPTER 5

WHEN CLIFF HARPER WAS TEN YEARS OLD HE HAD A PAPER route. He had wanted a bicycle, and his father had made the down payment but told him he'd have to earn the rest himself. It was really for the joy of riding the bicycle as he delivered the papers that Cliff took the route; he delivered the *Evening Herald-and-Express*. He would fold all the new, ink-smelling papers tightly, tucking the ends into the fold so they would fly through the air without fluttering. With his canvas sling-bag on, he would ride close to the curb in the afternoon when sprinklers were snapping on the lawns of the houses and dogs were playing and the men were just beginning to come from work and the women, who had put off their marketing till the last minute, would be going to and from the neighborhood stores.

This was his favorite time of day. Thinking about home from the Pacific combat zones to which he was later sent, he thought about the little houses as they looked at that hour, standing in quiet rows. The houses had been like letters and the blocks like the words of a quiet statement often read and finally committed to memory in the days when he had ridden past them on his bicycle, delivering papers.

Cliff rode like a circus acrobat. He seldom touched the handle-bars. Without looking he would reach into the bag and yank a paper out. He would do this lazily, as if he had all the time in the world. Suddenly he would throw the paper, throwing right- or left-handed depending on which side of the street he was on. His arm would flick across his body with a motion almost too fast for the eye, and the paper would zoom through the air in a beautiful flat trajectory and land on a front porch or lawn with a strong, satisfying thump that made the receiving of a paper an exciting thing for all his customers.

He made forty dollars that summer and had money left over from the bicycle. He got an Iver Johnson that was light, really stripped down. He could have had the kind the other kids were getting, with mudguards, headlight, horn and all that stuff, but he didn't like them and he got the kind he wanted, nothing fancy, but a bike that was built for action.

About this time his face changed in appearance. As a baby he had been round-faced and very serious; his mother had kept his hair long until his father got sore about it; she had dressed him in babyish-looking clothes to have his early pictures taken. From the age of ten on, however, his face got more bony and his eyes smaller. At the same time he was less serious. Quite early he rebelled against his mother's influence and began to imitate his father in every way he could.

At the schools he went to he was liked by the girls and fellows about equally. He was not forward either in his work or socially, but sometimes if an unexpected challenge were issued he would step up and accept it. Once, for instance, at the start of a school year, the geography teacher, Miss Carmody, made a joke. The last thing they had studied before school closed had been state capitals. Since she was sure that all this work was now forgotten, she asked, smiling, "Now, would somebody like to name the forty-eight state capitals?"

The class laughed, but Cliff calmly held up his hand.

29

He named the capitals with only two mistakes.

Though he had an exceptional memory for anything that interested him, he was not a grind. He was good at mathematics, geography, and physical education, but he didn't care much for languages or history. When he was fourteen an uncle gave him the engineer's drawing-set for Christmas. That winter Cliff made many drawings, reproducing patterns that were in his mind. They were not drawings of anything special, but they were finely made. He did them on thin sheets of the best onion-skin graph paper, and when he had a pile of them he put them away and the drawing-set with them and forgot all about them.

When he was fourteen he got serious and moody again, much as he had been when a baby. He would come home from school and go right to his room and lie on the bed, not asleep but not thinking about anything either. His mother, in the somewhat worried way she had, would open the door and look in.

"Are you all right, Cliff?" she'd ask. "Do you want me to bring you a sandwich and a glass of milk?"

"No thanks, Ma," Cliff would say, hardly looking at her. "I had my lunch."

In an hour or half an hour he would suddenly get up. He would go outside and whistle for his dog, Speck, and the two would roam away together. Cliff would come back at suppertime with a ravenous appetite, his strange mood completely gone.

He was the youngest fellow who ever played quarterback for Hoover Street High. He was big for his age, not chunky or fast, but heavy-boned; a football, when Cliff's palm and fingers folded around it, seemed an insignificant, easily maneuvered thing, and so it was. In the games, Cliff did the passing; he ran the team cleverly, but several times Coach Folger reproved him for letting the other backs do so much of the ball-carrying. He told Cliff to take it oftener himself when just a yard or two was needed for first down. Once Cliff, thus harangued, made an explanation which seemed strange for an up-and-comin' high-school back.

"I don't like to get under a pile. I get a bad feelin' when those guys pile up on me."

Like many Los Angeles boys, Cliff did not limit himself to any one or two sports. There was always the beach to go to, spring, summer, and fall if you wanted to, but again like the people of his city Cliff Harper took the beach for granted. One year he got very busy in the garage with some tools and made himself a surf-board, and it was a beauty. Then he took a fresh joy in the beach, learning to ride the board. It was often cold even in the summer, straddling your board, lying offshore with the little fleet of surf-board riders, waiting for a wave, with the sun shining and the salt drying on your skin and the ocean flat as your hand, not a wave in sight. Then a few little ones would come, and just when every one had given up hope, somebody would yell "There she is," and off to the west would be a dark line, ridging up higher, an untouched lovely big wave riding in from China, maybe, strong and green with shimmering, rustling edges, the foam folding over on top, running down in tiny silken waterfalls, and the wave coming nearer, nearer, pushing its salt breath in front of it, the riders getting ready, starting to kick for momentum as the huge wave arched roaring above them. The whole world would be wrapped in the lacelike salt mist of the wave, and the riders would be straining in the act of balance, standing up, and then, at last, the fearful and precarious moment of the first shock gone, tearing ashore with the live board under their feet and the wave back and under it.

Quite often when the weather was hot the entire Harper family went to the beach on Sundays, taking a picnic lunch; they would go in their own car or double up in a larger sedan owned by Mr. and Mrs. Edward Tracy. Ed Tracy was president of the T-B Construction Company, for which Cliff's father worked, and the Tracys had a house over on Hall Street a few blocks away. They had a lot of kids, and the older two—Patricia and Jim—were about Cliff's age. When a picnic was on the horizon Mrs. Tracy would phone Mrs. Harper or vice versa and the women would reach an agreement on the share each was to take in the preparations, one making the sandwiches and the other the drinks and the cake or pie which was to be dessert. There was a family joke —often proved wrong in actual practice—that nobody would eat Mrs. Tracy's sandwiches or Mrs. Harper's lemon pie.

For Cliff and Mr. Harper the beach outings were varied by trips to Wrigley Field, the local ball park. Mr. Harper was a baseball fan, and when watching a game he would keep his own box score. Baseball was never one of Cliff's best games, but he enjoyed spectator ball and certain memories of games he had seen were milestones in his life. Once in a spring practice game he saw Carl Hubbell pitch a one-hit, one-run game. It could easily have been a no-hit, no-run game and gone down forever in the record books except for a Pittsburgh batter who knocked out a home run in the eighth inning. Cliff never forgot the scene, the Big League Diamond and the Big League Pitcher's arm flashing and flicking forward and the batter swinging, then the crack of the bat and the ball tearing out in a huge arc toward the outfield and an outfielder, tiny in a beam of late summertime sun, running back and back, looking over his shoulder, back and back and back, trying to catch the ball against the outfield fence. The crowd was standing up and shouting and Cliff jumped on the bench beside his father, yelling, and his father just sat there, a cigar between his teeth, grinning at him.

Later that year the T-B Construction Company handled a bridge job down in San Diego, and Cliff's father took him down there for a month. Cliff, who was fifteen at the time, worked on the job at half the regular union pay rate; even at that figure he made enough out of the San Diego job and other jobs to buy himself a Model A Ford, the motor of which he hopped up and the springs of which he cut down until it was a racy-looking job. His friend Jimmy Tracy had suggested that he put a sign saying, "Here comes Cliff," on the front of the car and, "There goes Cliff," on the back, but Cliff rejected this idea as being too corny. He didn't like to make too much of a show out of his car; nevertheless, he took pride in its appearance and the fine roar which its motor made when he started up Hoover Street that summer and the next going to get Jimmy Tracy and his sister Pat and take in a dance or a picture show.

The year he got the car was the first year he had taken Pat out on dates. He sometimes thought that summer was the best he had ever spent; the nights especially were wonderful, warm and black, the gulf wind blowing and the palms bending and the kids going to parties in the little hopped-up cars. Jimmy's folks had a house up at Lake Arrowhead, and Cliff visited him there. The Tracys' house had a rock garden and a small private dock and boathouse, but the Tracys' didn't have a motor boat, just a canoe. Everett Kester, a panty-waist who lived across the way, had a Chris-Craft that the kids all used—Cliff and Jimmy and Bud Sholes, Lucien Garfield and Joy Chandler, and Pat Tracy. Right next to the Tracys lived a boy named Pinky Winston who had freckles and was always tinkering with machines, and whose older brother, Arch, had joined the Army, training for a pilot's commission. The Winstons had been sure that war was coming; Arch, home on leave, believed it. No one else up at the Lake thought so. Anyway, it was a great distinction for a scrubby kid like Pinky Winston to be brother to a guy who was a full lieutenant.

Patricia Tracy was by far the best-looking girl in the crowd. She had long red hair and never wore a bathing cap; when she went swimming her hair would stream out in the water, which turned it a much darker color in marked contrast to her hard, white, lustrous skin—not a bit mushy-looking like some red-headed girls' skins. Pat had odd-shaped, laughing, scrutinizing eyes that always seemed to be asking some question of Cliff. One day Pat's halter came off while they were in swimming, and Jim Tracy's girl, Joy Chandler, went up to the bath-house to find her another. There had been much squealing and giggling, and the deep dark secret was confided. Of course it had been supposed to be entirely a woman's secret. Joy had swum to the dock and gone up to the bath-house, but Pat just kept on swimming with her beautiful smooth stroke, not caring, and he'd seen the strong curve of the way her back molded around her side and formed into her small, smooth breast. Once she had looked up at Cliff, who was standing on the dock, and smiled at him, swimming lazily around till Joy came back with the halter.

Pat and Cliff had gone together ever since they could

34

remember. Perhaps, in the beginning, it was just going to the same school and living so near each other, in the city of Los Angeles, and Cliff and Jim Tracy being such friends, that started them. Anyway, it had worked out that by the time they were sixteen it was taken for granted that they were a combination.

Pat and Cliff were the same age. If Pat seemed older, it was not that she was more intelligent—Cliff got higher marks in school. It was just that a girl grew up faster than a fellow.

Pat had a good temperament: it took a lot to upset her. Having a lot of brothers had made her very practical and used to the ways of men. She had no mannerisms, the way most Hoover High School girls of her age had: she did not keep tossing her hair back a certain way or using some verbal expression till it got tiresome, and she was not always trying to conjure flattery out of a handbag mirror.

She had been mature since she was twelve, like most girls in that climate, but she did not wear high heels to school or use mascara on her eyes for dates. Yet she was a long way from being sloppy, a hell of a long way, and she could take care of herself in almost any situation. Her father, a scrappy, sarcastic mick, had started as unskilled help on building jobs, and he had risen in the world. He had taught his four sons to box and had included Pat in the instruction.

After Pat was mature she weighed a hundred and fifteen pounds and stood five feet six; her legs, though well-formed, were none too long, and if it had not been for the smallness of her waist she would have looked too strong for real beauty. It was the shape and expression of her eyes and lips and the way the bones set in her face that made her so good-looking. Her eyes shifted somewhat in color from brown to green, the change depending less on her moods than on the cycles of her body. Her brother Jim, though a fine athlete, was extremely temperamental, easily roused to anger and subject to upsets and colds, but Pat was rarely sick a day. She had by no means forgotten her father's instruction in the art of self-defense, and one day at Arrowhead when Everett Kester had picked on her in a stupid, annoying way, she told him quietly to cut it out or she would hit him. He did not cut it out, and Pat finally kept her word and hit him a short punch in the stomach that knocked him right off the porch steps into the rock garden.

Jim was the oldest, and Patricia came next to him; after them were the three mighty midgets, as Pat called them—Dennis, Gavin, and Brod. There had been a five year gap, mysterious in a proper Catholic family like the Tracys, between Pat and Dennis, with the other two punks following a year apart; as a result of this frivolity of the Lord's will, Mrs. Tracy was a very busy woman and Pat had to share her burden. From the age of seven Pat would be lugging along some solemn-eyed, fat-hammed mick baby who could not be left at home. Mrs. Tracy always said that Patricia was as fine a daughter as a mother could wish, a real help with the children. Pat could cook and clean up without giving out a saintly air of suffering the way the average good-looking girl would do. And she knew other useful things. Jim, due to his breakability, was continually getting hurt in games, and if he had a Charley-horse that really bothered him, Pat would rub it out with Sloan's Liniment. Several times, the last year that Cliff played at Hoover High, he got himself bruised up in games and Pat rubbed out the soreness for him just as she did for Jim.

That was the fall of nineteen forty-one. Neither Pat

nor Cliff was a great reader of the newspapers; Cliff read the sport page and Bill Henry's column in the *Times*, and Pat read the motion-picture page. She was not an honest-to-God fan, like some of the Hoover High kids, but she liked to go to shows and to read about the pictures that were being made so she could look forward to seeing them. There had been the war for two years and more in the papers, but that was in the papers. President Roosevelt had said on the radio he hated war also. The American people hated war and sent bundles to Britain, and everything was well under control.

The fall of nineteen forty-one was cool and pleasant in the city of Los Angeles. Hoover High had a good team and won most of their games, taking two trips, one to Pomona and one to Pasadena. After the games the kids drove riotously through the streets of the conquered cities in their hopped-up cars covered with bunting streamers and displaying the school pennants, blowing the horns like crazy.

That fall Cliff and Patricia had been together more than ever before. They had an air of preoccupation which was new to them. New also was the tone they used in speaking to each other. Neither was given to using many words, but there were important things to be discussed: it seemed important for each to probe the other's views on any subject clear through, to discover either agreement or disagreement. Thus a dialogue began, less a series of separate conversations than one conversation, continuous and rather serious, or at least grave, which ran all through the days and evenings of that season. If they were separated for a while, one would telephone the other and continue the dialogue, shortened now so that it was almost a code. It would have sounded senseless to a third person if one happened to be listen-

37

ing. At the Harpers' house Mr. Harper would become grouchy if forced to listen, and at the Tracys' Mrs. Tracy, that busy woman, would stand it as long as she could and then say fiercely to her daughter, "Patricia, you've been on that phone long enough," and Patricia would put her hand over the mouthpiece and say tranquilly, "Ssh, Mother," and go right on talking.

Patricia's good looks increased during that fall. She lost some weight, and the bone outlines of her face became clearly defined. She and Cliff went dancing at least twice a month, and when they danced their manner was withdrawn and serious like the dialogue.

Early in December the weather became brisk and there was snow in the mountains. Mr. Tracy said he would open up the Arrowhead house for the Christmas holidays, and Pat and Jim Tracy, Cliff, and a boy named Hugo Wrenn and several others planned to go up there. None of them knew how to ski, but there had been a lot of pictures in the magazines about skiing back east, and Jim and Cliff said they were going to learn. Naturally, if they learned, Pat wanted to learn, too. She wondered if she ought to buy a pair of skis first, and save up and get the outfit of ski clothes later, or buy the clothes first. It would be a lot of fun at the Arrowhead house with the gang there, and she hoped that there would be a lot of snow.

As it turned out, there was no party in the snow. Pearl Harbor was attacked, and Cliff and Hugo enlisted in the Marines. Jim had wanted to enlist also but could not because his father would not give him a letter saying he was seventeen instead of sixteen. Jim did not look seventeen, but Cliff and Hugo did and they got away with it.

The night before Cliff was to report to the enlistment

38

center, Pat stayed awake all night. She was worried. She did not want Cliff to go away without having really been with her. Often before they had been near it, though never so near as that last night. But they had no place to go to make love properly, and somehow it just hadn't happened, and now it was too late.

While Cliff was in boot camp Pat wrote to him every day and he answered as often as he could. He hoped and prayed, he wrote her, that he'd get a furlough before he was shipped out. Pat was terribly disappointed when he didn't get it. She wrote and told him how badly she felt about it.

CHAPTER 6

"... PERHAPS I SHOULD NOT SAY THIS, SON, BUT I BELIEVE that girls sometimes do foolish things in wartime. . . ."

Some girls, maybe, but certainly not Pat—not the Patricia Tracy who had written him those letters. Not that girl.

But there hadn't been any letters from Pat for three months. And his mother had enclosed the clipping from the "Vital Statistics" column of a home paper, saying that Patricia Tracy was married to Lieutenant Rorick Klim. Nobody at home, his mother wrote, had seen Lieutenant Klim. Pat had met him on a visit back east, where he had been in flying school.

Mrs. Rorick Klim! Sweet Faust, what a name—Mrs. Klim, the former Patricia Tracy!

Cliff, this is my husband Rory or Icky or whatever the hell I call him. That good old lieutenant from back east. I want you to meet the former Clifford Harper, private first class. Cliff and I are old friends. Yes, indeed. We used to go to the same school, and all that sort of thing.

Sure, girls did foolish things. They got all set to go to bed with one guy but he left and so they went to bed with another guy. Very simple. Naturally, his girl, Pat, wouldn't do a thing like that. She was his own true love and she would wait for him till hell froze over. But this Mrs. Rorick Klim would do it every time, the lousy stinking tramp.

Cliff had read his mother's letter and the newspaper clipping several times, as if in hope that by constant perusal he would discover something in the words which would change their meaning. Deciding they meant what they said, he came to the simultaneous decision that the best thing to do was forget all about it. Put the whole thing out of his mind. Which, except for about eighteen hours a day—the hours he was awake—was practically a cinch to do.

It didn't even bother him that he had heard the news from his mother instead of Pat—or rather Mrs. Rorick Klim. A tramp like Mrs. Klim would naturally not have the guts to write herself. Better just forget all about her.

On the outside chance, of course, that there might be some explanation of the matter that had never come to mind—or that it wasn't true or something—he had kept one contact with his love. For several months, in the breast pocket of his tunic, he had continued to carry a snapshot of Pat. Having the picture was stupid, but guys also did stupid things in wartime. Sometime, Cliff knew, he would get rid of it. And he had finally done it; he had torn up the picture and buried the pieces where no son-of-a-bitch would ever find them. Lying on the stretcher after the rest of the patrol had moved away he fished the picture out of his pocket. It was wrapped in oil silk in order to keep it from falling apart with the rot which destroyed almost anything in that jungle—firearms, clothing, records, and the fortitude of men. Clifford Harper folded the picture and tore across the folded halves, folded and tore again, and kept folding and tearing till he had reduced the picture to the smallest possible particles. He then made a small hole with his finger in the jungle earth, and he put the pieces of the picture into the hole and covered them with earth.

At this point the morphine began to affect him. He lost consciousness for a while, tapering down an endless tunnel into a shallow but oppressive sleep. When he woke again his mind was confused. For some time he fancied he was back in camp, then for a while he remembered where he was but imagined the rest of the patrol was still near-by, lying close to him in the jungle.

When the knowledge of his real plight came to him it was like the memory of a nightmare. For a while he struggled forlornly to dismiss his knowledge of it. Then he gave up the struggle and despair seized him.

Christ, don't let me die. Sweet Christ, I humbly pray thee, do not let me die. I beg you, Christ, don't do it. Get me out of here. (Now isn't that the hell of a thing, Cliff thought, disgusted; isn't that something, praying and hollering to God just when you had your thoughts under control and everything was swell. And what good did praying do, lying on your pratt. You had to pray in a reverent attitude, if at all. Why pray? How would you like it if you were Jesus and some chincy son-of-a-bitch, brought up by a woman to believe in you and taught to pray in church, never gave you a thought or prayer till he was in a jam and then, blaa, blaa, please God, please Christ, do this or that. Why can't you be a man, he thought, addressing himself. If you've got to die, then die like a man and earn some respect from God.)

But this is no kidding. Being a man and sportsmanship and all that stuff, it's all baloney. This is no crap. This is me, Clifford Harper. This is it. You start sometime and it's a mystery. Are you going to say it isn't God who starts that seed of life? What puts life into it? And the universe, the earth and sun, how do you account for that, Mr. Big-Shot, if there is no God. And if there is a God, then religion is a natural part of it. You believe in it, you always have. You believe in Christ—he was human, too, wasn't he? Go on and address him. Lying on your pratt, so what, how are you going to assume a reverent attitude with a slug through your insides? Do you want to start the bleeding again?

Don't let me die. Let the detail come back. Let them get me out. Let the bleeding stop. Please, Holy Jesus, hear my prayer. Don't turn your face away from me. Don't let me die. Please, Christ, don't let me die, please, Christ, please, Jesus, let me live, please, Jesus, save me, hear my prayer, please, Holy Jesus, save me, let them come and get me, Jesus Christ, don't let me die....

CHAPTER 7

PRAYER IS ADMITTEDLY A POWERFUL FORCE. ITS RESULTS may not always be perceptible, but in Cliff Harper's case they were quite satisfactory. Soon after he finished praying, the enemy landing party on the beach had been liquidated, causing the retirement of the Japanese flank and clearing the area between the jungle valley in which Cliff was lying and the American position on the ridge beyond. During the following day Sergeant Watrous led a stretcher party back into the valley, and shortly before sunset Cliff was delivered to Doc Smart at his dressing-station just below the ridge.

Doc Smart, a Johns Hopkins man, decided Cliff was still alive. This in itself was a decision which took more than ordinary perspicuity: many doctors, working under combat conditions, would have disagreed with it. The patient was in absolute shock. His hands and feet were very cold, and his face already had assumed the grayish pallor of the newly dead. His nose was thin and waxy, like a dead man's nose. You could not feel his pulse.

It was getting dark on the ridge, and Doc Smart knew he would have to work fast. He yanked off the emergency dressing on Cliff's abdomen and took a look at the wound. A bullet from a Jap .25 leaves a small hole, since the gun is designed to wound rather than kill. Doc Smart was encouraged by the fact that Cliff, though he had lost much blood, had not bled from the rectum. This seemed to indicate that there had been little internal bleeding. Also, the position of the hole induced the doctor to think that the bullet had not touched any vital organ. Plasma, lots of it, administered immediately, had brought back to life a number of corpses which Doc Smart knew of, and while giving plasma with a coral ridge for an operating table with night falling fast was not what had been taught at Johns Hopkins, the doctor took a chance. To bring the patient out of shock, he wrapped him in the ponchos of the corpsmen who had brought him in. Over his own head and shoulders and those of the men assisting him, he rigged another poncho as a sort of tent. He had to use a light, and if the light were seen the dressing-station would not long remain in a state of function.

Doctor Smart was a nervous and absent-minded man. He was a fine technician, but whenever he operated in the field he had a habit of reciting in a mumble every move he made, like a diagnostician dictating an examination to a nurse. Exhorting himself thus, in a steady sibilant undertone, the doctor got Cliff ready for the transfusion. The doctor's assistant, a pharmacist's mate, stood in great awe of Doc Smart, believing from the doctor's way of talking to himself that he was mad.

Doc Smart held a flash-light in one hand and a transfusion needle in the other. He was gratified to perceive signs, after the first unit of 250 cc. was in, that the patient was coming out of shock. By the time the second was in, Cliff was able to speak. By morning he was strong enough to be driven back over a bulldozed road to the field hospital near the beach.

Two weeks later Cliff was removed to the base hospital at New Caledonia. Physically, he was already much recovered, but he was troubled with a nervous ailment which had set in as a result of shock, exposure, and prolonged strain. He stayed in New Caledonia six months, and while there his citation came through on a White House scroll, signed by Frank Knox for the President, and he heard that all the guys on the patrol had received one and that all of them, for one reason or another, were going to be discharged. Cliff's citation stated that while in service against the enemy in the British Solomon Islands, Private First Class Clifford Wain Harper had volunteered for a dangerous patrol. Above and beyond the call of duty he had passed through the enemy lines and assisted in the destruction of an important objective.

CHAPTER 8

THEY HAD BEEN LUCKY ABOUT THE DISCHARGES. BEING returned to the same area was not, of course, a matter of luck but the result of having enlisted in that area: the luck was in the timing. Matt Klein and Perry Kincheloe had both been wounded in the final trip across the ridge. They had been in base hospital while Cliff was there and, like him, had been discharged for disability.

Gunny had come through unhurt, but shortly afterward the blow which he had feared so long had fallen upon him. Colonel Brennerhan had been transferred, and the new colonel, an Annapolis man, hadn't wanted any fifty-three-year-old gunnery sergeants in his command. Rather than go back to training boots, Gunny had asked for retirement.

Being together was luck, real luck. If they had come straggling back separately there would have been less chance of what Cliff was dreaming of—a continuance of their existence as a Group.

Five guys could surely do it. They could find ways and means to operate together. It would make the hell of a big difference.

Cliff had thought about it a lot on the *Solace*, coming back, and at Mare Island. But the first time the full advantages and practicability of his scheme became apparent had been during the twenty-four hours that he and Matt and Gunny spent in San Francisco, before taking the train south. That day and night, which had been swell except for one or two brief moments, showed what a bunch of guys could do, the kind of time they could have if they strung along together.

That had been their real homecoming, their first real contact with the good old U.S.A.

San Francisco was entirely different from the cities in the southern part of the state; it had a different feeling. What struck Cliff most about it, at first glance, was the girls. Not that the San Francisco girls were so much better-looking, but they were such snappy dressers. There was something elegant about them, something brisk and stylish and yet friendly and inviting.

Oh, how they walked, the girls in their summer dresses, the San Francisco girls on the streets of their city. Each face was different, the hat, the hair which they wore this way or that, their eyes, their bright mouths laughing and talking or serious and compressed, yet all one, all united somehow in the pattern they made.

Cliff, strolling along, watched them, entranced. He liked the way they walked and looked at the sights of their city or the people they were with; he studied, like a stranger in a foreign land instead of a man come home again, the new look the girls had, different from when he went away; perhaps the fashions had changed, or the mood of the girls, or perhaps he had changed—it did not matter. Just to see so many women, to be part of their lives even remotely, was partially satisfying. These girls came and went so unconcerned, so separately seductive yet each absorbed in her own affairs, just as if women were to be found everywhere and were not rarities unknown in that part of the world from which he had recently come.

It was fine to look at them and to breathe the air; it was fine to listen to the million noises of the city, blended into one low, incalculable noise to which he himself contributed his mite, thus being knit into its welcome. The little cable-cars reared back on end and charged up the steep hills, their conductors tramping valiantly on the old-fashioned bells. Automobiles slid along, parked, turned, jockeyed for position, gave out the choking, disagreeable, wonderful smell that is part of all American city streets.

Leaving the outfitters, Cliff, Matt, and Gunny had turned down Bush Street. They had no place particular to go, it was just a walk to put themselves in touch with the great day of homecoming. This day they had begun by shedding their uniforms, which they left at the store to be picked up later, having replaced them with brand-new civilian clothes. Cliff had bought a tan Stetson, so light it was almost cream-colored, a striped shirt, a light gray suit with socks to match, and box-toed shoes with a glossy store shine to them. The effeminate clerk in the store, somewhat contemptuous of such crude, loud-talking customers, had nevertheless folded a gray handkerchief for Cliff in a complicated way which made four sharp points perk out of his pocket. Matt was dressed with equal swagger, Gunny more conservatively in a tweed suit and darker hat. Yet Gunny had changed most of all. At Mare Island he had shaved off his full beard, and this made his face seem half the size it had been. In manner he was more subdued, apparently not being sure how to behave when disguised as a civilian.

To get the full feeling of being together in a homeland city, the three men walked abreast, unconsciously forcing passers-by to give way. Their cockiness, not unaccompanied by a slight bewilderment, was partly that of returned conquerors and partly the assurance which goes with possession of unlimited resources. What they had spent in the gent's furnishing store, though quite some dough, had not perceptibly reduced the roll of long-accumulated back-pay which each man carried on him.

Cliff could feel his roll making a bulge in the pants pocket of the new suit. He was sorry now he hadn't bought a wallet for it. Conscious of his finery, he kept moving his shoulder blades experimentally and taking deep breaths.

He had forgotten what it felt like to wear human clothes again. This suit was without weight or substance, almost as if he were nude; no belt to pull against his stomach, loaded down with canteen, sidearms, clips, knives, or God knew what; no pack, no tin hat to make him feel as if he was dressed. Just to walk down a city street in such an outfit was a swell sensation.

Matt Klein was preoccupied, but Gunny, like Cliff,

was on top of the world. His face was wreathed in a big smile, and his voice, which had growled like a six-inch gun in combat and cracked like a bull-whip in boot camp, had gone good-natured. No matter what anybody said, that old Sarge had a topper for it.

"Boy, what a number!" Cliff commented as a tall blonde girl dodged around them, smiling. "Did you get a load of that?"

"If she got a load of you," Gunny said, "she'll run for a cop."

"Oh, yeah?" Cliff said. "Listen who's talking. Listen to the dude sounding off."

"Alongside you," said Gunny, "I'm dressed like a preacher. You look like a pitchman. If you had three shells and a pea you'd be in business."

"Not with you," Cliff said.

"You're derned right, not with me. If you were, I'd lift that roll off you."

"Where we going?" Cliff demanded, not feeling a match for Gunny at the art of repartee. "Where we bound for? That's all I want to know. I'm not interested in pounding these boon-dockers on the pavement."

"Now he's beefing about pavement," Gunny said. "One month ago, if it was mud up to his knees, he thought he was in clover. Just so long as it wasn't over his head."

Cliff stood still and burst out laughing. It wasn't that Gunny's remark had been so funny, but to-day everything that anybody said seemed brilliant and apt, everything that happened had a hidden glory in it.

"Boy, that's no kidding."

"Maybe you've got something, at that," Gunny said as the stroll was resumed. "We could do worse than stop and buy ourselves a smile. I'm about ready."

"Hell, we can't do that, Sarge," Cliff said seriously.

"Why in hell not?" Matt demanded, speaking for the first time.

"They won't sell a service man a drink till five o'clock in this state," Cliff said with an oracular air.

"Are you dead sure you have the dope on the situation, kid?" Gunny enquired.

"Why, sure, Sarge. You know that."

"Is that right, Matt?" Gunny said.

"I guess so," Matt assented gloomily.

"Boy, what a brain-trust I'm traveling with," Gunny said disgustedly. "So they won't sell service men a drink till five o'clock! What kind of clothes have you guys got on? As of to-day you guys quit being Marines, in case you don't remember. What do you think you're out on, a three-day pass?"

Cliff looked sheepish. "Well, I'll be dogged," he said.

"You'll be dogged is right," Gunny said. "With a head-piece like you got, you don't have to be afraid of M.P.'s—only truant officers. Brother, you're a civilian. You can be served liquor at five o'clock, eight o'clock, or two in the A.M. All the problem you got is to walk up and name it, and then pay for it."

"Okay," Cliff said, recovering. "What's holding us back? You want a snort, Matt?"

"I don't care," Matt said, "Whatever you guys say."

He walked along somberly, sunk in depression as he had been all day. "I don't get it," he said at length, following the thoughts in his mind. "Something has happened, sure as hell. I wish I knew the answer. This has me all screwed up."

Matt's companions interpreted without confusion the sudden switch in topics. Bonds of their long comradeship enabled them to change effortlessly from light-hearted celebrants to sympathizers.

"Maybe she never got the wire," Cliff said hopefully.

"I wrote her twice," Matt said. "Once V-mail. And I tried to phone her from Mare Island, but the number had been changed. If she's still there she got the wire all right."

"Should have," Gunny said.

"What I'm thinking," Matt said, "is, maybe, she's *not* there. Maybe she moved."

Neither Cliff nor Gunny made any reply. They shortened their paces, slowing down with Matt, whose mental burden had rendered his progress dilatory.

When they had boarded the ferry at Mare Island a few hours earlier, Matt had been the most exuberant of the three; since then his spirits had turned to dismal brooding. His wife, whom he had wired to meet him at the ferry slip, had not shown up. Only under pressure had Matt joined his friends in their shopping excursion; even then, he had impaired the occasion by his conjectures about the absent Mrs. Klein.

It was bad. Not having a wife show herself at the place where, after a long absence, that wife was expected to be—this was a problem which would have depressed any one. But in Matt's case there were complications. On the island, and even on the transport outward-bound, Matt had kept up a flow of confidences about this wife of his. If ever a husband had seemed happily enamored, Matt was that husband. He had produced several snapshots of his wife—a full-bosomed blonde with a happy smile, seated on a photographer's plaster bronco, wearing a cowboy hat. Only when Matt's first pang of worry occurred—at the time when, from Mare Island, he had failed to get an answer to his letters—had he confessed his marriage was the fruit of sudden impulse. He had met his bride in the Seven Seas Cocktail Lounge; the wedding ceremony, crowning a whirlwind five-hour courtship, had been performed the day before the transport sailed.

"I got an idea, fellows," Matt said suddenly. "This address where she's been living, it's over in Oakland. That's only over the bridge. Maybe if we go over there they'll have some dope on her. Then we'll know where we stand."

"Why, sure," Gunny agreed. "Why not take a ride over there? Then we can get the cold dope. Okay by you, Cliff?"

"Okay by me," Cliff said.

They were still together, all three of them, still a unit. They would operate as such. If the present mission concerned one of their number slightly more than the others, that was a mere accident. Nor would Matt at the moment have had it otherwise or indeed regarded any other attitude as reasonable or possible.

"Swell," Matt said. The vast riches in his pocket made his choice in transportation automatic: though Matt had seldom in his life ridden in a cab, he signaled authoritatively to a passing yellow.

"Hey, hack!"

The cab driver had failed to stop at once, a circumstance which Matt found annoying. The curb between pavement and street was packed solidly with parked cars, but Matt solved this by climbing over the nearest one. His next leap—taken square in the path of a truck—put him on the cab's running-board. The cab driver, who had turned in time to see these antics, stared at him in terror, unable to conceive what manner of man this was who would risk his neck with these capricious acrobatics in the midst of rushing death.

"Pull over, hacky," Matt said with good-nature. "Me and some pals are gonna take a ride with you."

◆ CHAPTER 9 ◆

THE DRIVE TO OAKLAND WAS A SERIOUS ONE. THERE was little talk. Cliff and Matt got out cigarettes and Gunny lit his pipe, each occupying himself with the sights to be seen through the cab window: the huge suspension-towers of the bridge rearing above them in the air, the sea-gulls flying over the traffic stream, and the boats on the steel-like slab of harbor below.

Once across the bridge, a faint note of festivity was revived: at the direction of his passengers, the driver stopped at a liquor store. Here a bottle was procured and passed from hand to hand. Even the hacky himself was allowed a couple of swigs, offered less as an honorarium than as a tribute to his skill, the back seat having solidly agreed he sure as hell could handle a jaloppy. By the time the travelers had reached their destination they were well equipped to deal with any situation which might have arisen in regard to Mrs. Klein.

The house was a disjointed frame affair located in a

neighborhood which the city had bypassed: a sign on the beaten-down yard made clear that rooms could be obtained inside. Cliff and Gunny stayed in the taxi, appointing themselves a kind of reserve-line; their suspicions were the worst, but it was still too early to pass judgment. Matt was talking to the landlady, a slatternly woman who stood half in and half out of the front door. When he came back his steps were slow. He climbed into the cab and slammed the door.

"Let's go on back," he said.

"She's moved, huh?" Cliff inquired after a period of silence.

"Yeah," Matt said. "She moved." He spat with precision out of the cab window. "She moved," he said, "the day she got my V-letter saying I was coming home."

"How'd you find out?" This time it was Gunny who asked.

"Landlady told me. Those landladies in a place like that get smartened up. She was kind of suspicious on account of Doris getting letters under another name, Mrs. Dobrowsky or something."

"Another name," Cliff said slowly. "That's not so good."

"You said it, it's not so good. She told the landlady she was taking letters for her sister, but the old dame suspected the hell out of her. That's how come she remembered about her."

Gunny cleared his throat. Through a haze of pipe-smoke he voiced the question no one had yet ventured.

"Was she getting your allotment, Matt?"

"I'll say she was," Matt said bitterly. "Fifty-seven fifty a month she was getting, from me and from how many other goddam fools. Mrs. Dobrowsky, Mrs. Klein and

54

Mrs. Godknowswhosky. Mrs. Allotment Wife! That's what she was. Oh, boy, am I a sucker! What a chump!" He began to swear, repetitively and mournfully, in a slow strained voice. At that moment Matt Klein, the betrayed husband, was not in the least like the boastful and carefree Klein of boot camp or island base, or the Klein who had once walked up to a Jap cave and blasted it with a bomb he'd made out of three sticks of dynamite.

"Meet Mr. Klein," he said, "the original pigeon! Fifty-seven dollars and fifty cents a month, and a letter every week. Sometimes twice a week. Honeysuckle! Babydoll! Ittybittums. Am I a cluck! Am I the original dope!"

Cliff and Gunny exchanged a rapid glance. How many times in camp bull-sessions had this been discussed, the harpy-women who married fellows to get their allotment. Some of them, known cases, had married ten or twelve guys before they were finally caught. But how many had never been caught? Hundreds, thousands, probably. Cliff and Gunny had heard men say, and said themselves, that death was too good for such women. They were the lowest things that crawled on earth. Allotment wives! And here was Matt with one. Sure, he was a cluck just as he said, but what a break, hell, what a lousy stinking break to run into the day you got home.

"Maybe there's some explanation," Cliff said unconvincingly.

"You know there's no explanation. A dame getting mail under two names, maybe picking it up in post-office lock boxes, under two or three more. And moving out the day, the minute she finds out one of the guys is coming back. What I'd give to get my hands on that dame. Just for five minutes, no, for thirty seconds."

55

"I'd settle for one-tenth of a second myself," Cliff said. Suddenly he was as mad as Matt or even madder. He and Matt seemed like the same person. "I'd give her the works."

"The works!" Matt said. "The works is what she's gonna get." His eyes narrowed with menace. His face looked sharp and thin. "I'll sic the F.B.I. on her," he said. "I'll run her down, Dobrowsky or whatever she is, I'll ketch her. And when I ketch her, boy, I'll cut a notch in her she never had before. I'll cut a spare one for Dobrowsky."

In contrast to the savagery of his outraged husbandly threats was the weary rhythm of his voice. His tone had in it all the lamentation of a race persecuted and self-persecuted: the voice of an *ahvail*. And Matt's actions, even as he threatened, suited his voice. He had thrown his new fedora on the spit-pocked floor of the cab. He gripped his head with both hands, rocking back and forth; the awful sorrow, agony, and hurt masculine pride that tore his vitals seemed to call for an expression which went back through untold generations.

"Wedding bells!" he said. "Orange blossoms! Mrs. Klein's John Henry on the dotted line, and three days in the Hotel Clift. Fifty-seven dollars and fifty cents a month," said the *ahvail* who had once been a Marine. "Oh, brother, wait till I get my hands on that dame."

"Have a shot, guy," Gunny said, shoving the bottle into Matt's fist. "You sure need one."

In the moment of crisis Gunny was once more the soldier-father of the jungle. He was taking care of a hurt son.

"Go ahead," he encouraged. "Finish her off!"

Matt glared at the three-quarters-empty bottle. Then he grabbed it and drained off the contents. Abandoning his rôle of *ahvail* he entered more profane spheres. He began a consideration of matrimony as an institution; on it he poured the riches of a surprising vocabulary, not one word of which would have been printable. With no small amount of clarity he made it evident that he regarded his connubial career as finished; he embraced the prospects of permanent bachelorhood.

"Amen, pardner," said the hacker in a rich bass. Since he spoke without turning or even seeming to open his mouth it was hard to be sure that the words came from him.

The men in the back seat stared.

"Huh?" said Matt.

"I said, 'Amen, pardner,'" said the hacker. "I been hitched to two of them, and I'm with you. I'm through, finee."

"Amen, pardner," Cliff echoed. The phrase delighted him, though why it did was hard to say: its charm depended on the exact moment, on the way it had been spoken, and on the amount of liquor which he had drunk—and perhaps also because it condensed into a battle-cry the instinct in all males to be free, to be unencumbered by tribal-made sex and petticoat-begotten contumely.

"Amen, pardner," he chanted. "Amen, pardner."

Matt was shaking hands with the driver. "Amen, pardner," he said. He shook hands with Cliff and Gunny, sealing them with the new-found catchword like fraternity initiates. Even Gunny, a married man for many years, forgot himself: standing on the seat he pushed open the cab roof, which could be thus divided by unclasping clasps. With his head thrust out he yelled the magic slogan at a bus-load of shipyard workers, who responded joyously, not hearing what he'd said

57

or caring, but delighted at the sight of the gray-haired, tough-visaged man who stood in such a wild posture, his head through the roof of a cab, roaring with laughter and shouting words to the sky.

By some wonderful alchemy of comradeship, laughter, liquor, or the spirit of the day, Matt's suffering was gone. It had spitted his soul on a red-hot spit and scarred him with an eternal brand and now it was forgotten and gone forever and he was whole again. "Amen, pardner," he gasped, doubled up with Gargantuan mirth, crumpled in a corner of the cab seat while Cliff behaved similarly in the opposite corner and Gunny stood up in the midst with his head through the roof, yelling at the workers, and the cab—driven by the threadbare hacker now completely sober, thin, bereft, friendless, and gloomy after his one burst of poetry, his one immortal, burning sally —zig-zagged through the bridge traffic toward the city.

CHAPTER 10

SOMETHING HAD HAPPENED TO THE DAY. IT HAD BEGUN by being a day designated in enormous capitals in the mind of each of the three men: just as in combat the hour of an attack was always known as H-hour, and the day D-day, so this day of homecoming had its special identification, differently conferred by each man, but determined long ago, months in advance.

Now the day was almost gone. What with the suit buying, the sight-seeing, the trip to Oakland and the glorious ride back, hours had mysteriously slipped away. More time was occupied by a restaurant meal of steaks, overpriced but thick and wonderful, washed down with beer and accompanied with appropriate fixings. As yet the history-making bender which was to have glorified the day had not yet taken place. Warmed by the food and drink, the three comrades set themselves to correct this apparent oversight. Oddly enough it was Matt rather than Gunny who assumed leadership. Though abused by fortune, Matt had something of a reputation as a connoisseur of shore divertissements. Furthermore, he had intimated more than a passing knowledge of the possibilities of San Francisco, having worked in this city for a while before entering the service.

Single file, since the alcohol they had consumed brought out the hidden idiosyncrasies of each man's gait, Cliff and Gunny followed Matt on a considerable journey. Striking out with confidence, he led them away from the commercial areas of the town; he turned off Powell Street on to a smaller thoroughfare, so narrow that cars could hardly pass; mysteriously lighted bars, little juke-boxes and cafés lined each side of it. Fire-signs were winking in the evening air, and a player-piano up in an alley somewhere was plunking out an old song.

In the same tone he had used that morning, Cliff demanded, "Where we going?"

"Just keep your feet moving," Matt advised him. "I know the spots, brother. All you got to do is string along and I can find you stuff, any kind you want. Chinese, yeller, American, Australian. Anything. . . ."

"Whyn't you say so in the first place?" Cliff said, mollified. After some thought he added. "I don't want any of those other kinds. Only American."

"American, huh?" Matt said with an air of shrewdness, evaluating this choice. "Okay, then. I'm the guy can find it for you."

"Good old Matt," Cliff said warmly.

His depression was lifting. He no longer could have told what had so recently made him feel bad. From his breast pocket he extracted his cigarettes and after some difficulty managed to get one of them lighted. His interests of the morning began to revive and he looked appraisingly at the women who went by. Among others there were quite a few Eurasian girls, some of them wearing sequin dresses under their cloth coats, bound for their evening's work at the tourist cafés to be found in this part of the town. They were exotic, sultry-looking women, heavily made up; some of them exuded faint whiffs of disturbing perfume.

Cliff reconsidered his announced preference for an American consort. He wondered whether Matt was kidding or if he had means of contact with these aloof orientals. To make love to one of them would be quite an experience; it would be like some kind of Arabian night's dream!

"Hey, Matt," he said at length, "you honest to God know where we're going?"

"Keep your dogs moving," Matt counseled, "and you'll find out."

"Because, anyhow," Cliff said, "if you can't locate the American stuff, I'll take the other. I can be broadminded as well as the next guy."

60

"Now you're talking sense," Matt said approvingly.

"You don't have to tell me that, you jerk," Cliff said.

"You just string along with me, bud," Matt advised. "I've been around."

Feeling that his sophistication needed some defense, Cliff said, "Down home I could show you a couple of spots myself, only I don't know so much about this town. It's kind of rugged."

"You'll make out all right," Matt affirmed. His air of assurance was impressive.

"I sure hope so," Cliff said fervently.

A dark-eyed girl who looked like a Mex went by, and Cliff thought of Lolita Ramos. Lolita was the first girl he had really made love to. That had been in his boot camp days when he and three other fellows had rented a car: Matt, Hugo Wrenn, and a fellow named Jed Marsh who was killed on Tulagi. They had rented this car in San Diego and driven down to Tia Juana, across the border, where Jed knew about a place. He said the Mexican hook-shops were a hell of a sight better than the ones in San Diego. A bell rang in the kitchen when you opened the front door, the way it did in little neighborhood and country stores. Mrs. José, the lady who ran the joint, sent four girls in, and one of them had been Lolita.

Cliff would have undergone torture at that time rather than admit to any one that he had never been with a girl. He had been a virgin when he joined the Marines, and this secret had bothered him badly. He figured he was probably the only virgin in the United States Marine Corps. It was not his fault, he reasoned; before he enlisted he had only gone with one girl, Pat. With a girl like that you didn't just go out and jump in the hay. It was sort of serious. Still, he could never explain this to anybody, and if the secret were known he would have been disgraced. He wanted desperately to be with a woman both for himself, for his growing needs as a man, and to put an end to his secret shame.

The strange thing was that although he had wanted a girl for himself as well as for the secret, he had not at first liked anything at Mrs. José's place. The Mexican brandy they drank downstairs had a sweet, sickening taste, and upstairs the room smelled of some kind of soap he didn't like. Lolita sat on the bed, and the bulb swinging on a cord back of her sent sumptuous glints and shadows moving across her body. She was bored, waiting for Cliff to get over his shyness; when he did not, annoyance and then a joyful suspicion woke in her. She came over to him and asked him something in Spanish, looking at his eyes for an answer, and suddenly she laughed, not mockingly nor in the mechanical way she had laughed downstairs, but warmly and marvelingly as if she had just discovered something very valuable.

Downstairs, Cliff had thought Lolita was rather homely on account of her flat-looking face and the bulge her lips made. Now he changed his mind. Lolita was a wonderful girl and very beautiful; above all, once she was no longer bored, she had great powers of receiving joy and of giving it. Some womanly instinct or else a sharpened awareness gained through her trade had enabled her to guess Cliff's secret, yet this did not make her dislike him or have contempt for him, as he might have supposed it would. Instead, her knowledge had made her a person of importance in her own eyes. She was a special delegate, ambassadress of a domain to which Cliff would often return. In some way, because of her new status, she stopped being a whore; she was more like a sweetheart or a wife. She was a welcomer.

Lost in thought, he had straggled far behind Matt and Gunny; he saw them up ahead pausing in front of a huge plate-glass window. Feeling they must be near the end of their quest, Cliff quickened his pace—but the façade at which his friends were looking revealed no hint of femininity. On a big wooden sign above the window were the words

FRISCO PALAIS
SERVICEMEN WELCOME

Cliff had never seen a place of just this type. Inside, it was a kind of miniature midway. A calliope was pounding. At the back end where the place branched into a T were a bowling alley and a shooting gallery; at one side of the door was a photograph gallery where a photographer was taking pictures of some sailors. An aisle ran toward the back, and on each side of this aisle were electric slot-machines—but what machines!—not the penny-peep machines of old-fashioned midways but glorified military games, electrically operated. Each machine had a gun fashioned like some standard arm; when you dropped a coin in the slot a target-picture was revealed in the glass frame inside and you could shoot at the target with the electric gun. The pictures were of many kinds, gaudily colored: some showed Messerschmitts, wheeling in fiery attack formations; others represented Japs or Germans piling out of assault boats, swarming up hills, climbing over barbed wire. If you aimed correctly, a big X would indicate a hit; you got a free game for a certain number of hits.

Matt was immediately tempted. Stepping up to the nearest machine, he dropped in a coin and the target lighted up—a Jap carrier with planes taking off.

"Shoot you for a buck," Matt announced. He gripped

63

the handles of the imitation ack-ack, letting an electric blast go at the planes.

Cliff waited his turn, ill at ease. The second he had stepped into the place he knew something was bad. Perhaps it was all the enlisted men, sailors, soldiers, and Marines, crowding around the fake guns, or perhaps it was because the .22's firing in the shooting gallery sounded so much like the high flat snap of Jap .25's, or perhaps it was the way some of the targets lighted up in bursts meant to imitate shell-fire. Or maybe it was the rolling of the bowling balls and the perpetual crashing of the pins. He couldn't tell. All he knew was that he should never have come.

He had begun to shake. His hands shook, then his wrists, elbows, arms, and shoulders. The shaking passed into his head and neck, and with it came the old feeling of helpless panic and rage that had grown on him so during the last weeks on the island. He reverted to his trick of gripping his thumbs, stiffening his back. At all the hospitals where he had been they had told him not to do this. The shaking, they said, was bound to come back from time to time. That didn't matter; the thing to do was just ignore it. He was much better, much, much better. In time it would completely pass away. He was much better but right now he had to ignore it.

Shaking all over, with sweat pouring off him in his effort to show how well he could ignore, Cliff took his turn at the machine, trying hopelessly to draw a bead on the planes taking off from the Jap carrier.

CHAPTER 11

CLIFF'S ATTACKS VARIED IN DURATION. A BAD ONE LASTED an hour, a light one ten or fifteen minutes. In time they would no doubt diminish. The doctors had all said so. All he had to do was be sensible and avoid fatigue and strain.

He was a young and healthy man and there was a good chance that the condition might not be permanent, as it might be with an older person. If he took care of himself and acquired a sense of security everything might be perfectly all right.

Cliff did not know what to do in order to acquire a sense of security. All he knew was that at times he got the shakes. This humiliated him. He would almost rather have been operated on, like Perry—he would definitely rather have gone round with a gimpy leg like Matt, whose left knee ligaments had been severed by a shell fragment.

Fortunately, the attack at the Palais did not last long. When his condition became noticeable, Matt brought him a glass of whisky from a bar next door. Within a reasonable time he felt well enough to visit a second-floor establishment which Matt knew about, near the Embarkadero.

Later they slept in chairs in the Bush Street bus station. In the morning it was raining. The three comrades took a bus out to Golden Gate Park and looked at Seal Rock, which was satisfactorily covered with seals. Their reason for staying over the extra day had been to travel south with Perry, who was being shipped from Mare Island to the Naval and Marine Hospital at San Pedro; a public relations officer at Headquarters had made train reservations for them which they called for early in the afternoon. Seeing them in civilian clothes, the officer asked them to resume their uniforms before arrival in Los Angeles. As members of a famous patrol, whose exploits had been reported by the press and whose members had all been decorated, they were now somewhat in the public eye. The officer had arranged for some newspapermen to meet the train.

Cliff had not slept well on the train. A weariness which seemed to have been piling up in him for months or years descended on him after he reached home. At first he did not even go to the beach but loafed around the house, reading Western Story and War Story magazines, the latter never failing to give him a kick because of the ignorance of the guys who wrote them. He slept late in the mornings, and his mother would not wake him up at any special time. Both she and his father were always telling him about friends or neighbors who wanted to talk to him as soon as he felt well enough. The people mentioned often proved pests, and their elaborate efforts to be tactful about his war experiences made Cliff embarrassed. To avoid such attentions he began to go out more, meeting Gunny for a game of pool at the Hoover Snooker Parlor or taking the trolley out to Wrigley Field and seeing the ball game.

Until now Cliff had never registered with the Draft Board. But according to instructions received at the time he got his discharge he went to the nearest Board and registered. Receiving a 1-C classification he was advised by the Board's re-employment chairman to record his discharge in the Hall of Records and that, further, should he ever be in need of a job he could secure one through the U.S.E.C.

Cliff wasn't sure about the job yet. He wanted time to think things over. When he made a move he wanted it to be in the right direction. No use rushing yourself and getting all tied up. It was a good idea to take a breather, have a look around.

During these weeks he clarified his thoughts about keeping a combat group together in civilian life. Naturally, the Group was small. It would have to be its own supply, artillery, transport, reconnaissance, and general staff. Everything depended on the will, the guts, the passion, the friendship, the closeness nothing could impair or shake. With an organization thus knit up you had one hundred and thirty million licked. You were an army of peace, small, ruthless, secret, powerful, loyal, wise, and trained. You were all men of peace. But just let some one start something. Just let some fink come around and put a paper on your door or take your car away or lay your girl. Then you might have to let it roll. You might find out the four and a half guys were twelve and a half million guys saying take it easy, Mr. Wisenheimer, these boys have a reasonable request. They want theirs. Let us skip the well-known double-cross this time. Okay with you?

Through summer Cliff grew more and more convinced that if the Group were really organized, if it ever started functioning the way it should, the first man it would go to bat for would be Gunny Watrous. That was peculiar because in the old days Gunny had been by far the strongest, smartest member of the Group. He had known everything there was to know about combat—and if there was something he didn't know, Gunny could improvise the necessary knowledge. He was the man who, when their shoes rotted in the jungle damp, showed them how to make moccasins out of their leggings. Just let something happen to a weapon—it didn't matter what kind—Gunny could tell at a glance what was wrong with it; what's more, he could fix it. On the island, with his beard and his big pot belly and fiery, sunken eyes, running an assault group, Gunny had seemed like a Biblical giant turned pirate. He had seemed indestructible like a kind of savage Marine god.

It was strange how in civilian life much of his old power had slipped away from the Sarge. With the shedding of his uniform he had become suddenly an ordinary person.

It was hard to tell just what had happened to the Sarge. Nothing bad, nothing definite, but even in July when they had been home only two months, Cliff knew something was wrong. He knew the Sarge. From the way Gunny acted, from the few hints he let drop, Cliff got the notion that things were not going as expected over at the Watrouses.

Once or twice Cliff went over to Gunny's house. He met Gunny's family and liked them, all except that pasty-faced Harry, Gunny's oldest son. It was a swell house and all, but somehow Cliff never felt at ease there. He knew something was going on, but what it was he couldn't tell—probably no one could except the Sarge himself, and he had always been a guy who kept his personal affairs strictly to himself.

CHAPTER 12

GUNNY HEARD THE RACKETING TROLLEY-CAR SOUND OF A big shell coming. Harrrrumpp, it hit; the machine-guns opened up, chattering like crazy . . . he rolled over in bed and pulled the covers over his head. There was something about the water pipes which made them sound off this way every morning. Emmy would turn on the tap in the kitchen to get water for the kettle and the big shell would go off in his dreams, then as he became conscious he would hear the stammering of the air as the water forced it into the tap-valve. . . .

No sense getting up yet. In the time he had been home, the Watrous family had established a routine about bath room priorities. At first, with the early-rising habits of a lifetime, Gunny had mixed things up badly by trying to be the first up. He had even shaved, humming to himself in a gravelly baritone while slippers shuffled in the hallway at the bathroom door and impatient fingers tried the knob.

Now he knew better. He drowsed, while daylight filtered through the sheet over his eyes as through the top of a tent. From the kitchen came the subdued clink and stir of Emmy's breakfast-getting . . . Emmy in her worn comfortable wrapper, handling pots, pans, dishes, with the quiet, creased, broad-fingered hands, familiar for nearly half a century with the lore of ministering to morning needs. At Tientsin, in the Compound, and in Panama where Bobby was born—in all the posts and sta-

69

tions where they had lived together—Emmy had been the first one up, and she was still. She was always cold in the morning; she would look a little stooped, just coming out of sleep and patient with the early-morning patience of a woman getting her befuddled menfolk ready for the day.

There were sounds in the front bedroom which Emmy shared at night with Dot, wife of the absent lieutenant, and with the baby, Sonny. Dot would already have whisked in and out of the bathroom; she would be dressed now, talking mother-talk to Sonny, giving him his orders of the day while she took off his night-shirt and put on his clothes, leaving his boots off so he could stay in his crib till Emmy brought his breakfast.

Gunny never knew exactly how Dot's mother-talk went, but he had heard Emmy give the same talk in her time. With the sheet over his head he could imagine that the woman in the other room was the young Emmy, love in her summery voice like the warmth of the womb.

Was it in Oregon, just before the First World War, that he had first heard that special voice? Harry or Bobby . . . no, it had been neither, it had been himself and the woman was his mother, when his father had the store in Oregon, getting him up in the early cold to go and see the Cavalry stand roll-call.

There was a thump in the second bedroom, then the splash of water running in the bathtub. Gunny grinned. That Harry, taking a bath every morning! To Gunny, there was something laudable though slightly effete in such frequent bathing. Yet who would do it the way Harry did, except Harry? Harry's bath was luke-warm, not a Spartan dash of cold the way Gunny had seen Old Silvertop, his colonel in the Haitian campaign, take it in front of a tent, standing there naked while his orderly dumped a bucket over him. Not even hot, as a luxury-loving man, spoiled by easy living, might enjoy it. Just lukewarm, no pain or pleasure of any kind, just a way to get clean and to get the plump, pale, washed look Harry had. Probably the lemon-juice that Harry drank before breakfast did the same thing for his insides that the lukewarm bath did for his skin.

Gunny was not happy in bed: would Harry never get out of there? Bathroom priorities might be all right for young people, but when you were fifty-three years old and it was time to get up, you got up! But Emmy had asked him not to start an argument....

It was strange when you came to think of it, how often Emmy was Harry's spokesman; if not that, she was his interpreter, explaining actions or ideas which Gunny, as Harry's father and head-of-the-house, objected to. It was almost as if she sided with Harry against him, as if Harry, his own son, had supplanted him.

That was a lot of bushwash. He and Emmy were as close as ever. Only, he had been away a long time— Emmy had to depend on some one and she had got used to depending on Harry. Why not? Harry was a good earner. He was a smart man in his own way. Gunny had dealt with the beefing of dissatisfied Marines too long not to know when a beef was legitimate and when it wasn't; there was no sense blaming Harry for unpleasant elements which were not Harry's fault but the result of outside forces—war conditions, for example.

Take his room, now. When he had known that his discharge was coming through, he had written Emmy to get ready. She had been living at the San Diego base, but she had moved up to L.A. where Harry was working, and with his help they had found the house, a five-room frame bungalow on a corner lot. The rooms were big enough and the house in fair condition, and the yard was perfect for a man who had come home from the wars to do a little puttering; there was a two-car garage, with a dilapidated tool-shed attached to it, and in the back of the lot was an arbor with a tangle of flowers, fast going to seed for want of care, and a dense little copse of trees which weren't supposed to be jammed up together—acacias and scrub eucalyptus and a handsome little pepper tree.

Emmy had the place painted dove-gray. She had written Gunny all about the house before she made the down payment, and though he had never seen it till the night he got off the San Francisco train, he could have found it, he thought, even without the address; if he had walked in the front door in the dark he would have known where everything was; he could have gone straight to the big front room, the one which he and Emmy planned to use as their bedroom.

That was just it. The house was plenty big enough for Emmy and himself. That was what he had been saving his pay for all these years, so that he'd have a place to live in when he got through. Plenty of room for both of them, and enough to live on coming in regularly; the small bedroom, the one Harry had, would have been the guest room. Emmy would have fixed it up pretty and kept it that way so that Dot and Bob could stay there, if Bob had leave, or Harry. Sure, even Harry, once in a while. But you couldn't foresee that Harry, living with his mother temporarily, would have become a substitute head-of-the-house. As for Dot and the kid, it was wonderful to have them, even if the baby had to have the most sun, the most air, and hence the big front room. Of course the two women had to be in there with him. Where else? Two old people couldn't live there with the kid, and put his mother in the hall-nook . . . and catch Harry, a high-wage earner like he was, taking the nook. How would that have looked?

If you had spent twenty-eight years sleeping in ship's hammocks, on the sand, in mountains, in jungles, on coral atolls, anywhere there was to lie down when the time came, wouldn't it have been a hell of a note to bellyache because you had a day-bed? Were there springs in it, or what? You're goddam right, there were springs. A room would have been better, no denying it, but in a town filled up with defense workers, army and navy paper-men, and wives of fellows gone overseas, the Watrous family was lucky to have bought the bungalow when they did. Whoever had built the place twelve or fifteen years ago had put in the nook as a whim, or because the architect had a few feet of hall left over, and the real estate agent who sold it to Emmy told her how handy it would be. The little window made it all right for a breakfast-room, if you put a table in there. Or you could wall it off and make a big hall closet out of it or even a maid's room, if you had a maid.

Thus Gunny, home from battle, found his allotted piece of Shangri-là the hall-nook in the dove-gray bungalow on the corner of Felicia and Hoover. Here, through the print drapes which served him as a door, he listened to the morning noises, hearing at last—and with enthusiasm—the click of latch and slap of bare feet on linoleum which meant that Harry was through with the bathroom.

CHAPTER 13

FRAGRANCE OF COFFEE AND BACON EDDIED THROUGH THE little house, producing marked reactions in one of the keenest brains therein—that of Robert Nelson Watrous, II, son of Bob. Sonny had never tasted coffee, but this made no difference, since to him, as to many people, the smell of it was more important. Further, Sonny knew all about bacon, nor was he indifferent to its charms. He began to yell for his breakfast. Presently, and according to a well-established routine, Emmy—because Dot had to eat now and get away, or else be late for work—took it to him. The yelling stopped with singular abruptness, and thereafter, from the front bedroom, came grandmother-talk, intermingled with the sturdier sounds of food consumption.

Gunny dressed in leisurely style. Shaving could go till to-night or to-morrow night if need be; during the past year, wearing his campaign-beard, he had got out of the way of daily shaving and was glad that the priority system gave him a good excuse for skipping it. As usual, he hesitated in front of his wardrobe, displayed on a row of hooks under the window. The choice was not unlimited, consisting of two uniforms, one very shabby, the other still good, also the herringbone finery he had bought in San Francisco, and the work-clothes—once of Marine issue—which he used when working in the yard. Besides these there was a suit which a Chinese tailor had made him many years before: a sturdy outfit of khaki drill, civilian in pattern but just enough like a uniform to give the wearer a good feeling. This, also as usual, he put on, donning with it a wash-faded service shirt, brown socks, and composition-soled sneakers. As he issued from his cranny he collided with Dot, rushing from the dining-room; Gunny slapped his daughter-in-law on the backside, and she, after feinting a punch in return, put her arm around his waist and planted lipstick on him.

"That's so Emmy will know the way you act."

"How about another?" Gunny demanded amiably, reaching for her.

Dot dodged deftly around him. She had on a denim work-suit, trim and shapely on her strong young body. Pinned in the V of the blouse was a defense-plant work badge. She smiled at Gunny, her eyes warm and the sun bright on her reddish-brown hair. Dot's face was round but kept from being heavy by the bright enticements which it offered: straight brows, red lips, gray-green eyes.

"Take good care of Sonny," Dot said.

The smile was for that thought as much as for Gunny. He and Sonny were pals.

"I'll keep him in line, don't worry."

" 'By now," Dot said.

"So long," Gunny told her.

Dot was gone, dashing out of the gate to catch her ride—three girls in a dilapidated car who came by for her daily. She was a stock-room checker in a tool plant on the east side of town.

Removing the lipstick with his handkerchief, Gunny entered the dining-room. Harry was sitting at the table, reading the *Examiner* and eating cereal and milk; he had taken the chair at the end of the table—at least, Gunny

75

secretly felt that the chair facing the door was properly the "end" and hence the chair of the head-of-the-house. Soon after his return he had expressed this belief to his wife, but Emmy, with her somewhat pathetic eagerness to avoid friction, had insisted that since the table was round it didn't matter, and that, anyway, the "end" was the chair facing the window.

So Gunny had that chair, and Emmy, when she wasn't cooking or with the baby or bringing dishes in and out or answering the back door, sat across from him. What was the difference? Were the walls going to be pulled away and the jungle rain let in, was the table going to be turned into a field kitchen and the food into G.I. rations because a man was sitting on the side instead of the end, or because his son got the first look at the morning paper?

Harry cleared his throat. " 'General Douglas Mac-Arthur advances in New Guinea,' " he read aloud for Gunny's benefit. " 'Planes raid Naru.' Say, that man is really on the move."

He looked keenly at his father; back of his thick-lensed glasses, Harry's eyes had a small-boy's mischief in them. He was ready for an argument, MacArthur being his idol, while Gunny was not among the General's admirers.

Gunny rose to the bait like an old bull-pickerel. He never could resist it.

"The Army may be moving, but not him."

"Heck, Dad," said Harry, "if they're moving, he must have something to do with it."

"Sure he has—sitting in a dugout somewhere, talking on a field-telephone."

"A man with four stars on his hat can't go up in the front lines and get shot at."

"He'll never be shot at, don't worry about that hombre. He's dug in for the duration."

On the subject of MacArthur, Gunny had certain long-established prejudices. He held him personally responsible for the fact that the First Marine Division, which had gone ashore at Guadalcanal with seventy-two hours' rations, had not been relieved, and scarcely reprovisioned, for six months. Also, like many old-line Marine non-coms, Gunny had an unshakable belief in the legend that the General, while Chief of Staff, had wanted to scrap the whole Corps and absorb it into the Army. Scuttlebutt held that the General had remarked at a staff conference that he could use the officers but didn't know what in hell he could do with the enlisted men. That was enough for Gunny; accepting it, he accepted anything derogatory to General MacArthur which had ever been invented or circulated. Disregarding well-established evidence to prove that MacArthur was as brave as any man living, Gunny seldom referred to him without attaching his Marine Corps sobriquet, "Dugout Doug."

"He's dug in deep," he appended. "The only way they can hurt that guy is when they invent a land-submarine."

The automatic egg-boiler—a Christmas gift from Dot—clicked to indicate that Harry's two-minute eggs had severed contact with the water. Gunny, peeling a banana, watched with some repulsion while his son unshelled his entrée. What gooey food the guy ate, mush really—and little else! To Gunny, no egg was really palatable until turned over and fried to the consistency of leather.

From the eggs, Gunny's attention switched somewhat covetously to the paper.

"How'd the Angels do yesterday?" he inquired.

Harry silently handed over the sport section, thus keeping his father quiet until Emmy, temporarily through with Sonny, hurried in to provide her husband with nourishment.

" 'L.A. Team Trims Seals,' " Gunny read, his face lit with interest. " 'Dolan's Two-Bagger Topples Lead in Seventh.' " It sounded like a swell game; he was surely sorry he had missed it. Maybe he'd take a ride out there this afternoon if he could get some one to go with him.

"So long, Pops. See you to-night."

"So long."

Harry, never in a hurry, stood up leisurely. He fetched his hat and brief-case from the hall table, then started toward the back door through the kitchen, where he paused for a low-voiced colloquy with Emmy.

This daily morning conference, always conducted at a pitch inaudible to Gunny—but only barely, tantalizingly inaudible—displeased the Sarge more than any other feature of his life as a retired hero. While it went on was the time each day that he really felt helpless, old, useless, and somehow defrauded and displaced, an outsider in his own home.

This talk was the daily Watrous staff-conference—but Gunny was not in on it. Harry stepped formally into his new and mysteriously-gained position as head-of-the-house. He and Emmy were talking over what to get to eat, or, rather, Harry was indicating his preferences while Emmy nodded and listened and made mental notes and sometimes a suggestion, while she looked with proud eyes at her eldest son arrayed for his day in the great world. There was a click as Harry unsnapped a special wallet, carried always on his person: he was doling out ration-stamps. With his vegetarian and mush-food tendencies, Harry would probably have made them all live

78

on greenery and canned stuff, his father suspected. Gunny knew that in this direction at least Emmy had stood her ground: the Watrouses ate meat every other day.

Breaking up toast and mopping up the last egg-yolk and bacon-fragment, Gunny heard Harry open the garage and start his car. A moment later he drove past the window, leaning out anxiously to make sure he was backing right. The car was spotlessly clean—a middle-priced car, bought just before Pearl Harbor; it had fog-lights, a radio, and plenty of chromium. Harry, also glistening and well-polished, also stream-lined and prosperity-bespeaking in spite of his glasses, his frugality, his mush-absorbing stomach, and the evident fact that even if he hadn't been "essential" he would have been 4-F—Harry, too, reflected credit on the family.

In that brief glimpse of his son, snatched as the car backed into Felicia Street, Gunny recovered from some measure of his chronic annoyance. Harry was plenty smart to be where he was at twenty-seven—chief accountant of the Nuway Plastic Corporation, with an assistant treasurership in sight. He knew his way around, that boy. His eyes had handicapped him all his life, making him play second fiddle to Bob, but he had turned the handicap into an asset. He had studied. He had risen. Harry might be an old maid in some ways, but he'd get married some day and get over it. He even had a girl friend, Miss Bopeep Lipsitch of Azuza, a female accountant. They had been going together since before Pearl Harbor and might name the day at the drop of a ledger. Meanwhile, he was a son to be proud of. A real help to his mother. By God, Harry would be somebody some day, there was no doubt of that in Gunny's mind, no doubt of it at all.

"Hey, Em," said Gunny, addressing his wife through the open kitchen door, "how about another cup of coffee?"

❧ CHAPTER 14 ❧

FOR GUNNY, THIS LITTLE EPILOGUE TO HIS REAL BREAKfast was often the pleasantest period of the day. Leaf-shadows flickered in the California sunshine, hot and bright at the window even at this hour; the new coffee sent out its beguiling message; in the front bedroom, Sonny kept up a brisk conversation with himself. This was the time when, if she was not too busy, Emmy would come as she did now and sit beside him.

This interlude was part of no arrangement, it belonged in no one's schedule and had been computed in no budget; it was theirs, Gunny's and Emmy's, the one moment in the thronging communal life of the dove-gray bungalow when the two of them could be together, just the way they'd planned it long ago. Now they could dally for a little while with ancient dreams; they could feel young because there were no young people present to remind them they were old. Some of the obedience to an inner bondage slipped away from Emmy: she looked more like the sensuous, handsome girl

80

who had followed Gunny on his sojourns at democracy's bleak outposts, who had slept on the hard beds and cooked on the drafty stoves and borne his children.

A piece of ham lay on a clean saucer beside Gunny's coffee-cup. This was Emmy's current favor, her clandestine betrayal of Harry's edict about conserving meat points. She brought the gift in absently, hardly looking where she put it, and immediately glancing in another direction as if the appearance of the ham and her husband's consumption of it were matters unrevealed to her. And Gunny, whose retirement from service had failed to civilize his table-manners, reformed completely as he ate the ham; he slivered it in tiny pieces and ate each piece with a fork.

Ordinarily, Gunny and his wife did not talk much when they sat over the breakfast table; talking could spoil the sense, important to both, of being together. But today Emmy picked up the paper, folded where Harry had discarded it on leaving. She read something which made her give a low, quick laugh—the kind of laugh that meant she wanted Gunny to ask her a question.

"What's that, Mother?"

"Oh, just a movie. A picture at the United Artists," Emmy said.

"Who's in it?"

"Those two. You know, the short fat one, and the other funny one."

"Huh?"

"Oh, I forgot. They're a couple of new ones. I don't think you've ever seen them, but they're very funny."

"Weren't they the two we saw that night in San Diego, just before I left?"

Emmy's brow clouded, then cleared. "Why, yes.

That's so. I believe they were. They were the two we saw."

"Some memory you've got, Mother. Abbott and Costello."

Emmy looked at Gunny, but as if she were looking past him.

"It seemed so much longer ago than it was. When you went away, I mean."

Gunny said nothing. He ate several small slivers of ham.

"What about this picture? You want to go?"

"Why, yes. I'd like it, Earl." She was the only member of the family who called Gunny by his Christian name—but now she used it without assurance. "I really would, sometime."

"What's the matter with to-day? We used to see pictures in the P.M."

"Yes, of course, Earl," Emmy said in the same half-dreamy and self-doubting way. "We did, but that was different. I—I don't think I could go to-day."

Regret mixed with the hesitation in her voice. If there was one thing Emmy loved it was a slapstick comedy.

"What's different about it? Why couldn't you go?"

"Why, Earl Watrous," Emmy said, forcing the tone now, abandoning the intimacy of the moment for her housewife tone and housewife face, "whatever are you thinking about?" She groped for some reason that would explain her refusal; at last she found it. "What would we do with Sonny?"

"Take him along with us," Gunny said. His voice was serious; he put his hand over hers where it lay on the table.

"Let's go, Emmy," he said. "What's the matter. You said you wanted to go. What's stopping us?"

Emmy took her hand from under his. Once more it seemed that she wavered between refusal and consent. Then the days she lived, the housewife days flowing and pushing her along in their endless bobbing current, re-asserted their pressure.

She rose decisively.

"I can't go, Earl. I laundered yesterday, and I have all that ironing to do."

"Couldn't the laundry pick up the flat-wash, one time, and iron it for you?"

"Now you know that costs a lot of money, Earl," Emmy said in the same absent tone as before but now without the hesitation. She had made up her mind.

"I can't stand waste," she said.

Gunny looked at his wife; he moistened his lips but didn't speak. The laundry, he knew, was three-quarters Harry's—Dot always took care of the baby's. Every day Harry put on a clean pair of shorts and a white linen shirt with a semi-soft collar, and the collars must be done just so. Harry was fussy about laundry.

"Maybe we can go some other time," Emmy said. "Some evening . . ."

Gunny looked at the plate where the ham had been. In the evening would be fine, but in the evening Emmy couldn't go because she had to get up in the morning.

"All right, Em," Gunny said. "We'll go in the evening." He stood up, a burly figure in the overtight, Chinese-made khaki suit. Feeling in his pocket for his pipe he walked rather heavily out of the dining-room.

CHAPTER 15

FELICIA STREET STIRRED WITH A GENTLE, SUN-WARMED bustle. The Beamy Bakery truck, bright in its blue-and-yellow paint, cruised past slowly, the driver setting off an automatic chime to remind housewives that they needed Beamy Vitamin-plus bread. A milk truck made its rounds, the driver running up the driveways of the little houses carrying bottles in a metal rack. Women talked across back fences, hung wash, chatted with the postman, gardened, dried their hair on porches, and occasionally yelled at kids who, since it was still school vacation, played on the sidewalks and in the thoroughfare, adding their share to the life of the street. Sprinklers tossed bright little crescents on the lawns, and a boy with a thick wad of grocery throwaways ambled along, negligently and importantly twisting the newly printed sheets and sticking them in mail-boxes or between the pickets of fences.

Gunny, pipe in mouth, walked downtown. His step, though firm and soldierly, was not the standard thirty-six inch stride; Gunny had shortened it in order to accommodate his grandson. Sonny was not a fast walker, depending on determination rather than speed. He refused all aid; he took Gunny's hand only at intersections; pumping his legs hard, he kept his eyes fixed on the lines in the pavement. Though acquaintances greeted the pair from time to time, Gunny alone took notice of the salutations; except when they met a four-footed creature,

84

Sonny was too much absorbed in his own progress to bother with other matters.

Between the two companions as they thus proceeded, now side by side, now single file, there was a curious resemblance: they rhymed in other ways besides their names. Sonny, like his grandfather, had a long waist, chunky shoulders, and a pad of flesh around the middle —even the modeling around their eyes was much the same. Here, however, the likeness stopped. It was clear that in mood they were far apart: Gunny was thoughtful, whereas Sonny had an air of stout adventure.

Sonny was acting a rôle. On his sweater was a gift from his mother—an unfranked worker's badge which Dot had brought home from the plant. Sonny wore this token only when he took walks with Gunny; it was to some extent responsible for his self-confidence, making him in his own eyes a gala and noteworthy personality.

"Watch it," Gunny cautioned as a large black dog, ferocious and affectionate, barred his companion's path. Sonny tottered momentarily but rapidly recovered poise and came back fighting. Pushing his fist into the dog's face he steadied himself, at the same time discouraging further interest; eyes fixed vigilantly on the pavement-lines he pressed on toward a destination which seemed clearly known to him, to him and no one else except his comrade, Gunny. For some weeks now, ever since this walk had become routine, Watrouses had speculated about it: Sonny had always been a walker for his age, he had been active in the yard, but never in family history had he been content to go off somewhere early in the day, have his mid-morning snack away from home, and come back at lunchtime refreshed and unrecalcitrant. It was uncanny—as if Gunny had a charm over the punk. Where did they go and what did they do? The Watrouses wanted to know, but Gunny, questioned, was evasive.

"We got a spot we like," was all he would say.

Had a member of the F.B.I.—or even of the Watrous clan—been following them, there is some likelihood that the morning walks would have been stopped or at least redirected. To-day they followed their accustomed route down Felicia, across Byrd to St. Cloud, and along St. Cloud to a spot where a market, a post-office and a few stores made a small business oasis. Here, next to a vacant lot, its board sign swinging over an unswept and unhallowed chunk of sidewalk, was an establishment which had long been regarded as an eyesore:

HOOVER SNOOKER PARLOR
BILLIARDS—SOFT DRINKS

The place had been there when the neighborhood was young. What with its dinginess, its mottled stucco outside streaked with rust from the tin gutter, and the brown gloom within, it had a stubborn, fleshy, guttersnipe appearance, as if its unsavory vitality would go on unchecked, drawing customers and detracting from rent-values until the fine, modern, decent enterprises around it fell to rubble and grass grew among their ruins.

You would not have expected to find a client in the Hoover Snooker Parlor at that hour in the morning, yet Cliff was there, knocking the balls around on one of the pool tables. From his greeting to the new arrivals it was somehow clear that he had been expecting them.

"Hi, Sarge . . . Hi, Sonny."

"Hi, Cliff," Gunny said. He addressed himself sternly to his comrade. "What's got into you, my boy? Can't you answer when somebody tells you hello?"

"Hi," Sonny answered obediently. He climbed into one of the high spectator-chairs against the wall. From behind the cigar-counter a pasty, freckled youth with a withered right hand came over, carrying a board which he set into slots whittled in the arms of the chair; he reached into his pocket and extracted therefrom a handful of bottle-tops which he put on the board. Sonny, thus provided with amusement and at the same time secured from mischief, began to play happily.

"Thanks, Posty," Gunny said to the freckled youth. He turned to Cliff. "Well," he began ruminatively, "chalk up, partner. What's it going to be? Myself, I'm kelly-pool minded on a day like this. Yes, sir, I might just be in the frame of mind to shake you loose from some of your spare change. What's eating you?" he said, surprised, as Cliff, instead of swapping cracks the way he usually did, just stood there, looking at him with an odd expression. "Aren't you going to set 'em up? Don't we get a little game?"

"Sure, Sarge," Cliff said. "Only I got something to show you first. Want to take a look?"

Gunny slowly laid aside the cue he had been balancing and chalking. "Okay," he said cautiously. "What's cookin'?"

"Wait till you see," Cliff said. He led the way to the back of the pool-hall, where a beaverboard partition formed another, smaller chamber, sometimes used for card-games. Here, on a battered iron cot which had a spring but no mattress, lay a man whom Gunny for a fraction of a second did not recognize. The man had a sweaty, yellowish face. He was snoring rhythmically, buzzing on the intake and whistling on the out. From the fumes filling the apartment, the incumbent was evidently sleeping off a drunk of fabulous proportions:

87

neither Cliff nor Gunny would have felt it safe just then to strike a match in his vicinity.

The sleeper's clothes were as prismatic as his breath, the most glorified imaginable version of cowboy splendor: a hand-tooled belt with a silver buckle, striped California pants, star-boots, slash-pocket shirt, and neckerchief. A brand new Stetson ten-gallon rested on the floor beside him; strapped to his waist was a huge hand-forged, silver-handled knife.

"Tabeshaw—if it ain't that Indian rattlesnake!" Gunny was delighted. "When in hell did he get to town?"

"Last night. I gave him my address a long time back, on the island, I guess, and he had it written down; anyway, he came by the house. He was so drunk I couldn't keep him there so I brought him down here and Posty fixed him up."

"Why, the lizard-eating red son-of-a-bitch!" Gunny said happily. "I didn't even know he was discharged. When was it, did he tell you? Where was he wounded? I never thought the bullet had been made that could nick that belly-crawlin' rabbit-chaser."

"No bullet did nick him," Cliff said. He still had the queer expression on his face. "He wasn't wounded."

"What in hell are you talkin' about?" Gunny demanded, puzzled. "He's out, isn't he?"

"He's out, but he didn't get a medical discharge. He didn't even get an Honorable."

"You're kidding!" Gunny was aghast.

"I'm not kidding. The guy had a Summary Court Martial. Look at his papers if you don't believe me," Cliff said. "Go ahead, they're in his wallet. Take a look."

Once more—so incredible was this news—Gunny glared at Cliff; he had to be sure that he wasn't being ribbed. Then, gingerly, he extracted a bulging note-case which protruded from the sleeping man's hip pocket: from the cellophane card-slot of the wallet he removed the discharge certificate. He unfolded it and studied it for several minutes. Then he put it back in the cellophane slot and put the wallet back where it had been.

Gunny looked sick.

"It's the McCoy, isn't it?" Cliff asked curiously.

Gunny spat. "I don't know."

"What do you mean, you don't know?"

"I was in the Corps twenty-eight years," Gunny said. "I had to recommend some guys for those. And I was there when some of them was court-martialed so they could be handed one—but that's the first one of the goddam things I ever had in my own hand, the first one—you understand—I ever laid my eyes on."

⋑ CHAPTER 16 ⋐

"I NEVER GOT QUITE THE STRAIGHT OF IT," CLIFF SAID, "but from what he said last night, it was all on account of his getting the Navy Cross. You know these Indians—once you make them think they're hot, all of a sudden they're boss of the world. With that Cross the guy must have thought he was as good as an officer."

Gunny studied the sleeping man. He said, "Yeah,

could be. The Cap would have given him a summary Court Martial, quick, his first offense. The Cap comes from Indian country himself."

A snore shuddered in the sleeper's nose. Sound rose in knots to a dreadful crescendo, when it was cut off abruptly, as if a heart-stoppage had occurred. The wheeze on the exhalation began faintly but it was not pleasant, seeming as it did to issue from the Indian's vital organs.

"Judas!" Cliff said. "I haven't heard a thing like that since I slept next to him at Elliott."

"It ain't good," Gunny said reflectively. He appraised the Indian as if examining a dangerous terrain. "If he keeps on, he's liable to strangulate hisself. Maybe it's time he got up."

"Now you're talkin', Sarge," Cliff said with energy. Seizing one of the sleeper's feet, he shook it vigorously. "Come on, Indian!" he commanded. "Snap out of it. Wake up!"

There was little reaction. The abused foot, on being released, twitched slightly, but the Indian's posture did not alter; the next crescendo swelled its horrid course much like the one before it.

"What in hell do you know about getting a guy up?" Gunny inquired mildly. Taking a deep breath he rose slightly on his toes in the manner of an operatic tenor taking a high note. "Reveille!" he roared in an enormous voice. "Five hundred! Reveille! Hit the deck, you bastards. Climb out of those sacks. Reveille!"

It was the bellow of boot camp days—the summons which a second later would inaugurate a stripping of blankets, plus tremendous clouts on sections of exposed anatomy.

The Indian's eyes snapped open. At the same moment

his torso jerked into a vertical position and he swung his legs over the side of the cot. He sat there blinking, looking around for the familiar features of the barracks in which he imagined himself to be.

"Hi, Gunny," he said without surprise. "Hi, Cliff."

The text of the bellowed summons prodded his mind, and he asked anxiously, "Five hundred. Is that on the level?"

"It's ten-thirty, Bill," Cliff said, "and you're back on white man's time. Remember? You got discharged. What were you drinking last night, gasoline?"

"Brother, I was drinkin', that's all I know," Bill Tabeshaw said with feeling.

"You're telling me," Cliff said.

"I been drunk for two weeks," the Indian said. "Haven't had nothing to eat in two weeks, neither. Only booze. A man can live on booze, I found that out."

"He can if he's half-rattlesnake like you are," Gunny said. "Posty!" he yelled through the open door into the poolroom. "Cup of coffee for this stinking leatherneck; he used to be a good Marine."

"Coming up!" Posty said. He rose from the chair next to Sonny, whom he had been helping to deploy the bottle-tops. "Grind one with it?"

"How about a hamburger?" Cliff said to the Indian.

Tabeshaw's tongue explored his mouth. "Not for me," he said.

"Grind one, heavy on the mustard," Gunny yelled through the door. "And bring in something for the baby, milk or something." As Posty left to fill the order, Gunny turned to the Indian. "There's an All-Night right next door and the stuff's plenty good. It'll snap you out of it."

"Nothin's goin' to snap me out of nothin', Sarge,"

the Indian said sourly. He flexed his knees to test them, but the operation was unsatisfactory and he sank back on the couch.

"Did you hear me tell you to get up? God," Gunny said mournfully, "how did I come to get mixed up with this ant-eating, red son-of-a-bitch? You're some fighting man, all right," he said savagely. "One hell of a fine-looking piece of man-power."

The Indian wasn't paying attention. His face had tightened apprehensively and he clapped his hand to his shirt pocket. What he felt seemed to relieve his feelings; he relaxed, ramming his stubby fingers inside the pocket. When he took them out he was holding a thick roll of money, a hundred-dollar bill on the outside of it. He put the roll on the floor and took out his wallet and put it next the roll; then he began rapidly to go through his pockets, taking crumpled bills out of several of them, in ones and twos and once in a great handful of high de-nomination. Wetting his thumb, he began to count the money while Cliff and Gunny stood at the foot of the cot staring at him.

The door of the poolroom opened and closed, and Posty's steps could be heard in the other room. "Here's your chow," Posty called.

No one answered. Tabeshaw finished his count.

"Fifteen hundred, twenty-three bucks," he said. This did not seem to include the contents of his wallet, which he now returned to its nook on his left hip. "Got my muster-out pay in there. I was scared maybe I'd been rolled. What you say, guys," he went on, no longer a drunken Indian jungle scout but a man with the execu-tive manner proper to the possession of great funds. "What about this coffee? We gonna eat?"

"You dropped something," Cliff said. He picked up a

ten-dollar bill which had somehow slipped under the bed and handed it to the Indian.

"Cops looking for you?"

Gunny's question was not facetious. The Indian, drinking coffee in scalding gulps, said, "I did it on the square, Sarge."

"You must have been sort of hot with those dice."

"I was playing red-dog," the Indian said. "Took eleven hundred one night in San Berdoo. Fellow I hitched a ride off took me in a little club and I picked up the rest."

"Mama," Cliff said, almost reverently, "fifteen hundred bucks and a bad conduct discharge. Some Indian."

"Who told you?" Tabeshaw said. "Who told you about that?" His voice was very low and his slack, leathery-looking lips hung open.

"You told him yourself, you goddam fool," Gunny interposed. He stepped quickly between the Indian and Cliff.

Tabeshaw avoided Gunny's eyes.

"They had me in the brig," he said. "They had me in the brig." He shoved a big hunk of hamburger and bun in his mouth and slowly chewed on it.

"Where else would they put you, acting like you must of." Gunny turned suddenly to his grandson; in a different voice he said, "Drink your milk, partner."

"You're a gamblin' man all right, Bill," Cliff said. A wonderful yet natural idea had come to him—a real inspiration.

"I was hot," Bill Tabeshaw said. He finished his hamburger, wiping his fingers on the seat of his pants.

"You must have been hotter than a pistol."

"Pistol!" Sonny echoed. It was one of his favorite words. From his boarded-in perch he cast a bottle-top which cartwheeled across the floor.

"I told you to behave yourself," Gunny said in the special voice he used for Sonny. He picked up the bottle-top and put it back on Sonny's board.

Cliff was chalking a cue. As Gunny straightened up, a look passed between them—the same look which the pitcher and catcher of a smooth-working ball club will exchange when a batter with a known weakness is stepping to the plate and formal signals are unnecessary.

"Ever play this game, Bill?" Cliff inquired. He stroked the cue-ball negligently, letting it slide across the green baize table.

"Couple times," the Indian said. He swished the last of his coffee around in his cup, watching Cliff miss the nine-ball.

"You ain't so sharp," he said. "Missed it, didn't you?"

"I miss plenty of them," Cliff said, "but me and the Sarge, we futz around with it and have some laughs. We were all set to have a game this A.M. What do you say, Sarge, still want to unload some of that small change?"

Gunny had taken down a cue. He had it all chalked, ready at hand.

"Set 'em up," he said.

"Okay, Posty," Cliff said. While Posty racked the balls, the Indian watched the Sarge slide the cue through his fingers.

"Ain't you fixin' to shoot with the wrong end of that thing?"

"What do you mean, Bill?" the Sarge inquired politely. "Think the other end would be better?"

"It's bigger, ain't it?"

"Well, I guess it is at that."

"Sure it is," Cliff put in heartily. "Say, if Bill wants to use the big end it's all right with me. How about you, Sarge?"

"It's all right with me," Gunny said.

"It ain't with me," Posty said. "Fun is fun, fellows, but if he hasn't never shot pool let him stay away from my table. I don't want that cloth all chivered up."

"Hell, I'll shoot with the little end. It don't make no difference to me," the Indian said. Taking the first cue in the rack he made an awkward bridge, jabbed at a ball, and miscued.

"Never mind me," he said. "I'll ketch on to it."

"I'll tell you how we generally play, Bill," Cliff said. "First we shoot the one ball, then the two ball, and so on, see? Each spot on a ball counts for two bits. For the eight, see, you win two bucks. Get it? We take turns shooting and on account you're new around here, you go first. Okay?"

"Okay with me," the Indian said. Once more he bridged, miscued, and swore. "I'll be doggoned," he said. "It's not as easy as it looks."

"You'll pick it up," Cliff said. He bent over so the Indian wouldn't see him laughing. He deliberately missed the next shot; Bill was temperamental and he might still get discouraged and quit; he wouldn't really be hooked till he'd sunk a couple of balls.

"You're way off, Sarge," he said as Gunny followed his example. "Nothing off the table yet. It's up to Bill here to show us the way."

CHAPTER 17

THAT INDIAN! OH, WHAT A RATTLESNAKE, OH, WHAT A crafty guy!

Many times, later, they discussed it at the Hoover Snooker Parlor, just what he'd said, and the way he miscued that first ball. He did make one shot, right near the start of the game, and Cliff, second-guessing, insisted he'd suspected something then, but heck, it was a power shot, four ball in a corner pocket, and any one could luck in a power shot.

Still, they should have known. Just on the kind of guy he was they should have known, but that was how your mind worked when you thought you had a pigeon—you gave him an imaginary character until he'd proved different. And by that time it was too late.

After Bill made that one shot, he said why waste time with a penny-ante contest? He said why not go two bucks a number, he was ready and he had the hang of the game now, it was a pushover. So no sooner said than done. He had that one shot and he didn't rack the ball. He put it in his pocket where he could feel it, he said, on account he was so proud of the shot.

They should have known then, he was overdoing it, but the game was set. Gunny and Cliff had a couple of low balls apiece, and the table had opened up. That was when the Indian went to work. He was the kind of pigeon who would sink his claws into a full-grown steer and fly away with it.

He took the seven ball and the eight ball on easy shots. Sonny could probably have made them, but the Indian was gunning. There was nothing shaky now about the way he bridged. And when he lined up a shot, it was like a 106 mm. getting the range. He powered a couple more, still keeping the table open, and he played a lovely carom shot of feathery softness to sneak in the ten ball —it was just as if he'd breathed on the ball or wished it in.

Cliff didn't want to look at Gunny. His insides had turned to jelly because he knew then what kind of pigeon they had hooked. This Indian could play pool like Willie Hoppe!

Gunny knew, too. He made a run of three and missed, Cliff had an impossible shot and scratched, and the Indian cleaned the table. He knocked on the floor with his cue for Posty to rack them up—and this was the guy who didn't know which end of the cue to shoot with. . . .

"You've played more than a couple of times, haven't you, Bill?" Gunny asked quietly.

"Maybe a few times more," the Indian said. "I sort of like the game."

"You got quite a talent for it," Gunny said. "I swear, if you studied, you could get to be half good."

"Just lucky," the Indian said.

He called for straight pool, a dollar a ball, and even that was letting them off easy after the cut-throat rotation. They had to go along with him; he let on he was out for blood, but why wouldn't he be? They'd tried to take him; hence pride demanded that they go along. On the third game, which was kelly, Gunny got hot, and that time he and Cliff almost broke even. But they never had a chance. At quarter to one, when the Sarge had to go because it was Sonny's lunchtime, the Indian had won sixty-three bucks from Cliff and over a hundred from Gunny. There was nothing to do but come across.

"Now that you've got the dough, Tabeshaw," Gunny said as he paid off, "do you mind if I ask you a question?"

"Go ahead, Sarge," the Indian said politely.

"That antelope range up where you come from, do they equip that with pool tables?"

The Indian grinned. He had divided his total wealth into two slabs of banknotes and had put one slab in each of his glossy new star-boots.

"I tell you, Sarge, in my town there's six saloons, one pool-hall, and they've got a law, my people can't go in saloons."

"It's a lousy law," the Sarge said.

But in spite of being the loser the Sarge bought beers all around. The Indian owed Posty for the coffee and burger, and since he was short of silver, the Sarge paid for that, too. He and Cliff stood outside the pool-hall watching the Indian stride up the main street of the little business section; he had an odd walk that they'd hardly noticed on the island but that was unusual on a city street, rolling forward on to the balls of his feet, his neck strained slightly ahead as if he were carrying a hunting pack with a head-sling on it. He'd have to make time now, he had explained, if he was going to thumb a hitch north.

He was on his way home to impress his folks.

"You know," Gunny said slowly, as the rolling figure in its garish finery receded in the sun, "I don't mind his winning all that dough."

"Huh?"

"How long do you think it will stay with him—the whole roll, I mean? How long will he keep it?"

98

"Christ," Cliff said, "he'll snowball it. He's a sharp-shooter. Or isn't he?"

"He can play red-dog," Gunny said. "And he can shoot pool. Maybe a couple of other things. But everything he wins in six weeks or a summer, he'll lose in one night. Then what's he going to do?"

"Go to work, I guess," Cliff said. "What's eating you, Sarge? How can you be sorry for that guy? He's richer than Rockefeller."

"Rockefeller don't play red-dog," Gunny said. "Listen, boy, I wouldn't be in that Indian's shoes if he had a cold million. Did you say work? Where can he work? The first time he goes to get a job they'll ask to see his discharge. Do you think they'll hire him with what he's got?"

Cliff took thought. "They don't ask you for it every place."

"Nowadays you have to have a social security number. And when you put in for that, you fill out forms. Besides which, in any kind of factory you've got to show your draft card, and they fingerprint you. Brother, a Bad Conduct Discharge from the service is about as easy to hide as a third arm. It's just like the Silver Star—they gave him something, but they didn't tell him what it meant."

"He'll make out all right," Cliff said.

"Maybe. . . ."

Gunny made a grab at Sonny, who was trying to get out into the street. Sonny began to bawl.

"Take it easy, partner," Gunny said. "You're hungry, that's all. You and me are going home."

In the poolroom, Posty, for something to do, had turned on the radio.

". . . *bombers*," said the tinny voice of the announcer,

"*plastered the entire area, dropping two hundred tons of explosives Saturday. Sunday they returned at invasion time to lay down a smokescreen through which the Marines are reported to have landed unobserved....*"

"I'll bet," Cliff said.

Gunny jerked his head for Cliff to keep quiet. He and Cliff stood listening, their faces suddenly different, strained, mindless, vigilant, lost, wild, and set—the faces of combat.

"*...casualties are understood to have been reasonable for the objectives achieved. General Douglas MacArthur had barely completed the first phase of the operation when he recalled the amphibious craft and reloaded them with fresh troops and supplies....*"

"Turn it off, will you?" Gunny yelled suddenly.

There was a jumble, then soft, pleasing dance-music.

"Where was that they landed?" he said after a moment.

"I didn't hear the first part. Sounded something like Saidor."

"Saidor," Gunny said. "That's on the Huon Peninsula."

He looked yellowish, old and tired, standing in the poolroom doorway with the baby, thinking of the beaches of Saidor.

"See you to-morrow, Cliff?" he asked.

"Sure," Cliff said. "See you to-morrow."

CHAPTER 18

THAT WAS THE WAY THEY WOUND UP EVERY DAY, CLIFF thought. See you to-morrow, and then to-morrow it was see you to-morrow, and a game of pool and a bottle of beer, and then if Gunny could make it they'd take the street-car out to Wrigley Field and see the ball game.

They were hanging on to something and were both afraid to let go.

Someday he or Gunny would break off the pool, but he didn't want to think about that yet. Seeing Gunny every day, even if both were bored with what they did, kept him going.

Still, it was a lot of phonus-balonus. Did you need something like this when you were home, and everything was fine? As the doctors had said, it was just a question of getting your bearings, you had to relax. Things had been happening too fast, so goddam fast you couldn't keep up with them. Everything was swell, and above all, you mustn't worry.

Half-past one. Cliff ate a frank-on-a-roll from the All-Night and drank a Dr. Pepper, standing Posty a coke. Posty never stood anybody anything, not even a free rack, but Posty had a tough time making ends meet in the little poolroom. Posty's brother, a married man, had been drafted, and Posty was looking after his brother's wife. Nearly every guy you met was doing something like that, it was just the way things were.

What to do now? He could go up to the Y and work

out or maybe take a swim, but he had been staying away from the Y because Jimmy Tracy was there every day, working out to get in shape for football.

Jimmy was a right guy, of course. Nobody could say different. But what was the sense of hanging out with a guy whose sister you had buried in the jungle? Buried and gone where no son-of-a-bitch would ever find her, and all thought of old old days buried with her.

Here lies Patricia Tracy.

He had put the earth back into place, pressed it down with his hand.

As for this Mrs. Whosis, whoever it was Pat had become, Cliff wanted no part of that. When people used her name they were not talking about any one he knew.

"Clifford, I heard something to-day—about a friend of yours."

His mother always picked up gossip in the market, chatting with the neighbors as she trundled her wheelbasket along little aisles of groceries.

"That so?"

"Patricia Tracy. Her husband has gone overseas. She's living in Beverly—working there, I think."

Cliff let the matter lie. But his mother, not taking the hint, went on with it.

"I never asked you, Clifford, but I couldn't help wondering—whatever happened between you two?"

"Nothing, Ma. Not a damn thing happened."

"Patricia was always such a sweet girl. When I heard about her marriage, I—"

"Forget it, will you, Ma?"

"Now, Son. There's no need to get riled up. I only said . . ."

"Judas, what's the use. . . ."

To end the conversation, Cliff went out into the yard.

Later his mother looked at him reproachfully because he had been rude to her, but this he couldn't help.

He didn't want to talk about a person who did not exist—a person who was buried.

Once at the Y he and Jim worked out in the gym and swam a few laps. Cliff hadn't meant to get roped into it, but Jim had seemed so glad to see him that he couldn't refuse. Later, while they dressed, Jim said offhandedly, "Pat was asking about you."

That was all. Jim would have left it, but Cliff felt his throat get dry just as if Pat were still Pat and not some one buried in the jungle dust.

"She living here?" he asked. The words had popped out before he could think.

Jim shook his head. "She's got an apartment with another gal, both of them working for the OPA."

"That's swell. I'm glad she's working." He bent over to tie his shoe.

"The guy she married got a tough break. He was wounded overseas. Tunisia...." Jim turned from the small mirror as if a bright idea had come to him. "She was asking about you, just the other day. Why don't you give her a ring sometime?"

Cliff said nothing.

"She'd like to hear from you," Jim said.

"Thanks," Cliff said. "I'm kind of busy right now."

So there was a number. All you had to do was pick a 'phone up and you could be talking to somebody: Mrs. Whosis, working for the OPA.

Rain on that number. There was nobody there he wanted to talk to.

CHAPTER 19

CLIFF BUMMED POSTY FOR A CIGARETTE, NOT WITHOUT resistance, and inhaled deeply. An idea had come to him. Instead of going to the ball game or taking the bus home and hanging around the house, he could walk uptown, which would take half an hour, and see Abbott and Costello at the United Artists; when he got out he would go over to his father's office and drive home with his father in the car.

Small residential streets petered out into a network of large boulevards, interspaced with handsome buildings—hospitals and luxury hotels—set in landscaped enclosures. Finally the central portion of Los Angeles loomed up. Cliff walked along Figueroa, looking at the skyscrapers, wondering how men could create a thing like a modern city. How was it possible? Sure, they told you in school how the pioneers arrived and all that crap, you learned the history of your own city and the steps by which it had progressed from an adobe pueblo so that in a short time, not yet even a hundred years, it had become a place such as it was.

All that information told you just exactly nothing. It had happened—you knew that yourself—not only here but in many parts of the United States where modern cities had grown up. But *how?* Ask that, and people would decide that you were ready for a boob-academy. People took such things for granted, which was swell, provided that you had a place in all this so that some of it, if only one tiniest corner or process or detail of it, was completely known to you.

But suppose you had no place? What about that? Suppose you had no part in anything? Did you have to think and wonder until you went nuts? If you wanted an answer and a process or an operation of your own, where did you begin? That was what he wanted to know. Where in hell did you begin?

Take the city. Take what you could see, the buildings, churches, theaters, take the insides of them, the contracting work that went into them, the pipes, wires, plastering, the towering decks of the steel floors, the elevators sliding soundlessly in stony chutes, the clocks, the floors, the furnaces. And take the whole organization of the city, all you couldn't see, the huge intricate utilities, the courts, the telephone exchanges with their millions and millions of wires, each one hooking a life into the city and each put in and maintained by experts—how did men have the brains to make such things, how did they have the guts, where did they get the ideas? And if you had no ideas, if you got confused, if you weren't even sure that you had any guts but just the same you wanted to belong and be something, when was the time to start?

What was the countersign? Was it a code or something? Were you, you alone, ruled out, were you an exile, unfit for any share? Had you forfeited your citizenship here—taken out your final papers in a land five thousand miles away, a place of rain and awful growth and rotting and death in many forms, all terrible, but still the only place on earth that you belonged, where you could be with guys who talked your language?

Was that it? If you were once out, were you out for keeps?

Cliff crossed Third against the light, turning toward Broadway; his face was screwed up with thought, and his broad, bony shoulders hunched in the faded high school sweater.

He was considering what he could do in such a city as this. About building, about constructing or linking together what had been constructed he knew nothing; he had never been a part of any organization whose function was constructive. This was itself a kind of defeat. But if, on the other hand, he had entered a city not as a citizen, to make his home in it, but as part of a force which had assaulted and captured the city, then he would have had a place in the scheme of things.

Walking along Spring Street, on his way to see Abbott and Costello, Cliff thought about what he would do, merely checking as a mental exercise a technique in which he had been drilled.

To be sure, he had never campaigned in a country in which cities like Los Angeles were combat objectives; nevertheless, fellows were fighting in such zones, over in Italy, for instance.

There were modern cities there. First your long-range guns would blast them while aircraft knocked out key targets and provided a ceiling for assault troops. Then, once the city had been taken, part of it might have to be destroyed. Or there might be spots of resistance to mop up.

Suppose the captain said to him, pointing to a map, "Cliff, here is Building X. It's got to be blown up." Naturally an assignment like that would fall to an officer, but there might not be an officer to do it. Or it might be a reservoir, an ammunition dump, or this or that. No difference, except in technique. He would have the dynamite packed in the boxes and carried by the strappers. He would have a good fuse man and a good wire man. They would place the charge and get cover and let her rip. There would be nothing to it.

That was all he knew, but he knew that much; he wondered about the people who could build a city up, did they know how easy it was to build a city down? Knitting his eyebrows, he suddenly felt a tingling tremor, the first premonition of a shaking fit, start in his wrists. Tortured, he looked up at the sky. He stood still, sweat springing out on his lips and forehead. By a supreme effort of will he resisted the desire to grip his thumbs. If he could get inside the movie house in time and clear his mind, the shaking might not happen; it had not really taken hold of him. Buying a ticket, he rushed past the ticket-taker, dropped into the first empty seat. The audience was laughing at a gag, but although the laughter swelled and was repeated over and over at new things on the screen, it was half an hour before Cliff was calm enough to share the fun.

It was a good show, and he finally relaxed, staying to see a Popeye cartoon and the added feature. When he got out it was almost five o'clock. He walked over to his father's office, which was on the ground floor of a loft building on South Hill. Mrs. Fricke, his father's secretary, was alone in the outer office.

"How are you, Cliff?" she said, hardly looking up. She spoke to him as if he were a child—but then, she addressed nearly every one that way.

"There's a gentleman in with your Dad," she added, "but I don't think he'll be long."

Cliff took a seat. There was a *Life* on Mrs. Fricke's desk, and he took it and glanced over it, studying the pictures of the girls. Presently the door of the inner office opened and his father came out, ushering a stocky, neat man with dyed black hair and silver-rimmed glasses. Mr. Harper jerked his head at Cliff to get up and be introduced.

"Al," he said to the man with dyed hair, "this is my boy Clifford. He's just back from the Pacific."

"Well, you don't say, you don't say," the man exclaimed heartily. He shook hands with Cliff longer than necessary.

"How are you, my boy?" he inquired. "Why," he said, turning to Mr. Harper, "he looks sound as a dollar. You must be mighty proud of him."

"We think he's all right," Mr. Harper said. He put his hand on Cliff's shoulder.

Cliff looked at the floor. During scenes of this kind he could never think of anything to say.

"Glad to be back?" the man asked Cliff.

Cliff stated that he was.

The man was eying the Legion button in Mr. Harper's lapel.

"Two veterans in one family, eh?" he said.

"I guess that's about the size of it, Al," Mr. Harper said modestly.

"That's what I call real Americanism," the man named Al said, shaking hands with Cliff again. "Well, I'll mail in that confirmation."

Mr. Harper escorted his client to the door; he came back smiling.

"I'm leaving now, Mrs. Fricke," he said pleasantly. "Cliff, I'm glad you dropped in. Wait till I get my hat and we'll ride home together."

CHAPTER 20

THERE HAD BEEN TIMES IN THE PAST WHEN CLIFF HAD
been very close to his father. As a little boy, his mother
had been his whole world, but when he was still quite
small he had rebelled against this world. He had felt instinctively that there was no dignity in it.

At that time Mr. Harper, Senior, had been a courage-
ous, healthy, free-living American. He had a keen relish
for physical things and a proper indifference to the little
upsets which so often vexed his wife; he lived with some
pleasure, doing what he was fitted to do. In his phi-
losophy it did not make much difference how much
money a man made, provided that he made enough to
pay his bills, wear good clothes, and be accounted rea-
sonably successful. Unlike most Americans of his generation, he had no fear of losing his job since he owned a
part interest in the company he worked for—the T-B
Construction Company. This fact in itself was a form
of superiority; it gave Mr. Harper more independence
than many men who were both abler and wealthier.

C. W. Harper was by no means an unusual man, but
he was a fairly happy one. He liked to go fishing in the
spring and hunting in the fall, and he did. He liked to
drink, and he did. He liked the company of men and the
hearty, aimless jocularity of the numerous clubs and
lodges to which he belonged. Occasionally, he liked an
affair with a woman, not a secretary or another man's

wife but preferably one of the party girls who were procured to add zest to club entertainments.

The bond between father and son began when Cliff was nine. Mr. Harper responded to his son's appeal for aid against his mother's rule: out of the secret cabal of all males against females, he encouraged Cliff in many activities which Mrs. Harper disapproved. Thus, the next year came the paper route, and the buying of the bicycle; thus permission not to come straight home from school but to play sandlot baseball certain afternoons with some kids who called themselves the "Hornets."

That summer Mr. Harper took Cliff on a fishing trip to the High Sierras; they fished in mountain meadows, splashed with brilliantly green grass and surrounded by enormous peaks streaked with snow, through which small streams rushed with the speed of racing-cars. That trout could live and feed in such water seemed impossible, but Cliff, fishing with salmon eggs on the bank, saw his father in his rubber waders stride against the pull of the stream, flicking his line back sharply, sternly, then letting the pole straighten with a businesslike, high, swishing sound, indolently following through with his wrist as the heavy tapered line snaked out through the guides, the six-foot leader, so fine that it was almost invisible, straightening, and the fly dropping with perfect naturalness on the fast water. And again and again Cliff, sometimes with a little fish yanking ignored on his own line, saw his father's wrist make the oblique stroke which set the hook, and then the strong arc of the rod as his father played a fighting trout.

That fall they went after deer and repeated the trip nearly every deer season. Cliff shared certain duties around camp, and they had a routine of hunting together which was very companionable.

It was Cliff who broke the companionship. The year he was fifteen he asked permission to bring along Hugo Wrenn, the fellow who was later a casualty on Cliff's last patrol. Mr. Harper said all right, bring him along. Hugo had no gun, so he and Cliff agreed to hunt together and take alternate shots with Cliff's 30-30.

That was when Mr. Harper made a gesture which Cliff never forgot. After Opening Day, on which nobody got a deer, Mr. Harper said he didn't feel like hunting, he would stay in camp and fish. He lent Cliff his 30.06 with the telescope sight so Cliff could let Hugo use the 30-30. The companionship was broken, but in a way it was not broken; it was as if Mr. Harper had known all along that the day would come when Cliff would not want to hunt as a boy with his father but a young man with another person of his age. His father had helped make a new generation of hunters, and now without regret but with a sure and quiet pride he stepped aside for it.

No fellow could have liked his Dad more than Cliff did then. Even now, riding up Wilshire Boulevard in the car, there was a friendly feeling between them.

Only it was not the same.

Possibly, in getting older, his father resented being tied down; he would have liked to roam afar, cutting a figure in dangerous enterprises. The war, and Cliff's enlistment, had intensified this wishful thinking in Old Man Harper; as a compensation he kept harking back to the last war. Mr. Harper had served overseas, a corporal in a regiment of engineers, but he had been stationed in the south of France and had never seen action. Once he had joked about this, but he didn't any more; since Pearl Harbor he had gradually taken the position that he had been one of the saviors of his country, a true hero and a fearless warrior.

Maybe, Cliff thought, maybe so. Still, why did his Dad have to keep on about it? Mr. Harper never came right out and said he'd been in battles, but he let on that he had. This pose that he and Cliff were fellow-veterans —well, it was sickening. They weren't fellow-veterans. They weren't fellow-anything. What his father knew about war was zero. When he so much as talked about war Cliff wanted to throw up. All the stuff his father told sounded like something he'd seen in a movie and a lousy one at that; if any of it was true then that other war wasn't a war at all but some kind of musical comedy where the fellows all drank wine and horsed around and slept with French girls.

Maybe his father had brought something back from the last war that had been truthful and good to possess, but if so he had lost it long ago or spoiled it by talking and lying about it. The bragging was bad enough, but Cliff would rather have gone out on a patrol than stay home and listen to one of the boy-scout talks on conduct which his father now dished out. These were horrible. They ruined everything that had been decent in his relations with his father.

Cliff knew that his mother promoted the talks. His mother had always been his father's conscience: perhaps that was the basis of the secret feud between them. There were older married people whom you could imagine having been young once and in love and who still obviously belonged together; then there were others who, though they did not quarrel, were such strangers, so opposed on every issue that you could not conceive how they had ever had intercourse or what had brought them together in the first place. No doubt such people had been altered from the original pattern; they had slowly pushed, squeezed, pulled, worn, and whittled at each other through the years until it was impossible to tell what they had once been like.

Cliff didn't know what the feud was. All he knew was that his mother was the conscience and that when *she* thought it was about time, his father would lecture him or throw out hints about the things he ought to do.

To-night a lecture was coming—a special one. They had got home too late to wash the car, but Cliff had asked if he could take it, anyway. He wanted to investigate a place called Madame Java's, which Posty had told him about. They were finishing supper when he asked, and his mother gave his father a calm, monitory look.

His father cleared his throat unnecessarily and said, "I don't believe so, Cliff. I'd rather you stayed home to-night." He ate some of the canned cherries on his plate and then added, "Fact is, I want to have a talk with you."

"Okay, okay," Cliff said. In defiance of his mother's prejudice against tobacco he smoked one cigarette after another while the colored girl, Clara, was doing the dishes. His father read the evening paper, listening to the Jack Benny program.

God, if there was going to be a lecture, why didn't he get started on it?

At last Mrs. Harper excused herself. By family tradition she was never present at "talks"; her husband reported on them later, in the bedroom.

"I have a headache to-night, dear," Mrs. Harper said.

"I think I'll go up. Don't forget to lock the door when you come."

"I won't, Mother," Mr. Harper said.

He kissed his wife's cheek and Mrs. Harper kissed Cliff on the forehead. Then she went upstairs, taking the sock she was knitting for the Women's Auxiliary Aid for Russia. The old staircase creaked mournfully under her slight weight.

Mr. Harper turned off the radio, shifting somewhat uncomfortably in his big easy-chair with the battened-down cushions. He said, "Cliff, get my bourbon out of the breakfront and make me a highball, will you? Make one for yourself, if you want it."

No previous lecture had ever begun this way. In fact, it was the first time Mr. Harper had ever offered his son a drink.

These circumstances put Cliff on his guard. This might be a trap of some kind.

"I don't need one, thanks, Dad," he said. He got out the pint bottle and put the liquor in the glass, adding seltzer; Mr. Harper didn't take ice.

As Cliff handed him the highball, Mr. Harper said, "I don't mind your having a snort here in the house, once in a while. Told your mother so. Told her you had a right to smoke, too, if you wanted to."

His tone was slightly patronizing, as if Cliff had been petitioning for these indulgences. Since he seemed to be waiting for some reaction, Cliff said politely, "Thanks, Dad."

". . . But filling up with beer down at the poolroom," Mr. Harper said, frowning, "that's no good, Cliff. That's got to stop, right now. I know how it is when a fellow has done military service and gets out," he continued less sternly. "Went through the experience myself, you know, twenty-five years ago. I wasn't much older than you are now, so I guess I can tell what you're up against."

Cliff nodded, screens of hostility arranging themselves in his eyes. If his Dad only wouldn't get into that brother-veteran stuff!

"You feel sort of at loose ends," Mr. Harper went on, narrowing his eyes with a great air of shrewdness. "Isn't that about the size of it? I thought so ... but remember this, the longer you go on loafing in places where you shouldn't be and tanking up, as I just said, and doing nothing, why, the harder it will be to start when the time comes."

Mr. Harper took a sip of his drink while his son worked one big-knuckled hand against the other, waiting for his father to tell him what he was expected to start.

"How would you like to go to college?"

This was so unexpected that Cliff didn't answer right away. He had been sure his father was going to offer him a job with the Company.

"I hadn't thought much about it."

"Don't misunderstand me, I don't mean High. I was talking to James Tracy yesterday, and he said Jim was entering Cal. and Western. That set me thinking, is another man's boy going to get a fine education like that, and you miss out, just because you served your country? Not if I can help it, Cliff."

Mr. Harper put down his glass. Rising from his chair, he began to walk up and down the room; his step was buoyant and his rather heavy face glowed with animation.

"Not if I can help it, Cliff," he repeated. "And I *can* help it! I made some 'phone calls and I got the information I wanted. Cal. and Western wants to help you young veterans finish your education. Now here's the set-up."

Somehow Mr. Harper looked young, eager; he was seeing himself in Cliff's place, dramatizing the lanky youth of 1918, in ridiculous pants and tight-fitting coat, attending Cal. and Western. Cliff listened, the screens still in his eyes, noting the points as Mr. Harper ticked them off on his fingers: the University's willingness to waive entrance examination and provide a scholarship through the Student's Employment Bureau. Later on, of course, the Government might step in to help veterans get an education. Bills to provide tuition and a maintenance allowance were now pending in the House and Senate. Still, even without direct help, Cliff would be all right: with his disability allowance and the scholarship arrangement he would be dependent on no one. He wouldn't have to feel he owed a cent, but at the same time he would be getting the best education money could provide.

The proposition sounded pretty good. Cliff knew his father wanted him to be enthusiastic, and he did his best. But why did his father go on selling, emphasizing, explaining? It was unnecessary.

All he wanted to do was get started. He would have been glad, if his dad only knew it, to drive a truck or mix concrete, or sweep out an office, any damn thing just so long as he got started. Going to school might be all right. Maybe that was the way you had to do it, maybe that was the spot to begin.

CHAPTER 21

"THE COURSE WILL TRACE THE CORRELATION BETWEEN economy and politics, in medieval and modern times. . . ."

Professor Baird, a keen-looking, rather plump man with a glistening bald head and an eastern way of talking, sat back in his chair; his eyes moved over the class lazily and yet with penetration, as if he could tell by inspection which of his listeners would be able to absorb his teaching and which would not.

"In the light of what is happening to-day, events which took place several hundred years ago will not, to many of you, seem important. This is natural, but I believe that later they will assume importance; a knowledge, for instance, of the Treaty of Tilsit will give you a better understanding of that treaty which is still to be made and which will secure peace for our own world. You are all helping in some way to draft that treaty just as many of you may soon be shaping the course of history as members of the armed forces. Next term, when we study the crisis which produced the present war, I hope we can count on a report from a young man among us who himself has just come back from combat."

Professor Baird was looking at Cliff, and the students around him all turned in his direction, those in the rear desks rising to get a better view. Cliff, much surprised, kept his eyes lowered.

"At all events," the Professor finished, "Former Marine, Clifford Wain Harper is most welcome to History M and M."

There was a ripple of decorous clapping. For a second Cliff raised his head, wheeled his eyes around with a wild, shrinking stare. Though this was the first time attention had been focused on him quite to this extent, in every class he had attended in the three days since college opened he had been singled out in some way, generally by the professor taking him aside at the end of the session and offering personal assistance and advice. Though grateful, Cliff had the feeling that the teachers themselves were curious about him; that they wanted a look at a fellow who had been out there. With his identity thus quickly and publicly established, he often found other freshmen staring at him as he went around the campus.

His great hope about Cal. and Western had been that, once enrolled, he would no longer be a person set apart from others. Still, the campus was a pleasant place to be; he enjoyed getting his text-books at the Coöp, going to his first lectures, strolling from one class to another between the big spired buildings.

No doubt after a while the girls and fellows would stop looking on him as a curiosity. There was so much going on that surely he would become identified with some of it, be swept along, busy and absorbed, as others were.

In his eagerness to bring this about he signed up for several activities about which he knew nothing but which seemed to promise new horizons—round-table discussions, glee-club singing, and the school daily paper. Possibly there were untapped resources in himself which would come out if he made efforts in a lot of new directions.

For the first time in his life he worried about his appearance. He knew he had made a mistake in showing up for classes the first day in the clothes he had bought in San Francisco; they were too loud and citified. Earlier in the summer he had had a couple of crew haircuts; the G. I. cuts of service days had made him drop the habit of brushing his hair. Now he decided crew cuts did not look so well; it would be better if he could wear his hair slicked down. He started to allow it to grow out, annoyed that nothing made it slickable. Resenting discipline, the wiry blond bristles formed a matted mane, sticking out all over his head. This, combined with his averted face, his long, hurrying stride, and his big body, prodding in knobs of bone and muscle through his loose, shapeless clothes, gave him precisely the air of freakishness he was so anxious to avoid.

"Some of you presented Medieval History as an entrance subject last spring, but have not yet called for your papers. Kindly come up and get them as I call your names."

Cliff watched the clock. Ten minutes till lunchtime!

"Batterman, Bowman, Clemens . . . Clemens?"

A fellow in the back of the room spoke up. "Clemens is in the service, sir. He's been inducted."

Professor Baird put aside Clemens' pink-covered exambook. Many times, as he went through the list, he called some name to which nobody answered or about which somebody made the same report that had been made for the absent Clemens. Nearly half the men, it seemed, whose papers had been marked by the Professor were now in the service: the pile of unclaimed books was a kind of honor roll for History M and M. Idly, Cliff wondered whether this Clemens was the Link Clemens he had known in High School, and if so, where Link was now, whether he was still training or had been shipped out already, and where, and whether he was dead or alive. . . .

Prrrrrammmpppp.

The electric bell in the corridor announced the end of class, and Cliff, bounding out of his seat, rushed for the door, dodging and pushing through the students who streamed from the other classrooms. Racing across the quadrangle, he dashed into the cafeteria by the Employees' Entrance. He marked and racked his timecard, hung his coat in his locker, and put on his apron.

Two minutes later, panting slightly, he took his place behind the huge steamtable stretching down one entire side of the room. He had just had time to note that the day's special was pork chops when Cran Holt, the cafeteria manager, unlocked the double doors and a hungry mob charged in, grabbing tin combination plates from a stack by the doors. Cliff began working hard, plunking one or two pork chops, as requested, on each plate, while with his left hand he dug mashed potatoes with an ice-cream scoop, flattened the potatoes in their right partition in the combination plate, swished gravy on top, added a spoonful of stewed tomatoes mixed with breadcrusts.

Hot, succulent food-smells climbed around him, mixing with the steam which gushed up whenever a table-tray was lifted out so that a full one could replace it. More and more students, many of them in the uniforms of the various campus training units, crowded in, and from the dozen rows of tables in the center of the room came a great clashing of knives and forks on the tin plates, the scrape of chairs and feet, and a babble of cheerful, high-pitched talk.

Cliff did not mind the cafeteria job. The only thing

that was tough about it was comparing himself with the fellows in the R.O.T.C. It would be different, of course, after Congress passed those bills his father talked about, but meanwhile—well, those guys had the best of it. They didn't have to pay a cent for their tuition; they got basic pay from the Government while they were studying. And their books, food, clothes, rooms, all provided. More than eighty per cent of all male graduates were in V-12, the Naval unit, or the Marine Reserve or the Army Specialized Training Program, and all these fellows wore the uniforms of their branches: they streamed past him now, Navy blue, khaki drill, and olive-green, fresh kid faces showing above them, faces you could hardly believe, so unlined they were, so unlike the faces of the guys Out There.

They slid their combination plates along the rail in front of the steamtable and Cliff took the plates and filled them up.

"Hi, Leatherneck."

Harley Grenacker, a fellow he had played football with in High School, stood in front of the table; he had on the uniform of a Marine private. Harley knew about Cliff's combat record and his slightly tense smile showed his embarrassment at wearing olive-green while Cliff, a veteran, stood there in a white apron to serve him.

Cliff grinned. He knew why Harley had called him Leatherneck. It was a kind of salute. Boy, it sure sounded good to hear that again for a change.

"Hi, Harley. How's the old appetite?"

"Rarin' like a litter of panthers."

"Try some pig on it. Gravy, Harley?"

"Thanks, Cliff. Comin' out for practice?"

"Haven't made up my mind yet."

"Better had. We could use a good quarter."

"Well, maybe I will. Got to think it over."
"You better come out. So long, Cliff."
"So long, Harley."

❧ CHAPTER 22 ❧

NO, THE JOB IN THE CAFETERIA WASN'T BAD. HE WAS
glad he had strung along with it, even though he'd had
a chance to change it for a better one. The second day
of the term, after he had finished his meal at the waiters'
table, three undergraduates had come into the almost
empty cafeteria: one of them was Malcolm Riggs, manager of the football team, a very handsome, red-haired
fellow with an aquiline, mocking face.

Of the other two, one had a face you could never
remember because you had to look at his clothes: the
immense padded shoulders of his tweed sport coat, his
weird suède shoes, his floppy English pants turned up
at the cuffs so they bagged like a clown's.

The third fellow, slim and quiet, wore the jumper and
bell-bottoms of an apprentice seaman. This man reminded Cliff of some one, he was not sure whom. With
Riggs in the lead, they stalked down the length of the
room like gangsters in a movie, their heels ringing on
the tile floor. They walked up to the waiters' table, up

to Cliff who was staring at them, dipping into a dish of rice pudding, never dreaming that he was the object of their visit.

"Aren't you Clifford Harper?" Riggs said in a light, cultivated voice.

A smile like neon came and went in his slightly contemptuous, poised face.

"Riggs is my name. This is Grosvenor Guild, and John Moffat—Former Private Clifford Harper. Have you got a minute, Harper? Mind if we sit down?"

"We're fortunate in finding you here," Guild said. He was the one in the weird clothes. He sat down beside Cliff, the others facing him across the table.

Moffat made a pattern with the salt cellar and a spoon. He said nothing, but his eyes pushed hard at Cliff's face, moved up to his bristly hair, then down over the sweat-shirt to his hands, reddened with the heat from the steamtables.

Riggs said, "How do you like it, here at Cal. and Western?"

"I haven't been here very long," Cliff said.

Guild laughed as if this were very witty. Instantly, he was serious again.

"Good man," he said, glancing significantly at Moffat.

"He's all right," Moffat said. The way he said this made Cliff wonder once more what person out of the past, somebody close and dear to him, Moffat resembled.

"Harper," Riggs went on, showing no annoyance at the interruption, "we've been looking for you. These gentlemen here and myself, and more of us down at the house—we've heard about you. We'd like you to come down to the house to-night and eat with us."

This entire speech Riggs uttered without inflection, in his light, assured, patrician voice; he spoke with a certain pomposity which was not, however, affected, but seemed proper and ordained for what he said. His ironic, reddish eyes continued to dwell mockingly on Cliff's.

"Well—uh—that's mighty kind of you."

There was a silence. Cliff took a sip of water. He scraped up a dabble of rice pudding with his spoon.

"I generally eat home, nights," he said uncertainly.

He did not know what "house" Riggs had referred to; it was one of the campus fraternities, of course, but he had no idea which; since the three had apparently taken it for granted that he knew, he didn't like to ask. Maybe in a minute they would mention it.

Moffat leaned forward. "Harper," he said with emphasis, "you'd better think this over. We never pressure a pledge, but I'll say this—there's not a better chapter on the campus."

"That's straight from the shoulder, Harper," Riggs put in.

Cliff blinked. To "pressure a pledge"—what kind of talk was that?

"Sigma Nu has a strong crowd," Moffat said. "And so has Chi Psi. But we're close to either one in prestige members, and in some ways stronger. You've heard of Kent-Allsup Tires? Donald Kent is in the house. So is Jarvis Bell, son of J. V. Bell who donated Bellcal Hall."

"You played football, didn't you?" Grosvenor Guild asked suddenly.

"I played some in school," Cliff said.

"That won't do you any harm with us," Riggs said.

All three now had their heads over the table. It was clear they construed Cliff's uncertainty as sales resistance.

"No harm," Moffat conceded, "though as a rule we don't go for athletes. If you bid a man for being an athlete, you may be bidding a jerk. We don't operate that way. We want a crowd that's regular and congenial. As for money, we can get you a house managership that pays as much as you make here, or more."

A ball like wire tightened in Cliff's stomach. He had suddenly remembered who Moffat looked like. Hugo Wrenn! With his thin face and black, curly hair he looked like Hugo, but only enough to make you sick.

"You've got quite a rich crowd, then, I gather," Cliff said slowly, looking around the group. Small hollows had appeared in the flesh under his cheek-bones.

"I'd say it was a well-backed crowd," Moffat said. "We're solid in a money way, but we don't advertise it like some houses I could mention."

"Every one's regular, you don't have to worry about that," Riggs said.

Cliff could not take his eyes off Moffat. Yes, he looked enough like Hugo to be his brother—but this guy was alive and Hugo was lying out there on the island, dead. Moffat was about the same age as Hugo had been—and Moffat wore a uniform too, sitting there talking like a fool.

"I'm not so regular," Cliff heard himself saying. "Maybe I wouldn't mix well with a crowd like that."

Moffat's eyebrows rose humorously; Riggs looked blank. Only Guild showed no reaction.

"Then I take it," Guild said in his phlegmy, indolent way, "that some other house has pledged you?"

"No, sir," Cliff said. He added, after taking thought, "It's been good of you gentlemen to think of me."

Anger crawled inside him. For no reason that he could explain he wanted to kick Moffat's face off so it would stop looking like Hugo's.

Guild looked at Riggs and Moffat, motioning with his

head, and the three rose. Riggs held out his hand: "No hard feelings, Harper. If you'll take a tip from me, I'd say think it over. I believe you'll find you're making a mistake."

"Maybe," Cliff said. He took no notice of Riggs' hand. Picking up his spoon and pudding dish, he took them over to the busboy's wagon.

❧ CHAPTER 23 ❧

RIGGS MIGHT HAVE BEEN RIGHT. POSSIBLY HE WAS MAKING a mistake.

If it had not been for the chance resemblance of that one, that Moffat, to Hugo Wrenn, the proselytizing might have seemed flattering; he might not have insulted the committee. Then, if he had been accepted by the "house" and finally "pledged," he would have had a definite rôle in university life; as it was, he knew he had condemned himself to isolation. Most of the activities of the campus these days were military, only about fifteen per cent of the undergraduates being out of uniform and these because they were refugees who had not yet taken out papers, or because of mental or physical unsuitability to service. No wonder girls on the campus seldom made dates with men who were not members of some military body.

In the first weeks of university life, Cliff had come to a conclusion about the campus girls. They were all beautiful.

At first he thought perhaps he might be kidding himself about this; it might be an idea which had come from being away from women so long. Hadn't he thought the same about the San Francisco girls, his first day ashore? It stood to reason all the girls in a city as big as San Francisco could not be beautiful. All the girls in Cal. and Western could not be beautiful—nevertheless, they were. He had seen a lot of them and had seen none who did not have something that was beautiful in their faces or bodies, in their eyes, their bare legs, their hair, their clothes, their skins. Those who were not training as WACS or WAVES wore a kind of informal uniform consisting on class days of sweaters and plaid or plain wool skirts, bobby socks and saddleshoes; it was a smooth way for girls to dress, and it made a sharp contrast to the way they dressed for Saturday night formals. Then, seeing them in frilly and puffed-out dresses of frail material, brightly made up and wearing little artificial flowers in their hair—then, paired off with fellows, coming out of the sororities and getting into cars to drive to a hotel or country club, or hurrying across the campus to some fraternity where a band was playing and the open doors and windows, yellow in the evening air, showed girls and fellows dancing, laughing, talking, then you would never have known them, then there could not be any argument about the beauty of all of them.

Cliff was not worried about the girl situation. He knew that sooner or later he would get a girl of his own. There was no sense in being in a hurry about it. That was not the way. If you tried to press your luck and force it you might not get the right girl. Sooner or later without any effort on your part you would find one that was right.

That was how it had been when he had begun going with Pat Tracy. She had been right for him even if she had never been wholly and truly his girl. There was no sense thinking about that or trying to find a girl who looked like Pat; to do that would have been to substitute an imitation for something real, it would have been fair to no one.

Besides, there was no such person as Pat. She had been buried out in the jungle.

There were plenty of other girls, millions of them. There were a hundred and thirty million people in the U.S.A. and probably half of them were women. Of these at least a tenth were girls. What was the problem? What was all the worry? There were plenty to go around and sooner or later he would get one. You didn't have to hold out for a special face, a special voice—not unless you were a goddam fool. There were other faces, voices, other girls by the hundreds of thousands and any one of these could make the world look different if you liked her and were going with her.

So the heck with mooning about girls.

There was one girl in his chemistry class whom Cliff admired greatly. Her name was Priscilla Alderman; she was not a good student but was popular and attractive and she had a way with her; she was an officer of her sorority and while in High, a fellow told him, she had just missed being voted Spring Carnival Queen.

Outside of her figure there was nothing flashy about Pris. It was her style, not her beauty, that made her notable. If she had on a sweater, hers would be different from any other girl's; if she greeted any one, recited in class, did her lab work, or just walked along a path, looking up at the fellow with her in the flattering, attentive way she had, she didn't do it in an ordinary fashion. Pris had been born in Texas but she did not have one of those irritating Texas drawls—just a barely perceptible lengthening of certain vowels that was pleasant rather than otherwise. She had ash-blonde hair, but her eyebrows were dark and thick and she did not pluck them.

Cliff often watched Priscilla in the chem lectures; he enjoyed watching her take notes. Completely absorbed, as if she were all alone in the lecture hall, she would listen absently, a slight scowl between her smooth dark brows, her lips pressed tightly together; suddenly remembering where she was she would bend her head and scribble furiously in her notebook, her handwriting spreading all over the page in big, ornamental curlicues.

Always, on the way to and from classes, Pris walked with a fellow and sometimes with two or three, and though Cliff intended speaking to her, he would never have done so when he was intruding.

They became acquainted by accident late one afternoon, back in the stacks of the library. Outside, the Gulf-Stream wind was blowing, gray September clouds flying, and the date-palms on the driveway moving and sighing, but no sound or movement from the outer world penetrated to the labyrinth of stacks, warm and dusty, where so many lives and thoughts were packed away in silent rows. The basement stacks of the library were almost a city block square, and here, crouching to look at the lowest row of books, her skirt pulled round her long bare legs and her whole body compressed into a small tight bundle, Pris was searching for a volume.

Cliff did not see her at first. He had learned his way around the stacks and he came down with his long stride between the shelves, almost stumbling over Pris as he turned a corner. She looked up at him without the least surprise; without moving from her cramped position she asked him where a certain index series, broken in the stacks, began and ended.

"Right over here, I think," Cliff said, outwardly matter-of-fact but secretly pleased by the meeting. It was strange to find a living, breathing girl crouched down here in this dead men's world just as if she had been accidentally shut in when a tomb was closed and had continued, self-sustaining, to live here her warm, intimate, indestructible life.

Almost immediately, with the pride of one who gives directions to a stranger, Cliff located the index numbers Pris wanted. By the time he had obtained his own book, Pris also was ready to leave and they strolled out of the library like old friends, walking into the September wind. When Cliff asked her for a date, the slight scowl he had watched so often appeared on her forehead: she was sorry, she said, but she was busy to-night. She had to sit in on a round-table talk in Bellcal. She was really sorry, she said, because she would have liked to go out with him; her hand lightly brushed his elbow, hoping he would understand.

"Well," he said, "see you in chem."

They had come to a division of the path, and Cliff paused, standing in front of Pris but not looking at her. Once more she touched his arm, and this time she let her fingers stay.

"All right," she said, "if you-all are in such a hurry ..."

"I'm not in any hurry," Cliff said. "Got to catch the bus and get on home, I guess. That's all."

Pris hesitated. "Listen, Cliff. I'm not doing a thing Saturday night, and I just hate to sit home. But I guess you're busy. If you are, I don't mind. Honest. So you tell me. Are you?"

Cliff said he was not busy. On the way home that night he made a number of plans. He would have to get the car for Saturday; that might not be easy since his father liked to drive up to the show Saturday night. Still, he might get it. If he didn't, he and Pris could go on a walk-date. The important thing was, they were going out Saturday night: not a dub-date night, but the best date night of all.

This was just the way he had figured it would be. When the time came for him to have a girl he would get one without thinking about it: it would just happen.

❧ CHAPTER 24 ❧

AS IT TURNED OUT, THERE WAS NO TROUBLE ABOUT getting the car: Mr. and Mrs. Harper were going out with friends to a Rotary Club dance. As a special dispensation Mr. Harper even parted with a B gas coupon.

Cliff dressed carefully in gray slacks, a white shirt and a brown sport coat he had bought recently, taking the money out of the nest-egg of muster-out pay. After fifteen minutes of combing and plastering, his bristly hair, loaded with pomade, stayed down pretty well. He thought he looked pretty fair when, on the stroke of eight, he drove up to Pris's sorority.

Cliff was by no means sure of the etiquette for calling for a girl at a sorority. He supposed that he would have to park the car and go inside to ask for her—but Pris had seen him, she had been watching for him through the window; she came running down the steps just as he pulled up. Before he so much as had time to open the door for her, she was in the car, and she moved right over in the front seat and sat close to him as if they had gone out several times before.

Pris's mouth made a round, smooth O as she blew out cigarette smoke.

"Cliff," she began at once, "do you like Tomlin's? You know, that little dance place out on Crenshaw, where the kids go. I kind of like it," she went on with a little laugh, as if such a taste in dancing places might be amusing to persons of such sophistication as herself and Cliff. "It's kind of fun. We could drop in there for a little while, and then if you don't like it, why, we could go somewhere else."

Cliff took thought. He welcomed the suggestion, yet it seemed to him unworthy of a knowing escort to accept feminine guidance without some examination.

"Is that a juke-box place?"

Pris nodded. "In a way it is," she said, a slight anxiety tinging her voice. "Only, they have keen records. Lots of Frank Sinatra's, and some dreamy stuff. It's not a joint," she added firmly. "But if you don't like juke-places..."

"I don't mind," Cliff said tolerantly. Now that his authority was established he could ease up. "I don't mind a juke-spot, if it's not a joint."

Tomlin's neon topped a small slate-roofed building built in imitation of a French châlet. Inside, the walls were paneled in dark wood; a bar covered one side of the room and stained-oak dining booths the other three. Juke-slots were set in the wall above each table, and in the center of the room was a small hardwood dance floor.

Near the door, in a booth which had been extended with an extra table, sat ten or a dozen girls and fellows, most of whom Cliff recognized as members of the freshman class. The fellows, without exception, were in training uniforms, and they outnumbered the girls nearly two to one. What the women of this party lacked in quantity, however, they made up in beauty and, by campus standards, social importance: Cliff recognized two who had been pointed out to him as holding office in the class Council and Entertainment Committee.

Somewhat shy of this group, he had taken Pris's elbow to direct her to an empty booth in the back of the room when a fellow at the big table jumped up.

"Hi ho, Silver," he said solemnly. "Look who's here, kids. Little ole Texas."

"Don't be such a dope, Bert," Pris said calmly. She stood at the foot of the table, nodding and smiling first-name greetings around the group while one of the fellows placed two extra chairs for Cliff and herself. "This is Cliff," she said, rattling off a rapid string of first-name introductions, "Marge, Jack, Ernie, Dave—"

Cliff had no way of attaching the names to the individual faces, but Pris had already taken her place at the table.

"Well," she said, drawing a long breath of pleasure, firmly establishing herself in the group as she favored all equally with her expectant party-smile. "H'are y'all?" she said, burlesquing her own drawl and, at the same time, the fellow who had burlesqued her. The fellows laughed and the girls smiled politely, as if paying tribute to a person who was not considered easy competition.

"Where's Steve?" the fellow named Bert tactlessly inquired. "What did he do, Pris, run out on you?"

"He had to spend the week-end with his folks in Long Beach," Pris stated. She flicked a split-second glance at Cliff to see how he had taken this reference to an absent escort.

"Two cokes," she swiftly commanded a waiter who had just come up behind her. "Let's dance, Cliff."

Some one had fed the juke-box, and the strains of a hot band flooded the room.

"They're all dreamy kids, really a keen crowd," Pris said, lifting her arms in a stylized way to embrace Cliff, leaning the firmness of her body against him. "You'll like them when you know them. They're all keen about you."

"Me?" Cliff said, startled. "I never spoke to any of them in my life. I don't know them from Adam."

"They know you, though," Pris said positively. "Anyway, most of them have heard about you. You'll see. We'll have a swell time."

Cliff made a misstep. He had been a fair dancer before he enlisted, but he was out of practice; he knew that never, even at his best, had he been as good as the kids who were now cutting loose with specialties all around him.

"Couldn't we get out," he said, "and sort of drive around?"

"Why, surely, Cliff," Pris said somewhat coldly. "We can if you want to. Only, let's stay for a while. At least till we have a few dances. Isn't that all right?"

"Whatever you say, Pris," Cliff retorted gallantly.

They danced in silence till the end of the number, then started back to the table; becoming separated from

Pris in the crowd, Cliff found with some surprise that he was sitting down alone.

Pris had been cut in on by the fellow named Bert and was now dancing with him.

One man in an apprentice seaman's blouse and another in Army uniform were at the table drinking beer. Cliff beckoned to the ancient waiter.

"Bring me a slug of rum for this coke, Dad."

The sailor and the Army guy looked at Cliff speculatively. In collegiate circles hard liquor was seldom drunk: the hard stuff had been the prerogative of a past era, lacking in a serious outlook. It was not good form.

The Army guy leaned forward. "Pardon me, sir. Do you mind if I ask you a question?"

Cliff blinked. He was not sure at first that the fellow was talking to him.

"Weren't you in the Tulagi engagement? We were just having an argument about it, and I understood from Priscilla that you were in that engagement."

Cliff shook his head. "I was at another place down there."

But the fellow in the Army uniform went on to make his point. "My brother fought at Tulagi," he said proudly. "He's three years older than I am. He was wounded twice and got the Purple Heart."

The waiter brought the rum, and the sailor half-rose from his seat, pulling out his wallet. "I wish you'd let me buy this round, sir."

Cliff put thirty-five cents on the waiter's tray. "Thanks just the same," he said.

He didn't get this, the way these fellows talked. Evidently Pris had been publicizing him ... but the way they talked made him feel a hundred years old. Nobody had ever called him "sir" before.

He had felt like a dumb kid when the upper-classmen were patronizing him, trying to make him join a fraternity. Yet with these freshmen suddenly he was a "sir"!

Wasn't there any in-between age he could be?

All three sat silent, watching the dance floor. Pris was dancing beautifully with Bert, a smooth dancer: they did not cut loose but moved close together in a complicated series of steps, subdued in style but strongly rhythmed. Pris looked as beautiful as a girl dancing could look.

"My, I'm thirsty," she cried, stopping beside the table as the record ended. "Where's my coke? Did any of you thieves take it?"

Bert was mopping his face, but Pris looked as cool as when she had begun to dance. She drank a few swallows through a straw while the apprentice seaman came around and stood beside her chair.

"You and me, Pris?"

"Why don't you ask Cliff?" Pris said. "He's my date," she stated with a shimmering mock-severity. "Ask him. Maybe he'd like a dance himself."

She flashed a smile at Cliff, signaling him with her eyes to refuse the sailor's request, to say that he wanted the next dance himself. Thus she was making up for dancing with Bert but at the same time putting the burden of refusal on Cliff. This he rejected.

"Go ahead," he said. "It's okay by me."

With the sailor, Pris's dance routine was entirely different although just as effective as before, slower in pattern with long, swinging steps and spinning breakaways. She could really cut it. While Cliff watched, he had another rum and coke, and presently he had another. The Army fellow who had talked to him was also dancing and two other guys were at the table; Cliff ignored them, drinking without pleasure, feeling the liquor hardening inside him like a shell which cut him off from people. In an hour he had another dance with Pris, then sat the evening out with stubborn boredom, drinking one rum and coke after another, replying with bare politeness when talk was directed at him.

The party broke a little after twelve, by which time Pris had been dancing with scant interruption for more than three hours. When the men had paid the separate checks Pris took Cliff's arm, vetoing Bert's suggestion that they join those who were going to a drive-in for chili or sandwiches. As before, she slid over in the seat, pressed against Cliff's right side, but he did not respond. He drove silently, ignoring her chatter about the people they had left.

"What's the matter?" she asked at length, a slight ominous chill in her voice. "You're not mad at something, are you, Cliff?"

"What would I have to be mad about?"

"I don't know. Nothing, I guess. Only you seemed so . . . I don't know."

"I'm not mad."

"They're a dreamy crowd, aren't they? Isn't Marge Stevens too adorable?"

Marge Stevens, a striking brunette, was the only girl of the party except Pris that Cliff had danced with.

"She's good-looking. All those women are good-looking. They're all good dancers. So are the fellows."

"Gee, I'm glad you thought so. I was—I don't know."

"Go ahead. You were what?"

"I guess I thought you were mad."

"What would I have to get mad about?"

"Why, nothing, Cliff. Honest, honey, nothing at all."

The drawl, always noticeable when she was coquetting, was back.

"All right," Cliff said stiffly. "I'm not mad."

"I'm glad of that, Cliff," Pris said with coolness.

There was a pause of some seconds, after which she said, "But I think you're foolish to be mad." She left his side and moved over to her own corner, curling up with her legs on the seat.

When they reached the sorority Cliff leaned over and opened the door.

"Well, good night," he said.

"Good night, Cliff," Pris said. "Thanks for the evening. It was swell."

"Thank *you*."

Making no move to get out, Pris said in a direct voice, "Is that the way you want it to be, Cliff?"

"Is it the way I want what to be?"

"This. Aren't you going to 'phone me?"

"Sure," Cliff said. "I'll call you next time your steady has to go somewhere and you get stuck."

Pris sat silently, hoping Cliff would apologize and try to make up. He knew he could have kissed her, but instead he opened the door so that she could get out of the car.

Driving home, the liquor made him feel dull and angry. Jesus, what a dopy evening! He hadn't belonged, that was all. He didn't blame Pris. She had wanted a date and he had been a temporary convenience. It was his own fault that he had taken offense at her flirtatious ways; he had sat there like a bump on a log while the rest of them had a good time.

Well, if that was their idea of a swell time they could count him out. Those guys calling him "sir," and the gals acting stiff and formal as if he was a professor or something. Rain on all that.

He drove slowly down Wilshire, looking at the big lights blooming silently on their long stalks along the empty boulevard. Suddenly Cliff pulled over to the curb. He fumbled in all his pockets for his money, and when he had found it, he pulled it out and counted it to see if he still had enough to stop by Madame Java's on the way home.

❧ CHAPTER 25 ❧

MRS. KINCHELOE, PERRY'S MOTHER, FILLED THE TINY chair so that you couldn't see the frame of it, only the flow of Mrs. Kincheloe's body, encased in her black Sunday rayon dress, a mountain of descending folds. She rocked ever so slightly, eyes creased in the puckers of her ancient face, her ageless billowing body steeped in the Sunday lull of the hospital.

Watching over her boy Perry through the hot September afternoon, Mrs. Kincheloe kept on the outskirts of Perry's talk with the three white men. They had brought him magazines, a carton of cigarettes, a small potted plant which would flourish beside the high iron bed, its health betokening his own. Matt Klein, who came almost daily, since his place of business, the Klein

Super Market, was not far away, sat near the foot of the bed, listening to Cliff hold forth.

As usual Cliff was harping on his idea of the power that service men would have by staying together after combat. Sometimes when speaking on this topic he became a little wild. Going to college had by no means lessened its importance to him; rather he felt more than ever that these meetings, when he and his friends gathered around Perry's bed, were the best part of the whole week. The air would grow thick with smoke, as no sick-room ever should, and fierce but companionable arguments would often develop.

Sometimes Gunny would egg Cliff on. He would ask if Cliff meant to start a little war, and then Cliff would get hot. An unsuspected power of words would awake in him. No, he would tell Gunny seriously, he was not hostile to anything or anybody—all he wanted was to make sure no one was gypped.

"You're doin' all right," Gunny would say, winking at Matt. "Going to college like a little gentleman, aren't you? What have you got to complain about?"

That was when Cliff got mad. It was not a question of any one man's right, it was the question of all their rights. Twelve and a half million service men weren't going to be gypped this time. They weren't against anything but they were *for* something, and if any wisenheimer tried to slip over a fast one it was going to be too bad. Nobody wanted any trouble and a little war was the last thing in Cliff's mind, but if some smartypants in Washington commenced a double-cross, then, brother, let her rip. Get out the half-tracks, get the tanks, bring the grenades and hand them out. You didn't want a little war, but a democracy was of the people and by the people, and you were the people and never let any one tell you different.

Cliff tried hard to make clear what was in his mind. The trouble was when he tried to put it into words the idea lost substance. It became an old-fashioned, nihilistic scheme or else some chivalrous crap about one for all and all for one like the old-time musketeers. Still, there must be some way it would work—if only for the four of them (or the five if Bill Tabeshaw ever came back). They could still meet like this and talk things over, and it was a help somehow. It eased off the confusion bred in him because of his struggles at the university; it helped wipe out the feeling that he was a misfit, belonging nowhere, a member of no generation, and an exile in the land he had defended. Yes, sir, the old group was still a great combine.

All the time Cliff was talking Perry listened with great interest, his eyes glistening in his creased, black face. Suddenly his right arm shot up and gripped the iron bar over his bed. This bar was slung to uprights hung above the middle of the bed parallel to the sides. By seizing it Perry could move his body in the bed, shift it from side to side or even turn over without help.

"Cliff, you got something there," he said. "You got a right idea! You work it out good, and you'll get a lot of guys on your side. I'll be right along with you."

Perry's eyes were not those of a man who had met with defeat. His eyeballs were glistening white, not yellowish as they sometimes are in men of his race. They had the shadows of atrocious pain in them and were no longer like a young man's eyes, but they were living, bold, and soft, still vital with the comradeship and confidence which of old had made him an exceptional man.

Of his great strength, only one arm was left, a giant's arm, developed even past its former huge proportions by his daily task of pulling himself on the bar over his bed. Smooth-skinned, intricately corded, hairless, hugely veined, the arm might have been designed by Michelangelo; it served Perry's needs with an impersonal power which seemed self-generated rather than the product of the reduced body to which it was attached.

Perry had lost the other arm and both legs.

It was great to see old Perry feeling so well. The amputations he had suffered had not diminished him; rather they had constrained his fires in a smaller space, thus concentrating them for repair work. It was hard to think of him as a person who would never walk again. He was still a man, though only the hulk of one. Besides three limbs, he had lost only one element—his nickname: it was no longer possible to call him Five-by-Five because he had lost his former square dimensions. He was now, literally, broader than he was tall.

The three visitors sat smoking and talking, and all the while the vast billowing Negress with her ageless mother-face sat watching and listening, putting in a word when her son demanded it but otherwise silent, brooding with unsorrowful pride over the picture of Perry talking as an equal with his friends. Twilight glazed the glass sides of the solarium; the bedlight was turned on; Perry's supper was brought and he ate while he talked, relishing his food, glad of the presence of his friends. And all the while the huge, unsmiling Negro woman sat alone and silent in her pride of her son. So long as she was there, so long as her large body filled the shadows, rocking with an inner song, Perry would prosper, life would pour into him like plasma from his mother's strength; he would not die even if the doctors operated until nothing was left of him but a frame of ribs.

At last the nurse came in to say that visiting hours were over, the friends must go. Outside the hospital they stood shaking hands with Matt, asking him where he'd been keeping himself, why he didn't call a guy once in a while. What was the idea?

"I been cutting meat, that's where I been," Matt said. "Cut all day, and get up at five o'clock and go down to the wholesale market, trying to buy enough to keep my customers. What do I do nights? Close up the store and try to figure where I am on ration points. Boy, there are times I wish I was back in that jungle."

In spite of his complaints, Matt looked prosperous. He had put weight on. His fleshy face was now almost as red as his hair, and his light-colored eyes had lost some of their challenging glare at the world. Matt was doing all right.

"Been making any more allotments, Matt?" Gunny asked as the three strolled over to the parking lot.

Matt groaned. "Don't remind me of that."

"Listen," Gunny said, "I know a cocktail bar where you'd be right at home. They got one, two dozen B-girls in there every night. No kidding, it's a natural for you. A couple of hours there, and you could pick up some broad and settle down for the rest of your life."

"Okay, Sarge," Matt said, "I'll come over some night and get you to pimp me up a couple. If that's the line you're in now, I want you to make a living."

Cliff laughed until he nearly doubled up. It was like old times, to hear Sarge and Matt tangle.

"No kidding," Gunny said, "I was in the store the other afternoon. Figured I'd nick you for a bottle of beer. You weren't there, but there was a big blonde dame back of the cash desk. She had what it takes. Are you getting that?"

"That's a hell of a question for a used-up old bastard to be asking. I don't try to find out what you're getting, do I?"

"All I said was, she's put up like a brick outhouse. I figured maybe you was gettin' it—unless she's going with a couple of other guys with good allotments."

Cliff roared again. That Gunny sure could rub it in, but Matt just looked sheepish and said the blonde dame worked for him. She punched a cash register and time clock. That was all he knew about her. He said stop in any time, that beer was always on tap. They could go in the back room and the hell with the customers. So saying he climbed into the old-fashioned truck, lettered KLEIN'S SUPERMARKET, and plowed solemnly away into the ocean twilight.

Gunny's high spirits didn't last long. Lately he had lacked his old-time dash, his gift for devastating comebacks: Cliff had not been able to get to the poolroom much; when he had, his games with Gunny hadn't been so much fun. Sometimes the Sarge had been half lit up on beer; at other times he had been preoccupied and irritable.

Driving home, Cliff was thinking about something Perry had said—that he would get out of the hospital before long: he asked the Sarge whether there was any likelihood of this.

Gunny snorted.

"Get out?" he said with bitterness. "How would he get out? Do you think they'll send a nurse out with him to push him around in a wheel-chair like a millionaire? Brother, that guy is in for life."

"But Christ, Sarge, they can't keep him there forever. He's bedridden, that's all. He's not sick. He can't stay in a hospital."

"He might go to the Domiciliary."

"The Domiciliary? What's that?"

"Where they put disabled veterans when they got no home to go to and ain't sick enough to stay in hospital. Didn't you ever see that Home in Sawtelle?"

"Yes," Cliff said, a bad image rising in his mind, "I've seen that."

"Well, that's a Domiciliary. Only that's for Army guys."

"God, Sarge, they wouldn't put him in a place like that, would they?"

"Where else would they put him?"

Cliff shook his head, not believing it. The Veterans' Home in Sawtelle was a place he had passed often on the way to the beach. It was a large establishment, set back in handsome, well-kept grounds, yet there was something horrible, ghoulish about it. The big, old-fashioned, shingled buildings, built in a rococo style, were shabby and desolate as if existing in a stratum of lost time, erected for some purpose long forgotten by all living men. Once painted an orange color (as nearly as any one could guess), the buildings of the Domiciliary of Sawtelle were weathered to a natural wood shade; rusted screens gaped with holes, windows looked down from cracked frames on to the sleek modern boulevard crowded with pleasure cars.

Sitting in the rumble seat of some guy's car, glowing with health and carrying his lunch and bathing-trunks, Cliff had passed the Sawtelle Veterans' Home hundreds of times. Perry, too, since he was a Los Angeles fellow, was no doubt equally familiar with it.

Could it be true that Five-by-Five would now be put away in such a place?

Even chopped down to the bare, grisly stub of a fighting man, you could not imagine Five-by-Five among those shades. For the worst part of the Veterans' Home in Sawtelle was its inhabitants. No matter how fast, how light-heartedly you passed by, you could not help seeing them as they walked around the grounds with slow steps or sat on the benches returning the curious glances of the people in the cars. They were soldiers of World War I, fed and housed in what Gunny now denoted with this strange word—the Domiciliary. Those you saw outside could walk, but some had to be helped and often they would help each other, as the walking wounded Cliff had seen so often helped each other on a battle-field. In fact, around the men of Sawtelle stretched the perpetual boundaries of battle-fields now twenty-five years old.

Was there some dreadful potency about a battle-field? Once it came into being, did it continue, keep on claiming victims independent of the laws of time or the limitations of geography? Were the gray men of Sawtelle still citizens of a smoky place of carnage, still in some fashion living in it, far from the sunlight, the politely landscaped grounds, the iron benches, the sleek cars of beach-goers—as he, Cliff, and Gunny and Five-by-Five were citizens of the island jungle?

The men of Sawtelle, crawling with old men's feet on their shadowy battle-field, no longer looked like soldiers. They dressed in threadbare civilian clothes; their hands were uncertain, their skins a dusty indoor color; their eyes were not those of warriors. They pushed each other's wheel-chairs; they helped each other; sometimes with the raffish echo of their valiant wartime comradeship, they traded jokes, hopes and memories; they gambled for charity pennies, playing blackjack and poker with old packs of greasy cards.

Above all, they waited. Behind them, visible through a screen of trees, stretched the enormous cemetery where their comrades lay. It was a very handsome cemetery, splendidly kept up and adorned with a notable nickname: "The Marble Orchard." Nearly every day a new grave was dug there, yet the Marble Orchard kept increasing its crop. It took, apparently, an interminable time to get the harvest in; meanwhile, there were plenty of old soldiers in the Domiciliary of Sawtelle.

To imagine Five-by-Five in a place like that was awful. It could never happen, even if Gunny said it would. Cliff thought about it all the way home, trying in his thoughts to make a barricade which would prevent this happening to his friend. Surely, for a Marine like Five-by-Five, there must be some other destiny in store. There must be something somebody could do to keep him from entombment in a place like that.

CHAPTER 26

GUNNY OFTEN CAME DOWN TO WATCH FOOTBALL PRACtice. He got to be quite a friend of Mike Petrillo, the head coach. Mike was a bona fide veteran of the First War, having lost an arm at Belleau Wood. He would always find time to sit with Gunny for a chat.

Cliff got used to having the Sarge there. Waiting for the ball to be passed he would glance over at the stocky figure of the Sarge seated in the stand, pipe in mouth: if any member of his family had tried to watch practice he would not have liked it, yet having the Sarge on hand helped him to play.

Doc Damion, Faculty Adviser on Athletics, had suggested football as a therapeutic measure. When Cliff came in for the check-up given all freshmen, Doc had already looked into his medical discharge.

"Mind," the Doc said, "if you hadn't played in High I wouldn't be suggesting it, but from what I gather you were quite something. Mike Petrillo needs a bigger squad. Go down and report to him and tell him I sent you. How's your health, other than these symptoms we've discussed? Any headaches, nightmares, anything like that? How do you feel in general?"

Cliff said he felt fine.

"Thought so," the Doc said, running his eye over Cliff's big, lean frame. Built more like an oarsman than a football player, he reflected; a mistake to use him in the backfield. With legs like that he'd have plenty of speed.

Dean-of-Freshman Jervis Walters had not agreed with Doc Damion's recommendation in regard to Cliff. He voiced his doubts one afternoon a week later, falling in step beside the doctor as the two were leaving a Faculty Meeting.

Though the Dean expressed himself with tact, Dr. Damion bridled somewhat.

"I assure you, Jervis, I went over the boy carefully."

Dean Jervis said, "I think we've all been interested,

148

and for good reason. He's the first-comer of a pretty big flock."

Dr. Damion looked up at the huge electric clock of Bellcal Hall. One minute to four! Already, lined up in the corridor outside his office in the gym, the candidates for Aviation H would be waiting for examination. He needed at least four assistants and here he was, getting along with one—and only last week that idiot Forester had gone and got himself drafted.

"I agree, sir. Nevertheless, good healthful exercise . . ."

"It only occurred to me," Walters said, "that football with a play-pattern so much like combat might not be just . . ."

"It won't hurt him, Jervis. Take my word for it."

"Then his symptoms aren't psychic in origin?"

"Remotely," Dr. Damion said. "He has a peripheral tremor: it's an auto-hypnotic condition. Memories, suggestions bring it on. Down in the Southwest Stadium he can't go around brooding. . . ."

The Dean's light smile was not reflected in his eyes.

"Ah," he said gently. "That, sir, I can well believe."

As he turned up the steps of Bellcal, the big clock began to strike the hour.

The slow melodious strokes winged heavily over the campus, the last one fading in protracted ripples of sound. Cliff, late for practice, hurried toward the locker room, peeling off his sweat-shirt as he dashed down the gym hall lined with verdigrised trophies in glass cases, ancient footballs with dates chalked on the grainy faces, immolated on plush frames like flies in amber. In the steamy, chlorine-sweat-and-sour-clothes smell of the locker room the squad had already left the blackboard; a managerial candidate in a sweat-suit and baseball cap was rubbing off the O's and X's of the chalk talk.

Jimmy Tracy, standing near Head Coach Petrillo, jerked his head by way of greeting and Cliff winked a response. Working out with Jimmy in the backfield every day had relieved him of his previous uneasiness in the latter's presence.

Cliff put on a combed-yarn union suit and over this adjusted carefully the elastics of his pads, fixing them so they wouldn't chafe under the arms. Over the pads he pulled a gray sweater, its color the only designation which, this year, distinguished freshmen from the older fellows on the squad. Because of a shortage of material, League rules now permitted freshmen to play varsity ball, but Coach Petrillo had not as yet lowered tradition to the point of issuing gold-and-maroon varsity sweaters to unproven players.

Alone with three other late-comers, he jerked on his shoes, hastily laced the rawhide laces, then felt something hard in one of the shoes, unlaced it and shook it. Nothing fell out; must have been a wrinkle in his sock. As he ran up the tunnel to the field he heard the drum of a punt; in the sky above the field the ball rose in an indolent arc, a brand-new ball, unstained by grass, not yet spit on or handled, its clear brown-yellow skin as hard as metal. The ball hesitated at the top of its flight, then tilted toward the first-string quarterback, Eph Nirdlinger, who caught it without moving. Cliff ran out of the tunnel; he grabbed a helmet out of the manager's hand-cart and turned toward the backfield candidates standing near the bench, passing another ball around to warm up till Mike called a scrimmage. As he ran he pumped his knees high, getting the kinks out of his legs, feeling the cleats of his new Spalding shoes dig into the turf. One of the backs tossed him a slow pass and he ran out under it, caught it with perfect timing over his left shoulder; he feinted as if to dodge a tackle, then pivoted and whipped the ball back in a straight, hard line. His arm was right, and there was power and release in the act of throwing. It felt good to be playing ball again.

CHAPTER 27

"CLIFF'S IN THE STARTING LINE-UP," GUNNY SAID. HE folded the sports section carefully and put it on the table.

"Starting what, Earl?" Emmy asked. Bringing the coffee pot so he could have a third cup if he wanted, she sat down beside him in the nine-o'clock sun.

"Game down at the Stadium."

"That's fine," Emmy said. She poured a little of the coffee into her own cup, then asked with a curious timidity, "Are you going to the game, dear? It might be nice for you."

"I can't go to-day, Mother."

There was trouble in Emmy's face, the patient ledger on which life had written so much.

"Sonny could stay with me this afternoon, if you felt like going. I was just going to darn some of Harry's things."

Emmy had worried about Gunny for some time past. He had been unlike himself, irritable to the point of speaking roughly now and then—something that had happened seldom in the whole course of their life together. And at night, he had been restless: Emmy had heard him leave his cot bed in the hall annex and prowl around the living-room.

It had been nearly two weeks since they had enjoyed one of their after-breakfast chats; even the delicacies cadged from Harry's ration-budget had not tempted Gunny. She planned for the day when his strange mood would pass, when he would wait at the table after Harry's leave-taking for one of their gentle, aimless periods of idleness and talk, the last fragment left of their life-time closeness. Against this day, Emmy had saved some little sausages of a kind her husband liked especially; to-day she had cooked them for him, but they lay on his plate untasted. Gunny had eaten hardly any breakfast at all; he had on his herring-bone suit—the first time he had worn it since his arrival.

Emmy did not understand. With the same strained and touching timidity as before she asked, "Is anything the matter, Earl?"

Gunny did not look at her.

"I'm going out to Hilldale to-day, Mother."

"Oh . . ."

Emmy turned over this information without getting any clue from it. Hilldale, a suburb located in the San Fernando Valley, twenty miles or so from town, was a defense-plant center.

"What time will you be back, Earl?"

"I've taken a room out there, Emmy."

Emmy's expression showed no change. She peered uncertainly at Gunny in the morning light, waiting for the explanation which must surely qualify this statement.

"You mean, a room to work in?"

Once, on a furlough many years ago, Gunny had talked about retiring from the service, setting up a machine-shop. This was all that came to Emmy's mind now as a possible translation of what he said.

"No, Mother. A room to live in. I'm going to move out for a while." Gunny picked up a fork, tentatively touched the sausages with it. "I got me a job," he said, "out at Horizon Aircraft."

Now it was out: at last he'd said it. He looked heavily at Emmy, seeing pain lumber its slow way into her eyes like a dull, corrupt, and dark-winged bird.

"Horizon..." she said. "Way out there..." She moved her head weakly from side to side, but the dark bird would not take flight. "Going away from your home, Earl," she said with terror. "How can that be?"

Gunny waited. His next words would be the final test, the answer to his challenge, his stand against the strange betrayal of his years with Emmy.

He had thought it over a thousand times. He had gone to sleep with it and awakened with it in the night, sitting alone to think and smoke until he thought his head would split. It was the only way. Though far from being an inarticulate man, the gulf between words and his own emotions was not one that he could readily bridge. Even if he messed up what he had to say, if the test failed, he would still go away as he had said he would.

No other course was open. He could not tell Emmy that since coming home he had sustained a wound more severe than any he had suffered in his campaigns—the feeling, ruinous to male pride, of being supplanted. In his absence his son Harry had become the head of the house and he, Gunny, a tolerated, permanent intruder.

While he was unable thus to clarify it to himself, his reaction when it did come—as it had in recent weeks—was as clear as a battle directive.

He must go.

Here at home, destruction waited. To him, a man still knit together strongly, uselessness was ruin: he would be a nothing, an old some-one puttering around a bungalow yard, going to the grocery, minding a baby....A baby! Here lurked, possibly, the final ambush, closing tighter each day because of his possessing, ever-growing love for his grandson, Sonny.

Pretty soon he would give in to it, if he stayed home. He would get to exist for that baby, yielding himself to the mother-instincts which are also part of fatherhood.

If that happened he would be done for: no getting away then, no power for decisions. Then he would be really through.

So now the test. Gunny had planned this part of it. He knew he might mess it up, but he had figured in advance how he would make the test of his wife, Emmy.

He put his arm around the back of her chair, sitting as they had sat so often when there was a problem to be settled.

"Think you can come with me, Em?"

Once more Emmy's head moved in that aimless way from side to side. She had the air of a trapped creature—and Gunny was part of the trap.

She said gently and yet warily, "I don't know, Earl. ...I don't know just what you mean. Out to Hilldale," she said vaguely, trying to gain time. "How could I live out there?"

She too knew it was a test. And Gunny allowed no evasion.

"We could live together," he said. "Like we used to.

You could keep house there instead of here. It would be sort of a change, for both of us."

In Emmy's brain, the wings of the black bird spread wider. Once, perhaps even a few years ago, she could have met the test required of her as she had met all others in her life with Gunny, many of them no less torturing.

This one she could not meet. Something had gone out of her that would have given her the power. Until this moment she had not known that it was gone. Gunny, too, thinking of her as she was when younger (what man who has loved one woman will not do this?), had not been sure either.

In a slow and halting voice, abandoning her rights, yielding to the sickness which had turned her toward her son and away from her husband, Emmy made the rejection. "I would go, Earl. I would. Only, they need me here. . . . You can make out, but I have to be here or they couldn't get along. Couldn't you do some other way?" she said, groping sickly for a compromise. "Couldn't you ride out there on the bus? Or take a job nearer town?"

Gunny did not move for several seconds. Then, at last, he took his arm away from his wife's chair. He pushed back his own chair, rising to his feet.

"No, Em," he said. Mechanically he took out his pipe, fingered it, then put it back in his pocket.

"Well," he said, "got to be going. . . ."

Emmy took a quick step after him, and Gunny paused.

"Earl, you won't be gone long? You'll be home weekends, won't you, and some evenings? Won't you?"

"Sure, Mother, sure," Gunny said. He put his arms around her, feeling the small dry sobs knotting in her chest.

"Take it easy, Em," he said. "Nothing to cry over, just a job to keep me busy for a while."

"I know, Earl, I know," Emmy said, clutching him, her lips against his chin. "Only it's so different. I don't know. You going away like this."

"I'll get home as often as I can," he said. "I'll be home quite a bit. So just take it easy. Nothing to cry over, Mother. Nothing in the world."

CHAPTER 28

ON THE DAY HE LEFT HOME, FORMER GUNNERY SERGEANT Earl W. Watrous had some four hundred and fifty dollars on deposit with the Bank of America—a sum which was less by a hundred dollars than it had been a short time previously. The accounts of Matt Klein and Cliff Harper, each fairly formidable a few months back, also showed hundred-dollar deductions: the withdrawals had been lumped together and presented in a brown manila envelop to Mrs. Kincheloe. Before the end of the week on which the presentation had been made, Mrs. Kincheloe vacated a furnished room she had been occupying in the southeast part of town, paying a year's rent on a two-room bungalow on Mount Auburn Street. Here—after the place had been inspected by a Rehabilitation Officer from the Veterans Administration—she brought her son Perry home to live with her.

Old Five-by-Five was going to be all right. He wasn't going to any Domiciliary.

Getting the money had been the easiest part. It had been the first practical demonstration of what the guys could do by working as a unit. There had been many other conditions to meet, forms to fill out, Bureau officials to be talked to. For a man whose life was to be motionless, Perry needed considerable equipment: a wheelchair, various bed utensils, and a special bed, one rigged up with the bar on which he could pull himself around. The Outpatient Department of the hospital had supplied some of these items: the bed, for instance, and the wheelchair (which was returnable and had to be signed for), but the utensils had to be paid for out of Perry's hundred and fifty-seven dollars a month disability allowance.

A neighborhood plumber had made the bar for the bed and the trestles to hold it, refusing—when he learned what it was for—to accept any pay. The plumber was a Negro and a member of the Brothers of Jehovah Church, to which Mrs. Kincheloe also belonged: the afternoon Mrs. Kincheloe brought Perry home the plumber had come over to the bungalow to make sure the bar would properly serve its purpose. He had stayed to help Matt Klein and Gunny carry Perry out of Matt's car and put him in the bed. Later on Cliff had come over, and Mrs. Kincheloe, a welcoming song for her son swelling in her vast body, had cooked them all a roast pork dinner with boiled greens and black-eyed peas and a molasses cake which she had learned to make before she got sick and tired of cooking in other people's houses and went to work as a machine operator in the XLent Laundry.

It was a fine homecoming, fitting complement to the magnificent manner in which Perry had said his farewells at the hospital, the nurses and even the doctors coming out into the hall to shake hands with him. Other patients, the Marine and Navy veterans who had met and talked to him in the Solarium (and some who had never set eyes on him but had heard the fame of the black man cut down to a stump of bone and gristle who had nonetheless refused to leave in the Outpatient Ambulance, saying he would go out "under his own power") had shouted to him from the wards,

"So long, Five-by-Five." . . . "Good-by, Leatherneck. Good luck." . . . "So long, Perry." . . . "Take it easy, black boy." . . . "Keep punching." . . .

And to this last admonition Perry, being wheeled past the open door of the ward in the chair he was "borrowing" for life, had called back in his deep silky voice, "Only got one arm to punch with now, friend, but she's a good one. . . ."

This evening of the homecoming banquet in Perry's honor was both joyful and sad for Cliff. In one sense he was happier than he had been for weeks, secure in the solidarity of comradeship with his three friends; on the other hand, Gunny had told him that morning of his plan to move to Hilldale and work for Horizon. Cliff felt with the sureness of premonition that the four of them would never be together again. In the service their actions had been interrelated, their destinies inseparable, and until now this feeling of group identity, though thinned and impaired, had somehow persisted. Yet the feeling had been oriented around Gunny. With the Sarge somewhere else the unity was broken, and henceforth even the thinnest remnant of group closeness seemed to be denied them.

One strand, however, was laid down that evening which, through the autumn months, bound Cliff closely to Perry. Cliff had brought a special present to the home-coming banquet—a small, second-hand radio by means of which his friend could listen to the games; when the two were together in the bungalow on Mount Auburn Street, they would discuss what had happened in the Stadium the previous afternoon.

"What for you played so far up on that punt? How come you let that guy boot over your head?"

Perry, a student of sports pages, would make complaints, ask questions, hand out praise and compliments, and Cliff would come back with explanations, answers, acknowledgments.

"Heck, man, that Oregon full never booted that far in his life. The wind caught that ball."

At times Perry's laugh would spiral out of his chopped-off body, starting deep in the barrel of his chest and sliding up to a vibrating, velvety shimmer.

"You better git rid of that wind, Cliff boy. You better know how hard them backs can boot when you-all play S.C."

That September and October, playing the early games in the warm polleny sunshine, Cliff would think about Perry lying in the bed with the bar over it and listening. Sometimes after a good play he would grin to himself, thinking, "Old Five-by-Five will like that one...." And after a fumble by Cal. and Western or a run by the opponents, he would arm himself with an alibi. Football seemed to have more connection with real things when he remembered Perry lying there and listening to it. Also, this thought helped when, at times, in spite of all that he could do, the combat feeling took possession of his nerves while he was in a game.

CHAPTER 29

ANGULAR CLOUDS SHOULDERED EACH OTHER PONDEROUSLY in the sky which cupped the smaller oval of the Stadium. Now and then the masses of vapor parted, letting through a burst of brilliant cold light in which the field with its wide lateral strips seemed to expand like an accordion, only to shrink again as the fissure was closed. For almost an hour, veering up and down the quilt of stripes in calculated, savagely kinetic patterns, the two teams had played without a score, watched by a dispirited scattering of spectators who filled less than a third of the immense tiered stand. Cliff, who had hurt his ankle the week before, sat on the bench, a blanket pulled over his head; next to him, the student manager hunched in a raincoat, chattered incessantly, discussing every play as if he were broadcasting. Between the first and second quarters he took a folded newspaper out of his pocket and showed Cliff a story he had planted, naming "Harper, the Marine Vet" as a mainstay of the Cal. and Western backfield.

Cliff didn't care about press stories. In High School he'd had his picture in the paper several times and felt pretty big about it. What he wanted to do now was play ball, whether the papers wrote him up or not. Out on the field S.C. was kicking off, and Nirdlinger dropped back a step or two and made the catch. Holding the ball against his belly he stood motionless, his eyes sweeping the incoming tacklers, no strain in his face, poised with a bull-fighter's calculated insolence against the rush of bodies. Two S.C. men were already almost on him; like a man balancing on a diving platform, Nirdlinger swayed and the first tackler hurtled past, one outstretched hand clawing his knee pads. Nirdlinger took a side-step back, and the second tackler dove at his ankles and missed. Now Nirdlinger was running through the broken field spinning and side-slipping, down for a second on one knee and then up again, the ball never having stopped its forward motion. He was down on the S.C. 45-yard line and the team fell back into a huddle.

"Jesus, can that guy run!"

The student manager was bouncing on the bench, waving his arms like a high school kid, but Cliff sat still, every muscle tense, bunching his energy as if to push it out across the field. Cal. and Western tried two passes, one of them completed for a short gain. Tony Powers made a dash through center. Woodward dropped back on fourth down as if to punt but tried a pass instead. This fell incomplete, and it was S.C.'s ball on the 47-yard line.

The huddle unwound and the ball was snapped. An S.C. lateral was complete, and with the stands roaring like trees in a hurricane Ted Gross, the S.C. fullback, took the ball to the 18-yard line. Two more plays shoved it across. Pantomiming against the deep roar of the crowd, Mike Petrillo, his empty sleeve flapping, his usually calm face frozen in fury, motioned half a dozen substitutes into the game.

"Halsey, Dubowsky, Kodiac, Harper...."

The knot in Cliff's stomach slowly untwisted. He made interference for Tony Powers on a double cross-buck, taking out Gross. On the next play he dropped back a step and flipped a short pass, flat as a rifle's trajectory, against Nirdlinger's ribs. The ball was well out of his hands when he was knocked down by two S.C. players, one falling on top of him. The referee took no notice, but the Cal. and Western stands booed the play.

A few minutes later, with the ball deep in S.C. territory, Nirdlinger gave the signal for an end-around, with Cliff taking the ball. He was tackled without gain, and on the play three players piled up on him after he was down. This time S.C. was penalized five yards for unnecessary roughness.

Nirdlinger and Kodiac helped Cliff up; his wind had been knocked out. Nirdlinger held up his hand for time out, but Cliff heard his own voice, dry and faraway, saying, "I'm okay, I'm okay," and Nirdlinger called the team back to a huddle. Cliff hardly heard the signals as the quarter called them in the huddle; he was thinking of what one of the S.C. men who had piled on him had said as the referee burrowed for the ball.

"How you doing, Big Shot?"

He got it now: this was what all his publicity had done for him. Evidently the S.C. players had picked him as a dangerous threat, a man to be ganged up on, shocked into helplessness or, better still, injured and eliminated even if it cost a penalty. Fury choked him, and he put his hands against his ribs and pumped, bending over in the huddle, trying to get his diaphragm working again; all the confusion engendered in him by the failure he had made of college life bunched into hate.

If that was what they were doing he would show those sons-of-bitching guys. He made a hole through left tackle for Nirdlinger and, as the pile unscrambled, saw a face close to the ground, the big blond bastard who had jumped on him when he was down. He pumped a knee into the blond man's face, sending him sprawling.

162

This time the referee was looking, and the Cal. and Western team was set back fifteen yards.

"Watch it, you goddam fool," Nirdlinger said as they walked back to the huddle.

No other man on the Cal. and Western team would look at Cliff, all hating him for costing them the penalty. Outcast now by his own tribe, Cliff's hurt deepened; his was the resentment of the rogue male against whom all hands, weapons, thoughts are lifted, who has no place of sanctuary. He was alone now, fighting the world, and in the icy vacuum of his loneliness his brain stopped working. The combat feeling was so powerful now it washed out everything: reflexes learned in a world far from this imitation killing dominated him, purging all taint of weakness out of him, making his movements positive and sure.

Cliff went in on each play, and each time he was deliberately smeared; not only the blond tackle he had kneed but every one of the S.C. players was laying for him now. When he got out of the second pile-up he was bleeding at the nose and there was a cleat-cut on his cheekbone. This time S.C. drew the penalty, the stands howling their enjoyment of a football game which had taken on the semblance of a bar-room brawl.

On the sidelines the S.C. coach, puzzled and heartily irritated, sent in a substitute, yanking the big tackle who immediately trotted toward the sidelines and tossed his helmet on to the pile in front of the bench. At his coach's signal he moved off toward the dressing-room tunnel.

Head Coach Petrillo saw Cliff following the blond man off the field. His first conclusion was that Cliff, injured, had checked out of the game, forgetting in his groggy condition to report to the bench. Yet there was something odd about the way Cliff looked—and Mike

Petrillo suddenly knew what it was. In his brain was a memory-picture of men stalking forward, bent at the shoulders just a little as Cliff had bent just now, their faces turned into the face of combat.

Coach Petrillo did something then which he had never done before: he left the field while his team was in the middle of a game. Before he was in the tunnel he could hear from its stone mouth the unthinkable animal-like snarl and the thick bruisy blows of something made of flesh, yet hollow, being pounded on concrete flooring. Mike Petrillo lunged without perceptible result at the hunched figure partly crouched, partly squatting above the unconscious S.C. tackle, blood dark now in the silver-blond hair. Mike Petrillo bounced back, then stepped in like a fighter; his fist then caught Cliff on the point of the jaw, and as Cliff spun around the coach hit him again, then caught his sagging body and pulled him through the steel door of the Cal. and Western dressing-room.

Fists were banging on the door. When Mike stepped out again, alone this time, the Stadium corridor was full of men—the S.C. manager, two rubbers, the team doctor, an assistant coach.

Mike leaned back against the door.

"Just a minute, gentlemen."

"A minute, hell," the assistant S.C. coach said wildly. "What's going on around here?"

"This is a serious matter, Petrillo," the doctor said.

"One of my boys is sick," Mike said. "I can't discuss it with you now."

"One of *your* boys is sick," the assistant coach said. "I just picked up our man here unconscious, blood all over him."

"I'm sorry about that," Mike said.

"He's sorry," one of the rubbers said.

"Shut up," Mike Petrillo said. He pushed the rubber back against the wall. He turned to the doctor. "Is the man still unconscious?"

His eyes moved from one man to the next, his sweat-shirt sleeve dangling at his side like an empty scabbard.

"He's snapping out of it," the doctor said, "but I'm afraid of a skull-fracture. Were you there when it happened?"

"Would I have let it happen, if I had been?"

The doctor said icily. "Can you give me any details? I have to make out my report."

"The men had some difference on the field," Mike said. "They were settling it here when I came in."

"That Harper is a maniac," the assistant coach said. "Listen, man, he tried to kill our boy. The guy is nuts."

"He's sick."

"Sick, hell. He ought to be in a strait-jacket."

"Excuse me, gentlemen," Mike said. "I have to attend to my player."

CHAPTER 30

THE CROWD AND PLAYERS HAD BEEN GONE FOR AN HOUR when Mike and Cliff, with Jerry, the Greek rubber, came out of the dressing-room tunnel; the air was dark with just the faintest bloom pasted on the sky by the lights of the city. Mike's car was parked near the tunnel entrance; he switched on the lights and drove slowly out on to Santa Barbara Avenue, dropping Jerry at the bus-stop on the corner.

Mike said, "We can 'phone your folks and tell them that you're eating with me, maybe staying all night."

Cliff nodded, hardly hearing. He drooped in the seat beside Mike, no feeling in him of any kind. As they drove along, his brain kept skidding like a car on wet asphalt.

"Was the guy hurt?" he asked several times. "Did I hurt him bad?"

Mike's answer was always the same, "He'll be all right. Don't worry about that now."

But Cliff paid no attention. "I didn't mean to do it," he said. "Honest to God, Mike, I didn't mean to."

"Don't think about it," Mike said.

"What would make you do a thing like that? All he did was smear me a couple of times, and I . . ."

"Forget it, Cliff."

"I ought to be put away. They ought to lock me up."

"Shut up," Mike said harshly. "Will you sit there and relax?"

Cliff would fall silent with an almost childlike acquiescence, only to begin again a moment later.

"Is his skull fractured, like they said?"

"The guy is going to be all right, I'm telling you."

Cliff buried his face in his hands.

"I tried to kill him. I should be put away."

Mrs. Petrillo knew enough not to ask questions. She was cooking a big spaghetti dinner and she kept on with it while Mike took Cliff in the den and made him lie down on the day-bed. The coach—himself a teetotaler,

166

who invariably cut men from his squad if he smelled liquor on them—got out a bottle of whisky.

Cliff never got to eat any of the spaghetti. Five minutes after he had drunk his whisky he was sound asleep; he slept all night under an army blanket Mike spread over him. Mr. and Mrs. Harper were advised by telephone that their son would spend the night away from home.

Cliff woke with the ten-o'clock sun hot on his face; after breakfast he sat in the patio while Mike puttered around the yard, edging a path, pruning the vines, throwing an occasional question in Cliff's direction. Talking was easier now because Mike had 'phoned the hospital and got information that the S.C. tackle had spent a good night; he would be all right. Little by little the talk which had bunched in Cliff for months loosened and unrolled. He told how he had gone to the university to make a start: to make the switch from being on the side of tearing things down to the side of building them up, from the side of confusion to the side of knowing; from death, doubt, terror, to life, hope, assurance. But it hadn't worked, it hadn't made sense, he didn't belong. . . .

With his hands knotted around his thumbs and his face contorted with the pressure of his feelings, he told Mike of the fear which haunted him by day and night: that he belonged Out There, and only there, that he should never have come back home. . . . He sat in the wooden chair, blinking at Mike, begging for an answer which he felt did not exist, a reassurance which he would reject.

But Mike offered no glib comforts.

"What do you want to do, kid?"

"I don't know."

"Sure of that?"

Cliff thought a minute. "Except get out of school, and that wouldn't be so good."

"Why wouldn't it?"

"My folks . . ."

"You're living for yourself, not your folks."

"I'd like to get out. Oh, God, I'd sure like to."

"Got any place you want to go?"

"No." Cliff thought again. "There is a place I *could* go, though. Where I could get a job, maybe."

"You better go there, Cliff."

Mike quit pruning. He sat down and lit a cigarette.

Cliff said, "You think it would be okay, no fooling?"

Mike said slowly, "It's the only thing to do. Your folks will understand, and if they don't, they'll get over it."

"They wanted me to go to school."

"That would have been fine, only it didn't work out. There's no way you can come out of combat and be happy in a buster-brown collar, writing on a slate and playing hop-scotch at recess."

Cliff laughed. The thought of leaving Cal. and Western, where he had been such a failure, filled him with joy; till he had told Mike he wanted to leave, he had never admitted this thought to himself. Now he could think of nothing else. Oh, boy, if he could get away. . . .

"It wasn't that bad, Coach."

"It was damn near that bad. I should have talked to you a hell of a long time ago. I might have saved you all the grief you've been through. Sure, you tried to mash a fellow's head against a concrete floor. That may not be pretty, but the reasons for it aren't pretty either." Mike stood up. "Let's go over to the house and see your dad."

Later, in the room he had occupied since boyhood and which he was now leaving for good, Cliff emptied dresser drawers on the bed, then made selections from the bed and stuffed them in a suit-case.

From downstairs, through the floor, came the vibration of two voices: Mike's voice careful, patient, resolute; Mr. Harper's questioning, interrupting, protesting. Cliff heard his father call for his mother, and then the door of the parlor was closed. Suddenly the door opened; Cliff heard a sound like a muffled sob, then feet on the stairs and the slam of another door as his mother went into her bedroom. He could tell from the way she was crying that she wanted him to come to the door, frightened, and ask if he could come in, as he had when he was little and his mother had made scenes like this, made them for one reason or another but always a reason connected with him, with her possessing him and controlling his future. Cliff went on packing his suit-case, and when he had it full, he locked and strapped it and put on his coat and took the suit-case downstairs.

Mike and his father were standing in the hall. From Mike's calm face and his father's flustered one Cliff knew that Mike had won.

"I understand you intend leaving the university and looking for a job," his father said. "Don't you think a decision like that calls for more thinking over?"

"I've thought it over, sir," Cliff said.

"I don't know, Cliff, I don't know," his father said. "When I got out of the Army...."

Cliff took a deep breath. "You were never in the Army, Dad—not the way I was."

Mr. Harper's jaw sagged slightly. His eyes blinked, and then they were new eyes and a stranger was looking out of them. "I shouldn't have said it," Cliff thought, knowing that nothing else that ever could be said would make it right between him and his father.

His father had lived on that World War veteran routine, and now he had blown it to hell.

But he'd had to. He'd kept from saying it a thousand times, and finally he'd had to.

"You may need some money," Mr. Harper said, "to get you by until this job materializes. . . ."

He was taking out his pocket-book, the last instrument of power left over from the old father-son relationship. Cliff stood still, looking at the pocket-book, and his father put it back.

"I told your dad I'd drive you to the bus depot," Mike said.

Cliff and his father shook hands.

"So long, Dad."

"Good-by, Clifford," Mr. Harper said. He added in a hurried, flinching tone, another tone entirely, " 'Phone to-morrow, boy. Your mother will be worried."

"All right, Dad."

"Don't forget, now. And remember, Son, no matter what happens, you've always got this house to come back to. You've always got your home."

"Thanks, Dad," Cliff said.

Rain sprayed the bus windows, painted the concrete highway black and shiny as a snake's hide: under the enormous tires the rain sang a song of good-by to everything known till now and a high whining overture to new things coming. Cliff leaned back on the leather seat, happy to think no thoughts but only to relax in the promise of his journey. The fatigue which had been somewhat relieved by his sleep at Mike's was pulling at his insides like a cable—yet now it was not torturing but pleasant. By degrees the hissing sounds of the bus, its warmth and swaying motion blended with his thoughts;

from the tiny swaying lights set in the ceiling of the bus a mist pressed down into Cliff's head, and when he turned his face sidewise on the bus seat he was asleep.

CHAPTER 31

SQUEEZED INTO AN IRREGULAR WEDGE BY TWO RANGES OF mountains, watered by the snowfall and rain condensation of huge ranges to the east and cooled by the slow steady push of the Gulf wind from the west, California's San Fernando Valley is a good place to grow things. In early times the Jesuits built a mission and a vineyard there, the Spanish dons ranged their herds over it; later, settlers from the Middle West planted orange and walnut groves and built roads, schools, little homes, and truck gardens. Two or three motion-picture studios, seeking to avoid high rents downtown, pioneered in the Valley's quiet verdure, without, however, altering its character: now and then a famous face could be glimpsed early in the morning or at suppertime, hurrying to and from work in limousine or station wagon; now and then a "location" company pitched camp in a meadow or took pictures on one of the Valley's dusty dirt roads. But for the most part, in the course of years, the Valley had changed very little; its eggs, honey, nuts, fruit, and dairy products were trucked into town each day; its citizens paid off their mortgages, raised crops and children, went to bed at nine and rose at six or seven, swapped horses, yarns, and real estate, rocked on front porches, and voted any ticket that would promise fifty dollars a week and all expenses to a man or woman who had reached the age of fifty.

Thus the Valley had been, once upon a time. Now all was changed. A new era had swooped down upon the Valley's quiet dream and, in a few months, transformed it into a combined arsenal, manufacturing center, and boomtown.

There had been, it appeared, an airplane factory in the Valley. Nobody had ever paid much attention to it. Along with such staples as leeks and alfalfa, the Valley had lent its fertility to freakish, transitory enterprises: clairvoyants, dog hospitals, crematoria, mink farms, and institutes for colonic irrigations.

Citizens of the Valley took no stock in new-fangled inventions, but—like most well-nourished people—they possessed the quality of tolerance: they had accepted railroads, the bicycle, the automobile. They wished the aircraft factory no ill-fortune. Once in a while, to be sure, one of the planes manufactured at the plant fell into someone's backyard with a quantity of burning petrol and unhappy results to the rabbit-incubators. No matter. Accidents would happen, and the aircraft company always paid off. The factory jogged along for several years with reasonable prosperity; no one had any inkling that remote developments in Europe and the South Pacific would cause it, like an animal whose glands have been stimulated by some violent synthetic substance, to expand into a monster overnight.

A monster it certainly was. Oranges, nuts, rabbits,

alfalfa—these were now nothing: everything was planes. From a couple of modest tool plants and a few assembly sheds and landing fields, the factory had rampaged over a hundred square miles of perfectly good oat land. Hundreds of miles of track had been laid to haul its supplies in and out, and to protect it from invasion a division of troops—infantry, anti-aircraft, listening posts, and fighter planes—had been installed in its surrounding fields. Through the once sleepy Valley a six-lane concrete speedway had been built to downtown Los Angeles; three times a day over this military road a group of special buses with police motorcycles screaming ahead of them brought out workers and took back those who had finished their shift.

The Horizon Aircraft Corporation worked three shifts in twenty-four hours, thirty thousand men and women in each shift. Wages started at eighty-five cents an hour, scaled rapidly up to a dollar, a dollar twenty-five. The Valley's walnuts fell and rotted on the ground; its rabbits burrowed, unreproved, out of their hutches; its unfed poultry snobbishly refused to breed, but no one gave a damn: almost every Valley tenant over twelve and under sixty had followed the gold-rush trail to Horizon. And since even the prolific Valley could not provide enough workers to staff the titanic production line, builders financed with Federal loans had tossed up villages of box-like houses to give shelter to the émigrés who, driven by patriotism and a pay-rate past their wildest dreaming, had deserted Dakota wheat lands, Oregon orchards, Texas ranches, to give proof of hitherto unsuspected talents for plane-making.

The villages weren't much. Over them, as over the huge factory, breathed a deferred betrayal, a strange air of impermanence. At a whispered word, a siren's scream, a head-line in the paper, you felt, it would be all over—the walls of Horizon would melt like ice-cream; weeds would gently push aside the muscles of the speedway; trucks would come and take away the workers' villages. When that happened, of course, then would be the time to prune the trees, make the fowls copulate again; then there would be lots of time available, and maybe not much else. Meanwhile, incandescent gases burned all night in the ten thousand miles of neon tubing whose scrawled zigzags lighted the production sheds. Every half-hour a finished plane was trundled from the paint-shop out on to the testing field. There was a war to be won, and the Valley, by God, was doing its best to win it.

Gunny had rented a room in the prefabricated home of Mr. and Mrs. Conrad Rodd, on Nestor Street, Hill-dale—about two miles from the south portals of Horizon. Rodd was a shop foreman at the plant, and Gunny had obtained the room from the plant housing bureau. True, the room was not much bigger than his hallway cubicle at home, but he was sole possessor of it, with kitchen privileges—a free agent, dependent on no man or woman, empowered to eat when and what he liked, sleep when he wanted to, come and go at will except for the eight hours (from four-thirty in the afternoon till twelve-thirty at night) which he devoted to Horizon.

Yes, sir, Gunny was free. He had hung his extra cover-alls on a clothes-hook; he had put his shirts and service pistol in the drawer of the small wooden locker by his bed. He had moved in, begun a new life.

It was fine to be free.

Naturally, it took some getting used to. A man as old as Gunny had to adjust himself to the pleasures of free-dom. He had to drop a lot of weak and foolish habits in order to benefit fully from his freedom. Up to this moment Gunny had lived very stupidly; he had not properly appreciated the values of freedom or made the slightest effort to obtain them. Instead, he had lived always in the closest, the most intimate relationships with other people, conditioning every act, every decision to some demand made upon him. At peace with himself, he had asked no questions, made no criticisms of this mode of living; he had given himself unstintedly.

First, in the old days, there had been his pride as a Marine, his acceptance of authority for the men under him. Together with this, all through the early years at least, had been his inexorable love for Emmy and the kids, a pull in his bones, strong as the ocean tides. Always he had looked after every one who turned to him for leadership—his own family first, and then the beardless babies whom he had taught to shoot guns, and keep their noses clean, and whom he had finally led into the hell of combat on a rainy jungle island.

It was only the senseless gnawing of the outmoded and preposterous habit of taking care of others which kept him from fully relishing his freedom. A few week-ends he went home, saw Emmy and Sonny and the other folks, but that didn't do him any good, it only increased the loneliness which, in weak moments, made him think about getting a dog.

A dog was company. Every dog was a character all by itself, after you got to know it: if it had any brains you could always teach it a few tricks. It would be there when you got home at night. Gunny entertained such thoughts at times, but, with a proper resolution, he put them aside. Every old man in the world, living alone, had some dog he pampered, fed too much, and made weak and lazy like himself. Some of those house-dogs got so dumb they wouldn't even lift their legs. You would get all wound up in a dog and then the son-of-a-bitch would die. It was no good. Besides, having a dog was the real pay-off, it was the final sign that you were old.

Thank God he wasn't in that stage just yet. He would be damned if he would have a useless animal around day and night, smelling his place up. He had too much sense.

Though adhering to this line of reasoning, Gunny was quite absurdly pleased when, one morning about one o'clock (just after he got home from work and was lying on the bed reading the funny paper), his landlord, Foreman Rodd, told him that there was a guy out the front door, asking for him. Mr. and Mrs. Rodd, both of them worked day shift, had been none too pleased about the nocturnal disturbance. Foreseeing, however, a chance to raise the rent with two men in a room instead of one, they had produced a camp cot from the garage.

Cliff hadn't done much talking. His recent experience had exhausted him as if he had come out of battle. He mumbled something about leaving school, and then, still wearing his pants, he had laid down on the cot and gone to sleep.

That night Gunny could hardly shut his eyes because of pleasure, waking with the first light to make sure his friend was still there. He got up an hour earlier than usual so as to have the kitchen to himself; he let Cliff sleep till the coffee, scrambled eggs, and a big pile of griddle cakes were ready. Then, going to the bedroom door and rising slightly on his toes, he cut loose with his old-time shout of reveille.

CHAPTER 32

IT WAS A GALA BREAKFAST. IN ITS COURSE GUNNY GOT THE story of how Cliff had left Cal. and Western: Gunny drank coffee and puffed his pipe; now and then he asked a question, watching Cliff's face for the answers as much as he listened to his words.

"So this punk tried to get tough, huh? He got wise and tried to smear you up?"

Cliff looked uncertain. The awful guilt of his attempted killing still weighed heavily on him.

"It wasn't that, Sarge. Sure, he roughed me. But a lot of guys will do that in a game. I mean, Jesus Christ, Sarge . . . I tried to murder him."

"You did right."

"Don't say that, Sarge. I'm not kidding; I tried to kill him." Guilt rode Cliff's back like a witch's cat. "If I'd done it, I couldn't have gone on living. I'd have wanted to be put away."

"What about all those Japs you killed. You want to be put away on account of them?"

"This was a white man."

"White or yellow, he pulled a fast one on you. So you got sore. So you wanted to kill him. I'm saying you did right. Naturally, you didn't kill him. You could have, and I ought to know: I taught you how. You could have put your knee in his back and broke his neck when you caught him in that tunnel. Only you didn't. Something held you back, just like it holds me back when I get hot under the collar and decide to wipe some jerk off the earth. You had mercy on this wisenheimer, and what little you did to him he had coming for roughing you. Don't give it another thought."

Gunny's shaggy eyebrows, thick as snouts, poked at Cliff like a second pair of eyes.

Cliff, who for the second time in two days had confessed what he had thought could never be confessed, looked sharply at his friend to make sure he was not being ribbed.

"But Judas, Sarge, suppose I try it on some other guy. Then they'll put me away for keeps, but it will be too late. The guy will be dead."

Gunny struck a match on his pant's leg. "Your killing days are over, Cliff," he said. "You're an old worn-out Jap-butcher, just like me, but you won't kill no white men. You may get sore and think you're going to and you may try it, but you won't kill nobody. Take my word for it. I've been in four campaigns and I've killed guys in every one of them and thought no more of it than shooting me a forked-horn buck. In peacetimes, a buck is the biggest thing I ever killed. And next year I'm going to git me one of them again, and you're going along with me. What do you say?"

Cliff said nothing. He swished the cooling coffee around in his cup, trying to believe what Gunny said. More than anything he wanted to believe it.

"I hope to God you're right," he said, speaking as if to himself. "I sure hope so."

"I'm right," Gunny said, "so forget it." He began to stack the empty dishes, then desisted. "What about this job you talked about last night?" he asked. "Were you leveling? You want to go to work?"

"You know I do."

178

"How would I know what you college hepcats would want to do? For all I could tell you'd want to git you one of these here zoot-suits and go out jitterbugging."

"I might do some of that, too, after I draw me a couple of pay checks."

Cliff grinned, his black mood rapidly lifting. It was certainly swell to be back with the old Sarge; it was different from being with anybody else, even a guy like Mike Petrillo.

"Out where I'm working," Gunny said, "you don't qualify fer pay checks by winning dance contests. You're liable to get yourself covered with dirt and grits. Maybe a super-educated Joe out of the upper brackets wouldn't want to mix in a set-up like that."

Cliff took the dishes over to the sink.

"Why don't you shut your big yapper and give me the dope. Can I get a job there, or can't I?"

"We got jobs to suit all tastes. A while back they hired a man for twenty thousand bucks a year—and he'd never seen the inside of an aircraft plant! Captain Archer Winston. Now if you play your cards right, maybe you can knock over a spot like that."

"You mean Arch Winston, the ace?"

"Uh-huh. You read about his getting the Congressional Medal?"

"I read about it," Cliff said. "And it so happens, I knew him. I used to go to school with his kid brother."

Clear as a photograph he could see the face of Pinky Winston, Arch's kid brother, a nearsighted kid with freckles all over his face, always tinkering with engines. The Winstons had lived over on Lavelle Street and each had successively attended Hoover High. Arch had enlisted in the air force several years before Pearl Harbor: Pinky's one claim to distinction in school had been that he was the brother of an officer. Once, during a football season, Arch, home on leave, had come to the High School locker room after a tough game, wearing his uniform, and he had congratulated Cliff on his playing.

"Honest to God. You know Arch Winston?"

"Pretty near as well as I know you."

"If you're not ribbing," Gunny said, "we're going places."

Gunny knocked out his pipe. "Cliff," he said seriously, "this Winston is a big shot out at the plant. Think he'll remember you? Enough to let you in to see him?"

"Why, sure. I guess so," Cliff said, taking thought. "He was pretty regular, anyway when I knew him. I think he'd talk to me." He wiped a dish and set it carefully aside. "What will I ask him for, Gunny? What kind of spot could he get me?"

"Any doggone spot in the plant. He's what they call special relations executive or something like that. No one knows for sure just what he does, but he's got plenty of influence."

Cliff's head began to spin with plans.

"He would have," he said, himself becoming awed with the wonder of his acquaintance with this hero. "Fifty-one missions, and the Congressional Medal—"

"If he'll talk to you," Gunny persisted, "and he likes you, you won't be swamping in no store-room, no sir, nor standing up all day on the production line. You'll have a nice upholstered chair under you, baby, and your feet on a mahogany desk."

"Holy Pete," Cliff said. "You think so?"

The vision of himself in such surroundings was a dazzling one.

"I'll lay you six, two and even," Gunny said. He put

down the dish towel. "Now just let me tell you what to do."

"You name it, Sarge, and I'll do it."

In Cliff's tone there was an anxious dedication, bred of new, fiery ambitions. "I'll put the bite on him," he promised. "You see if I don't."

"Okay," Gunny said. "Now, when I go out to work this P.M. you take a ride out there with me. You take a ride and then you stroll around to the front office and you have a little talk with Captain Archer Winston."

CHAPTER 33

FLOOD-LIGHTS THREW A MILKY GLARE INTO THE EARLY fall dusk. Yellow buses were arriving in a long, fast-moving stream, stretching down the road as far as the eye could see. Cops straddled their motorcycles, one foot on the road, the engines idling as they watched the workers unload. Under the camouflage nets which covered parking lots, plant buildings, and runways, you could hear a low, persistent pulse made up of all the myriad production noises—the hiss of steam, the chatter of welders and automatic hammers, the hiss of air hoses, and the inter-mingled sounds of ventilator motors, airplane motors, trucks, trains, and cars. In the gateway areas, behind ropes, marshaled by plant police, thirty thousand swing shift workers waited for the gates to open while the day shift poured into the streets, their faces set in the expressions acquired at work but their thoughts already reaching for other affairs.

In this drama of the shift change, the masses of men and women, the machines, the synthetic lights and huge camouflaged buildings, and the orderly stream of vehicles, the faces of police, and the cavernous yet intimate, terrible and wonderful throb of the work, there was a cosmic quality like that of natural force, the change of the tides or the alternation of day and night.

Cliff had never heard about the camouflage. He studied the nets incredulously, trying to calculate how many miles of them had been required to make it all. Dotting the nets were artificial tree-tops made of spun and painted twists of plastic. Other trees and even hayricks, lawns and fences, were sprayed in paint on the plant buildings to give them a pastoral appearance, the larger structures being disguised to resemble hills sprinkled with small houses and indented with roads; the control-towers of testing fields and airports had been draped and smeared to look like cottages.

Thus, by the art of counterfeiting, two complete worlds had been created, one real and one unreal, one driven ceaselessly to secret ends by a savage unresting purpose and the other airy, charming, lost in dreams, spun frivolously from the warp of fairy tales.

Once the friends had joined the crowd in front of Gate 16, Plant A, Cliff found abruptly that the world of camouflage had no significance for him: he was required to deal with the real world—a task for which he was as yet but poorly qualified.

Driving over from their boarding-house in the pick-up

bus, the friends had carefully rehearsed the procedure to be followed. Now that the matter called for action, Cliff wasn't so sure of the sentiments which Arch might entertain for the one-time school-mate of his young brother, Pinky.

Gunny poured scorn upon such vacillation. "Would you ruther be making fifty smacks a week in an office, or bucking the assembly line? The worst he can do is toss you out—and if he does then he's a worse jerk than I figure him to be. . . ."

There was no gainsaying the argument that there was nothing to lose in talking to Arch. Still, it was hard. It took a lot of brass to walk in on a man making twenty grand a year—a former officer, moreover, and an ace at that—and ask for something.

You had to make a pitch. Think up a reason that made sense to the secretary who would ask you what you wanted, so that she could tell Arch Winston you wanted to see him. You couldn't just stroll in on a big executive the way you'd walk into a poolroom. Fellows like that were protected.

Well, it was a personal matter. Yes, he was a personal friend of Captain Winston's. Yes, it was important. No, he didn't have an appointment. . . . And when, after his name had been phoned to Arch's secretary, and the fantastic answer had come back that Arch knew him, yes, would talk to him, Cliff was required to sign a registry, a pledge to abide by the plant rules, and an affidavit that he was a U.S. citizen. Finally, a plant guide conducted him upstairs; somehow he found himself sitting in a big upholstered chair, looking at a pack of playing cards which occupied the middle of Arch Winston's desk.

No pen, no blotter, inkwell, ash-tray, or typewriter. No doodads of any kind. Just a pack of cards, well-thumbed, and a sheet of paper with some kind of score scribbled on it.

There was something weird about the pack of cards, something Cliff didn't get.

Arch was the same old Arch. A little heavier in the face, maybe, and a little thinner in the body. A handsome fellow with a keen face, wearing a pin-stripe suit which somehow emphasized his trimness and his look of vigilance and dissipation. How old was Arch? About twenty-seven, tops. The gray at the sides of his hair gave him a lot of dignity.

Cliff wasn't thrown by the hair. He had seen fellows five years younger than Arch come back from the islands with their hair gray all over, not just a couple of wing-streaks at the sides.

All this time Arch was chatting with him in really friendly style, asking him about his family, telling him about Pinky, who had been drafted. Cliff kept glancing at the cards, trying not to but feeling his eyes shift over by themselves as if Arch had had egg on his vest or a button open in his fly.

Finally Arch caught him and said in a new voice, with a rapid smile that Cliff did not remember.

"Want to play some gin-rummy?"

He picked up the pack and shuffled it.

"How about it, Cliff? Got some time you can kill? You name the bet. Or no bet. We can play for cigarettes or matches. Anything...."

Cliff was embarrassed. The request, so casually made, was as odd as the hard jerky twist of Arch's voice. It was as if, by inviting him to play, Arch had been making fun of Cliff—or of himself.

"What's the matter, fellow?" Arch demanded. "Wouldn't a little game appeal to you? It passes the time, believe me. Nothing kills time better than a friendly little game. Wait a minute—I've got something to attend to, then we'll play."

Arch flipped a dictograph-key. He spoke to his secretary in the other room.

"Will you check with Mr. Humphries' office and see whether they've heard from Senator Mahlon?"

"I just checked, Captain," said a girl's voice. "Senator Mahlon has not arrived. His plane is late. I'll let you know as soon as I get any word."

"Okay," Arch said, and closed the key. "I'm a hell of an important man, Cliff," he said. "You perceive that, I suppose."

Cliff did not know whether Arch was kidding him or not. He looked at his hands, wishing Arch would let him in on the joke.

"I'm sure sorry, Arch," he said, to change the subject, "but I can't play gin. I've heard about it, but I never played it. I—"

He was just about to say he would play poker or reddog, but Arch interrupted him, shuffling the deck with a sound like tearing silk.

"Never mind. We'll discuss topics of mutual interest, eh, Clifford? For instance, my brother's efforts to evade the draft. Or let's say your own experience in the Marines. We'll chew the fat. How will that be?"

"Why—fine, I guess," Cliff agreed, more uncomfortable than ever.

"Pardon me for suggesting cards," Arch said. "I spend a proportion of my time alone, and I play cards. This"—Arch held up the score pad—"indicates the progress made to-day. Twelve games for my right hand, fifteen for my left."

Arch took the scribble sheets from the score pad and

tore them up. He leaned back in his swivel chair and looked out of the windows at the vast stretch of the Horizon Plant, twinkling with lights and humming with activity in the smoke-colored air.

"Have you got any idea what I do around here, Cliff? I'll tell you," he said before Cliff could answer. "It's quite interesting. I shake hands."

"Huh?"

"I shake hands, Clifford. I am a greeter. Do you get it? Probably not. In the Marines, no doubt you operated crudely. There were no greeters, no high-paid receptional executives. Well, my boy, the president of this concern is a young struggling millionaire named Walt Humphries, employer of ninety thousand people. Mr. Humphries builds a war plane every half-hour, each plane costing from one hundred and twenty-five to three hundred thousand dollars. Mr. Humphries is a very busy man. Has he time to shake hands? Has he time to show visitors around the plant? He has not. That is my job, Clifford. I am fairly well known as an aviator, if I may say so. I have completed x number of maneuvers. I have received x decorations. When a stuffed shirt is hand-shaken or shown around the plant by me he is not resentful. Far from it. He is flattered. He has been officially greeted by Horizon's expert greeter, Captain Archie Winston, former combat ace. The rest of the time I play cards, my right hand against my left."

Cliff stared. The self-mockery in Arch's tone made it hard to listen to him.

"That's tough, Arch."

A network of small lines stood out in Arch's face.

"What's tough about it?"

"You made it sound that way."

"It's not tough, Cliff."

186

"Pardon me, Arch. My mistake."

"You want to know what's tough? Flying fifty-one combat missions is what's tough."

"I'll bet."

"No, you won't bet. I'm telling you. It's tough. How did *you* get discharged?"

"Disability," Cliff said.

"You were wounded, in other words."

Cliff nodded. Being wounded was the wrong thing to discuss. If Arch knew about that, there might be no job.

"Did your pals have to bring you back a thousand miles in a crate, with you bleeding all the way?"

"No, sir."

"That's the difference between land and air combat. Do you get it?"

"No, sir."

"It's this way. A plane is like a crate—we call 'em crates, and that's what they are. You and your crew are all jammed in together there, co-pilot, navigator, radio-officer, gunners, and so forth. You're the pilot. Let's say four or five of these guys get shot up over the target or on the way in or out; these fellows tell you about it on the inter-com. Or they don't tell you about it. They say they're fine, they're swell, when you check them, but from the way they say it you know different. Once in a while they scream but if they do they generally apologize —they're nice guys. You tell them to keep pounding. That's all you can do. Dish out a pep-talk like a dumb scout-master—and fly them back to base. You've always got to get them back."

"I see that part of it," Cliff said.

"Well, that's the part that's tough. So you get them back. And then the ground crew opens up the crate and finds it full of busted guts. Always the other guys, you

187

understand me? Never *you*. *You're* lucky. If your wings get shot off, you let down the wheels and taxi on the flak. You're that kind of a pilot. Naturally they give you medals every so often for being lucky. Brother, when you have medals enough so you rate a job like this, is *that* tough?"

"I guess not, Arch."

"Don't guess. You know it isn't. I'll take this, my friend. Even if they quit handing me the fancy salary checks, I'll take it. Just so long as they don't take away my cards."

The dictograph buzzed and Arch pressed the key. The girl's voice said, "Excuse me, Captain, but the Senator is coming in. Mr. Humphries' office just checked with me, and they said—"

"I'll be right over."

Arch closed the key. "Stick around, Clifford," he said, rising. "I've got to go to work. Be back in a little while and we can play some acey-deucy. If you get bored waiting, there's a bottle of liquor in the bottom drawer."

Cliff sat motionless, a sense of failure clogging his thoughts. He had messed up everything as usual: he hadn't asked for a job; for some reason which he couldn't define he would never ask Arch now. No sense sticking around; he had flopped again. The best thing to do was get out.

Arch's secretary, a frosty-faced blonde, looked up in surprise as he came out of the office.

"Captain Winston thought you would wait."

"Tell him I—had to see a fellow. Tell him thanks."

"Will you call him later?"

"Sure," Cliff said, "I'll call him."

Outside, the air smelled of dampness, burnt gasoline,

and paint. Cliff sucked in big breaths of it; he was feeling for a cigarette when suddenly his hands began to shake so hard he couldn't take the pack out of his pocket. He jumped back into the doorway, pressing himself against the wall.

From the other side of the executive building sounds continued, getting louder all the time—a bunch of .50 caliber machine-guns firing at close range, amplified by heavier blasts of cannon. In a second, Cliff knew well, bombs would start knocking the daylight out of everything. While the firing continued he crouched beside the door, shaking all over, his eyes staring, searching for better cover; he did not notice when the door beside him opened and a square-built man with a Horizon badge pinned on his shirt came out and stood there, watching him.

"What outfit were you with, pal?"

Right in the middle of an air raid was a hell of a time to be making conversation, but Cliff, not to be outdone, answered through chattering teeth.

"I was in Tunisia with the Eighth Air Force—Old Man Eaker's outfit," the square built man said. "Don't take any stock in that shooting. Just a routine gun-test, installations on the Navy bombers. You working here?"

Cliff shook his head. "Looking for a job."

He felt like a damn fool not to have known the guns were only testing—but now, even knowing it, he didn't yet have full control of himself.

"Come in on an interview pass?"

"Uh-huh."

"Roy Connors is my name," the fellow in the doorway said. "I'll tell you how to save yourself some time. Interviews don't mean a thing. Go around this building, past the test-field; go into the first door on the right, that's the Application Office. If you can write your name they'll take you—that is, unless you use a seeing-eye dog or done time for being a Red. And don't take no stock in that gun-fire. If it was what you think it is, I'd be high-tailin' over that fence."

❧ CHAPTER 34 ❧

CLIFF WROTE MIKE PETRILLO THAT HE "THOUGHT" HE had a job. He put the statement conditionally because he was afraid something might still go wrong with it. He had signed a sheaf of papers and been advised the F.B.I. would check his answers. He had been finger-printed and photographed and had submitted his discharge for numerous inspections. At least, he was safe in one respect: the discharge didn't mention any reason for the termination of his service except "disability due to wounds received in action." And he had passed his physical.

Several times the shaking came back on him. Once a group of fighter planes banked into the airport, flying so low their motors shook the ground: another time a truck-driver dumped a load of scrap a few feet away from him while he was sorting salvage. Several times Cliff escaped observation by going to the washroom and staying there until the fit was over: once or twice a straw-boss noticed his condition and sent him to the plant hospital, where he was treated and sent back to work. Horizon needed men, and if a guy wanted his job and didn't have the screaming mimies or something, he was not in much danger of getting fired.

Being in Salvage wasn't bad. It was the lowest-paid work in the plant, it was dirty, and it required little brains—but Cliff had no particular objection to any of these conditions: they were unimportant when compared to the fact that he was part of something, no longer an outsider.

Let the girls in Metal Process call the Salvage hands "Glorified Junkmen" and "Garbageers." Who cared? He was doing all right: besides, many a man had moved out of Salvage into the skilled departments: Assembly, Tooling, Tremletting, Experimental—even into Personnel, Research, and the hundred or so Special Engineering Fields. Those girls weren't so hot themselves, mostly just helpers to the men who ran the big hydros. Salvage got even with them by putting their names on soap-trucks and pick-ups: "Jessie," "Viola," "Tillie." On the sides of the vehicles was a company label which, in the minds of the Salvage hands constituted a devastating comment on the girls' names: TRASH ONLY.

Salvage had the run of the plant. Its trackless trains, towed by small gasoline engines known as "pigs," rattled through the complicated network of company streets, collecting slag at the Drop-Forge, garbage at the Canteen, cardboard, burlap, wood, and paper from Shipping, and the product of swampers' baskets everywhere. At an enormous terminal all the waste was dumped, sorted, checked, and placed in high-walled wooden bins according to class and specification.

Even in the dim continent of Salvage, the precisions

of Horizon were maintained: trackless trains ran on time-tables, sorting-bins were titled with big signs like circus sideshows, and all junk was catalogued, grouped, ticketed, according to an intricate system. The hegemony of dump and wrecking-yards, junk-piles, sheds, terminals, warehouses, loading-platforms was operated with the efficiency of a high-class clinic.

Men employed in Salvage were for the most part Negroes, kids, and old guys taken from relief-rolls. They moved slowly, worked slowly—the stuff wouldn't run away. Many of them, in depression times, had been hobos; they had roamed the highways or holed up in the rabbity tramp towns which were to be found on the outskirts of all big cities and were then known by a name which by degrees was to become the most elaborate monument ever erected to a defeated politician—Hoovertown!

In the depression days, the going had been tough in Hoovertown. A man kept alive by sifting stuff that other people had thrown away. Bindle-stiffs who didn't freeze, starve, or get beaten by cops, survived because they were experts in waste: now, due to Horizon's policy of employing experts, they had found their proper niche in life. Now they were paid wages to do what they had once done to keep from dying. They were lords of the biggest junk-pile in existence.

The men of Salvage were, after their fashion, veterans of an older war. For wherever junk collects, there gather the armies of wabbly-boned and filthy-handed men cast out by cities, charity hospitals, hard-working wives, and county jails, men who have had trouble with the law or been burnt out by factory production lines and are, as a result, no use at all. From the smell of such men, from the droppings of their tired bodies or the thoughts in their minds, or perhaps from the junk-piles that sustain them, there arises a strange culture, timid and profane, coloring the litter and discard of their lives like the paltry grass pushing its coarse stalks between tin cans on a city dump: a bitter culture, implemented by the law of fang and claw—the Hobo Code.

This Code explained many otherwise puzzling phenomena in the Salvage Department at Horizon.

For one thing, there was the stealing. Salvage Personnel used a separate gate and were examined, when they checked out, far more carefully than other employees. Guards watched perpetually for a bulge that could be a coil of wire, a power tool, or a piece of assembly equipment (all of which in Hilldale could be pawned like jewelry). But in spite of everything, the stealing went on: if they were kept from taking anything better, the bindle-stiffs of the Salvage Department just stole junk. Some of them had enough assorted scrap at home to build a bomber.

A bona fide bindle is a saving sort of man, and Salvage personnel were true to this tradition. They were saving with a purpose. Some, drawing ninety cents an hour, still lived in the local Hoovertown, out by the stock-yards; even those who rented proper homes elsewhere went back to Hoovertown once in a while just as anybody who has made a success in the world returns occasionally out of sentiment to visit his home town.

Horizon's hobos needed nobody to tell them that the Old Town was still there: from coast to coast it still flourished grayly, its population trimmed now to a mere million or so—a token population, negating the efforts of the nation to achieve total mobilization. The Old Town waited patiently, expecting a population which was sure to return. Against the day to come, the guys in Salvage hoarded leather, cardboard, metal trimmings, nuts, bolts, anything and everything that had a possible value. When they went back to Hoovertown they didn't mean to go back empty-handed.

An evidence of Hobo Culture, quite aside from stealing, was the names of the guys. From times beyond recall, perhaps when most bindle-stiffs were gipsies or whisky-drinking pot-menders, the nomenclature of the damned has been a colorful one. With a gaudy name a man has something to live by, a coin to keep even when he has been cheated out of everything else. At Horizon a man's name was inscribed, for convenience, on his badge, but if a Salvage worker had been baptized N or M, or had a legal surname, no one ever found it out. The names on the badges were Papago Kid, Popeye, The Gimp, Moon Mullins, Tucson, Dynamite, Slow Freight, Satchel Pants, The Killer, Ice Box, Red, Frisco Express, Dusty, Trigger Bill, The Senator, Ace, Mickey Mouse, Joe College, Fargo Frank, Wink the Barber, Main Street, Last Chance, and Johnny-Play-the-Queen.

The Personnel Department winked at this odd tradition of the Salvage guys' badges. Thus Horizon's sociology experts set out to humor Salvage—a notoriously troublesome element—with this easy flattery of painted tin.

Cliff, who had gone to work with a badge reading "Harper," got a new one that said "Slim." He had acquired this name one afternoon when, his crew having turned out one man short, the straw boss, addressing him, said, "You, there, Slim. You know how to drive a jeep?"

Cliff, sorting waste metal sliced from bomber bulkhead sections, let on that he did.

"Then climb on that there Goose and run it. Works just like a Four-by-Four, only for the hoist, and you'll git on to that."

The Goose was the most spectacular machine used in Salvage. Painted red, with big hind wheels, small front wheels, and a low body which contained a powerful gasoline motor, it was used to maneuver loads too heavy to be lifted by hand-power.

The Goose had the muscles of two hundred men. A pair of steel arms stuck out stiffly from the front of it, tracked in a vertical frame. A chain-drive gear-mechanism powered the arms so that they could be raised to the top of the frame or lowered till they scraped the ground. The Goose was not much bigger than a motorcycle sidecar, but it could pick up a case containing half a ton of metal scrap and toss it on a truck as easily as a man could lift a cup of coffee; its arms could nudge under a bag of heavy stuff and whisk it off the ground without so much as tearing the burlap.

The exuberant life in the steel arms of the hoist was hard to boss. Once Cliff almost tore the end-panel off a truck, trying to set a packing-case on it; many times he stalled the Goose by ramming its arms into the ground. But before the shift was over he was on his way to being an expert Goose-operator; as long as he remained in Salvage he did no other kind of work.

"Where's that Goose?" a lead-man would yell, working with some material that resisted ordinary lifting methods. "Hey, Slim, can you cut it?"

Then Cliff would look at the foreman for a nod and, if he got it, streak over to the guys and do the job. He was always pleased when he was summoned. He would grow very serious, perched on the high seat of his machine, figuring how to handle each new problem.

"You fellows get a crowbar under it. Lean on the bastard...."

His decisions, once he was the Master of the Goose,

were final: without waiting for an okay from their foreman, men would do as Cliff suggested. Backs bending in the sun would straighten a half-inch. With a snort the Goose would back up, sidestep for position like a boxer. Down would come its never-tired arms. The Goose would flash in, its red body gleaming and Cliff bouncing on the seat, checking its frenzied rush without the least hint of stalling. The Goose would plunge the steel arms under the object to be lifted; the sturdy motor would roar as its chain-driven hoist fought the compression. Then a flip, a terrific gunning of the engine: the soup-truck would be right side up, and Cliff, grinning, would wave to the guys and hurry to another job.

Driving the Goose was different from working in Assembly. Roy Connors had taken Cliff in there, and he had seen what happened.

In Assembly the machines ran the men.

A man who was run by a machine was nothing. But a man who ran a machine like the Goose had the strength of many men. He had importance, too. He was a troubleshooter, a position which in any industry is full of honor. Running the Goose made Cliff a key man in Salvage.

The day he acquired the name of Slim and was assigned to the Goose was the finest day Cliff had lived since his fourteenth birthday, when his uncle gave him the drawing-set. It was even better than the day when he lost his virginity or received the Silver Star.

A job he liked was a beginning, and a new name was also a beginning. It was swell, but he still had one great worry. The hard work often made him tired, and when he was tired he got the shakes. Back of all his good luck was the nightmare and worry that the plant would decide he was unfit for his responsibility and make him change his job. There were times when he was helpless and had to get off the Goose and wait until the panic in his veins, aroused by any chance occurrence, had subsided.

He felt that if the boss got wise to him and fired him, his life would be over. He would be doomed then to the invalidism he had feared when he was in the hospital.

All that stuff the doctors told him might be baloney. He had been out a long time and he had not got well. Maybe he was never going to get well. Maybe he'd end up like the spindly hobos in Salvage—just a relic that a war had left behind.

He felt a little better after being transferred to day shift. In the mornings when he strolled through the gate with the other workers his fears about his condition were far away. But at night they came crawling back. Fight them as he would, they were always there.

CHAPTER 35

"HEY, CLIFF!"

Cliff, just entering Gate 16, lunch pail in hand, turned at the shout. Arch Winston was standing on the sidewalk in front of the Administration Building.

"How're you doing?"

"Swell, thanks, Arch. I keep punching, anyhow."

Arch's face looked chalky in the sunlight. He was just as dandified as the last time Cliff had seen him. His tie and double-breasted suit looked as if they had been picked out of an ad in *Esquire*.

"I didn't even know you were working here till the other day—my wife heard it from your folks. We were talking about you."

Cliff fidgeted. He hadn't punched his time card, and if he stalled much longer he'd be docked. Arch, noticing his restlessness, strolled along with him toward the time clock.

Other guys from Salvage, hurrying past, gaped at the sight of Cliff strolling beside a big shot from the front office.

"Why didn't you tell me you knew Mrs. Klim?" Arch said affably. "She's an old friend of my wife's. Used to go to school with her."

"Mrs. Klim?" Cliff looked stupidly at Arch. The name meant nothing to him, yet there was a strange familiarity about it. "I guess you got me wrong, Arch. Did she say she knew me?"

"Why, sure."

The two had stopped in the sunshine by the time clock.

"She was in that Hoover Street crowd. Said you used to be a pal of her brother or something."

"Marriage of Patricia Tracy, daughter of Mr. and Mrs. Edward Tracy, and Lieutenant Rorick Klim..."

The memory was like a jolt in the belly.

Cliff had pushed the name of Klim out of his memory: there was no such person as Mrs. Rorick Klim. Only a girl named Pat who was buried out in an island jungle.

Arch's affable voice was saying: "We thought you

198

might drop over to the house some night. She's out there quite a bit. How about it?"

"Thanks, Arch. That's mighty nice of you, but I'm kinda busy these days. Really pounding it."

Arch patted Cliff's shoulder, thus exhibiting for the Salvage day shift the cordial spirit exisiting between Administration and Labor.

"Just a thought. If you get some time off call us. Number's in the book. So long, boy."

"Thanks, Arch. So long."

Rain on Mrs. Klim, Cliff thought, punching his card. This was the second time he'd heard of her through some one else; he remembered Jim in the locker room at the Y saying, "Why don't you call her? . . ."

That was a dame for you. Pulling a fast one and then asking to see you so she could explain. Give you a lot of fast talk to make herself feel she hadn't done anything dirty. The hell with it.

He would get along without Mrs. Klim. He was doing all right. He didn't have time to think about women, and if he did he could always make friends with some of the gals in Metal Process. He'd get along.

No doubt if he worked on Arch, went out to his house and everything, he might worm his way into some desk job. Still, this idea had little more appeal to him now than on the first day he'd come to Horizon. In three months he had secured two pay raises and was saving up to buy a car. A dollar-ten an hour was top money in Salvage, but he thought he had a chance to switch to Metal Process. Roy Connors had told him about a vacancy in this department. Roy's buddy was quitting to go back east, and Roy practically guaranteed to get him this guy's job on a two-man punch-press, cutting bulkhead sections. This job paid a dollar-ten; it would be a short-cut to accumulating the down-payment on the car.

One noon-hour, punching in a little early, Cliff cased the job.

The punch weighed five hundred pounds and was operated by an electric motor. Roy was the operator. The feeder, a girl, handed him a segment of aluminum and this he placed on the plate of the punch. His helper straightened the metal while Roy put his hands on one set of controls. The apparatus, for safety, had two sets, and both sets had to be operated at the same time. The moment Roy touched his set, contact was complete and the punch came down, moved about a foot, sliding soundlessly on its oiled journals: at the second when it struck the metal, a deep, powerful shock passed down through the cradle and mounting, into the floor, and its tremor shook the floor, clear down through sixteen feet of concrete.

There was power and precision in the operation, and at first, as you watched Roy and his helper work, their team-work looked fine. They seemed to be running the machine. It was only after some study that the truth would appear: the men were as much a part of the punch-press as the gears that delivered its power or the counterweighted wheel that pulled it up after the blow had been struck.

The punch-press was a metal brain; the hands of flesh which served it were subordinate to its own hot, oily, murderous intelligence.

Here the same thing was happening that Cliff had noticed in Assembly: the machine was running the men. If he ever took a job like that, he knew his shakes would come back worse than ever. After watching for a while he strolled out of the shed, and when Roy, follow-

200

ing him, asked how he liked the job, Cliff told him it was all right but it looked a little tough. He thanked Roy for thinking of him but said he would string along with the Goose.

Gunny, of course, didn't have the shakes. He had come out of the service healthy, certainly a tough old devil for his age. Gunny was a lucky man, and it was all right for him, from a health point of view, to get himself transferred from Bomber Assembly to Processing. In Assembly, it was drive, drive, drive—keep the stuff moving—and that pace was hard for an old guy even if he was tough. The old nerves just couldn't take it. Sure, a lot of girls worked on the Bomber Line, doing the same tube-assembly work that Gunny had been doing, but the girls were kids, some in their teens, many in the early twenties. They could take it better than an old war-horse like Gunny, worn down by the battle-fronts of three decades.

Not for the world would Gunny have confessed he couldn't stand the pace. Nor had his boss any complaints of him. "Excellent worker" was the phrase on Gunny's transfer slip, and after it the penciled comment, "Would do well wherever he is placed."

Gunny told Cliff he was changing jobs because the tube-assembly was too easy. Well, women could handle it. Gunny wanted to do more for the war effort. He wanted a *man's* job.

But although Gunny got the job he had requested, there was something wrong about it. Gunny was crabby, just as he had been before he left home. He was given to spells of brooding, and he was drinking quite a bit. When he got off work he'd go over to Swing Shift Row and lap up beer. Sometimes he'd get in a crap game and wouldn't show up at "Rodds' Lodge" till Cliff was getting up.

Maybe the new job wasn't any better than the old. Maybe not even as good, even though Gunny was now knocking down a dollar two bits an hour. Like Roy Connors, Gunny had been assigned to a punch-press, only his was a solo-press and the single operator was his own feeder. It was just a little hundred and fifty pounder, and it was completely safe. Any kind of punch-press, big or little, can cut off a man's hands as easily as a chef can slice a hunk of oleomargarine, and hands cost money. Far easier for a company to buy a new plate for the press, or even a new ram, than to pay for a pair of hands. Payments for hands may be stretched out as long as the handless man keeps living.

With this thought in mind, some whizz-bang designer of industrial devices had perfected a method of keeping the one-man press from causing loss. Gunny wore a harness called a Punch-Press Safety Harness—an arrangement of straps fitting over his back, elbows and shoulders. This contraption was connected with the press in such a way that, when the ram came down, the operator's hands were automatically pulled back out of harm's way. When he wore the harness Gunny's hands could not move far in any direction, but he could make the movements necessary for lifting the metal sections from a feed-box at his side and placing them correctly on the plate. Then he would touch the operating button, the ram would come down—and at the proper moment, Gunny's hands would be jerked back. So forth and so on, a gentle, beneficial cycle of activity which would be repeated several thousand times each day with little effort by the operator.

It was a very simple job, really, well-paid, and very,

very safe. It should have been flattering to Gunny, as a Horizon employee, to know that such meticulous consideration had been given to his safety: the harness was a poor excuse for him to go out and drink and waste his salary bucking the crap-table in clip joints.

Yet Gunny didn't like the harness. He talked about it in contemptuous terms and would have left it off had it been possible to do so and still operate the press. Having led men into battle, a task requiring initiative, he resented being hitched to a motor-brain. Finally he put in for another transfer, saying he would take less money to get rid of his harness.

This time the transfer wasn't issued: instead, an executive in Personnel dished a lecture. He said Horizon couldn't hand out transfers to every man who got bored with what he was doing. Two months on any given job had to elapse before a worker could be transferred. No exception could be made in Gunny's case.

Outwardly, Gunny accepted the verdict. But though hitched to the punch-press, he was not yet a true part of it: while the press jerked him back and forth, his brain was busy fighting its superior brain, trying to defeat its purposes or—if that was impossible—at least to escape them.

While this struggle went on in Gunny, there was no living with him. He was as irritable as a sick dog and at home would quarrel with Cliff at the most trifling provocation. Suddenly, however, this period passed: he became tranquil and secretive.

He had thought of a way of outsmarting the machine. Now he no longer got drunk, and he began to save his money again. He wrote for mail-order catalogues and procured some books from the Public Library. One day, in response to a money-order sent to Chicago, a camp tent arrived by express. Gunny took off the paper and string and stowed the tent under his bed: having it there afforded him a satisfaction which Cliff did not share. The tent was not in any sense an asset in the stuffy little room. Its canvas, or some water-proofing stuff on it, gave out a powerful smell.

"Couldn't we put it out in the garage?" Cliff suggested one day. "Judas, Sarge, we don't need it in here."

Gunny had not received this proposal with any grace. He seemed to feel that storage anywhere except in the closest proximity to himself would leave his new possession at the mercy of vandals.

"I'm gonna need that tent right soon now. Can't take no chances with it."

"What in God's name you going to do?"

Gunny assumed a mysterious air. "Kid," he said, "I been meaning to tell you, only I was waiting for the right time. As soon as I git two, three hundred dollars more, I'm going to shake the dust of this place off my feet. I'm going up north. If you want to come along, the tent will hold the both of us. That's why I bought a decent-sized one."

"Up north? What would we do up there?"

Gunny's crafty manner intensified. Reaching under his mattress he produced a volume taken from the Public Library. He showed Cliff the title: *Labrador Mink: Its Care and Feeding*.

"Take a gander at this sometime. You'll learn plenty."

Cliff said suspiciously, "Is that what you want to do? Hunt these animals?"

"Not hunt 'em. Raise 'em. That, and trap 'em. When I was a boy in Dakota I learned trapping, and this book gives the raising end of it. Up there you don't punch no time clocks. You ain't tied up in no harness like a coal-mine mule."

Cliff's mind dealt with this warily. The project sounded attractive but fanciful.

"It wouldn't be like having a job."

"You're damn right it wouldn't. Prime pelts bring a lot of dough, only you kin keep it up there—you don't have to spend it. We'd go fifty-fifty, use the tent until we built a shack. Then we'd run out trap-lines and start our breedery. No straw bosses playing Hitler on you up there, kid. Nothing to pay for but your staples—flour and bacon and tobacco. Game is free, and the air in the woods don't have to be pumped through a strainer. You kin breathe it the way it is."

"You sure sound like a resort ad."

"I know what I'm talking about. Tell you what started me thinkin'—that day we were planning to go deer-hunting. Ever hang a deer until it's aged just right, and then make a stew out of the haunch? And fish—brother, if your shack is by a stream, the way it would be, the trout'll wake you up in the morning jumping and splashing. That water's cold and those babies are hungry. They'll take a fly like a baby takes a titty."

Cliff was grinning. Gunny's words were like a tune—the dream of all American workers at one time or another.

"What about the nights? What would we do then?"

Gunny said the nights would be the best part of all. No movies to bother with. No bus to ride. Not even booze or cigarettes, because up there you'd lose your taste for them.

Nights you'd build up the fire. You'd light your pipe and lie back on your bunk; there'd be an owl hooting, way off somewhere, and the moon coming up, maybe, and—

"Want to take a chance, Cliff? Want to put in with me?" Gunny's tone was almost pleading.

"I don't know, Sarge. Sounds good, all right. I'd have to think it over."

"Better let me know, kid. Because I'm pulling out. Going to hit for the tall timber, and it won't be long now."

Gunny walked about restlessly, moving his arms as if pushing aside entanglements. Watching him, Cliff thought of the way he looked standing at the punch-press, laced into his harness. The chunky Sarge seemed small and helpless when you thought of him that way.

"You better come," Gunny said, "because I'm moving on. And you kin bet your bottom dollar, nothing's going to stop me."

❧ CHAPTER 36 ❧

SWING SHIFT ROW WAS A CITY OF BARS, WHOREHOUSES and gambling joints which had mushroomed in a desolate area near the plant. Curfew made its comforts taboo after twelve o'clock and consequently quite expensive, but the swing shift didn't mind the expense. The plant's insomniac pressure bred a corresponding fever in the men who worked night hours; few of them went to bed till dawn; they were driven to spend their money by the very weariness they had acquired in getting it, by loneliness and the feeling that the war might end at short notice and their jobs be taken from them.

Cliff had arranged to meet Gunny in a parking lot a little after midnight; they had borrowed Roy's car for the drive over to Swing Shift Row. Some rain was falling when Cliff reached the parking lot; he sat in the lean-to of the kid who parked the cars, getting dried out in the warmth of a kerosene stove. Outside, a circle of light showed in the misty night where a powerful light bulb dangled from a post; Cliff kept glancing at this spot, watching for Gunny. After a while he called the parking kid's attention to a man who had stepped out of the darkness and stood looking hesitantly around at the cars. While the two watched from the shack, the man tried the doors of several cars. Finding one unlocked he immediately jumped in and closed the door. Cliff saw a match flare as the man in the dark car lit a smoke.

The parking kid said, "He'll sit there now till your friend Watrous comes in. He's here every doggone Satiddy night."

"Who is he?"

Something about the man he had glimpsed out in the blur of rain reminded Cliff of a person he knew.

The kid said, "Some kind of a bum, I guess. Comes around for a hand-out—there's the Sarge now."

Gunny had just entered the parking lot, walking briskly, his head bent in the rain. He looked sharply to the right and left and then, having perceived the car in which the man was waiting, crossed to it and got in. In a minute both got out and stood beside the car, talking; the man's face was turned toward the light, and Cliff saw that he was Billy Tabeshaw. Excited, he took his feet off the stove and ran out of the lean-to.

At the sound of his hurrying steps Bill Tabeshaw whirled around nervously.

"Who's that?" he said in his deep voice, blinking in the rain.

"It's me, Bill."

Cliff moved into the light, and Bill relaxed.

"Doggone," he said. "I didn't recognize you. How are you, kid?"

"Just fine, Bill," Cliff said. He shook hands with the Indian, whose broad and chilly hand, wet with rainwater, felt like a slab of iron.

"Good to see you," the Indian said. Knowing that Cliff was studying him, he lowered his eyes. He was dressed in a thin, pawnshop suit, too short in the sleeves. Under the suit he wore a gray sweater instead of a shirt. He was clean-shaven but looked thin and sickly.

"Everything okay, Bill?"

"Sure, Cliff. Can't complain."

"That's swell," Cliff said. Feeling that Gunny had unfinished business to take up with Bill, he patted the Indian's shoulder and moved off. He sat in the car till Gunny got through and joined him.

As they drove out of the parking lot there was no sign of Bill Tabeshaw; he had moved back into the folds of the rainy night.

"He's only been around a couple of weeks," Gunny said defensively, as if replying to a criticism. "I didn't see no use in telling you. You got better uses for your money than to let him drink it up."

"Are you so loaded down with cash I can't cut in to help a pal?"

"When I need you to cut in, I'll let you know."

They drove for a while in silence. In Cliff's mind was the figure of Bill as he had looked a few months ago—

striding up the street, resplendent in his western finery. That day he'd had close to two thousand dollars folded in his star-boots—and now he was dead broke, on the prowl for hand-outs.

"Where's he living?"

"Got himself a bivouac in the hobo jungle, over by the stock-yards."

"You always said he'd lose that dough."

"Know how he lost it? Went in the used-car business. He'd have made out better if he'd stuck to red-dog. Matt's been helping him, and with the few bucks he shakes out of me he makes out all right."

"I'm going to get him a job in Salvage," Cliff said tensely. "I'm going to talk to the Supe. We've got a couple ex-cons on the shift, one of them did eleven years for manslaughter. I guess if they hire cons they can hire Bill."

"Most any defense plant will hire a con," Gunny said. "They'll hire dwarfs and rummies and bindle-stiffs. But it's like I told you—they won't hire a guy with a bad conduct discharge. He's an outlaw every place he goes."

"What'll become of him, Sarge? We can't leave him in that jungle."

"There ain't nothing you kin do."

"There must be something. There's got to be some kind of job he can get."

"An Indian can't take every kind of job. He can't be a bus-boy or a swamper. He's too lazy and too hot-headed. If an Indian takes a job like that it eats his insides out till he starts in to brood, and after he gits brooding then he tries to kill his boss or something. It's no good. There's just one hope for Bill—he might git starved down till he's ready to go home and check into the Reservation."

"Won't he do that?"

Gunny swung around to look at Cliff. "What do you figure?"

"I figure he's got to."

Gunny jammed on his brakes to make a stop-light. "You saw the way he got himself rigged up, before he went home the last time. He's got to be a hot-shot to his folks. Do you think he'd go back the way he's looking now?"

For another stretch of road neither man spoke: the raindrops pelted like glass bullets into the cone of the headlights. They were near the turn-off leading to Swing Shift Row when Cliff said, "Maybe I should feel like getting drunk, but I'm damned if I do."

"Git your mind off it," Gunny said. He made the turn, slogging along on a dirt road now.

"You go on in. I'll wait for you in the car."

"The hell you will," Gunny said. "Waiting in the car won't help Bill none, and a couple of beers right now will help you plenty."

CHAPTER 37

YET CLIFF WOULD NOT ACT AGAINST HIS INCLINATION. Sitting in the car while the rain poured down, he thought of the nervous, hunched figure of Bill, once such a hell of a Marine, stepping out of the night to collect a hand-out and then vanishing into the toils of his obscure and terrible destiny. Many times on the island Bill had saved them all; instincts keener in him than in white men had told him when danger threatened.

Now many of the jungles were captured. The big ships had rolled up to gun-range of the atolls and shelled them to pieces. Nowadays they shelled for two days without stopping instead of a few hours as they had done before. And when the boats went in now, the fellows in them had been trained for eighteen months instead of three. Present-day assaults, he had read, were organized: the guys didn't need to pray so hard while they circled around in the dark in the mêlée of boats, jerking and swinging to avoid collisions, all lights out and the engines blubbering in the pitch dark and the coxswains yelling to each other, "What's your number? What's your number?"

Things were different now and the war was being won, but when he and Bill and Gunny had been out there the war was on its way to being lost—and who had turned the tide if not such men as Bill? In those days an outfit that had an Indian scout assigned to it had been considered lucky. An Indian didn't stand out in the rain in those days hoping for a five-buck hand-out.

Cliff went to sleep in the car, waiting for Gunny to get through his fun and drive him home. During the week that followed he was nervous and depressed, and once, when a motorcycle pick-up jammed into the Goose at a plant intersection, he got a fit of the shakes. Next day he laid off work and in the afternoon rode out to Hoovertown to see if he could find Bill, but he had no luck. On Saturday Gunny reported Bill hadn't come around for his hand-out.

Cliff decided Gunny's advice had been right—a few

beers once in a while might not be such a bad idea. There was no sense getting in a mental rut. He made several trips to Swing Shift Row, staying away from the crap tables but enjoying himself in other directions; he struck up acquaintanceship with some of the girls who worked in an establishment called Happy Landings.

There was one girl there, Mona Harris, who reminded him of Lolita: she was a small brunette, lively and vivacious, with an easy, joking way about her.

Mona was a very busy young woman. Early in the evening she worked in a strip-tease act in a Hollywood café; she did not, she confessed to Cliff, personally strip, but she stood on the stage and caught the garments which the featured strip-tease artist tossed to her as she removed them.

At Happy Landings Mona had a strip-tease of her own. The clothes-catching was done by a patron whom Mona picked out of the audience.

On the night when this assignment fell to Cliff, Happy Landings was jammed with swing shift workers who demanded that the clothes-catcher improve the act by stripping also.

"Take 'em off, take 'em off," they chanted. "You, too, big boy."

Laughter sprayed like water from a fire hydrant, bouncing from the walls of Happy Landings.

Mona—as Sarah Bernhardt was once rumored to have done—turned to her audience and reprimanded them.

"If you guys don't stop your foolishness, I won't take off another thing."

Later, Mona apologized for the ribbing he'd had to take. "They'll carry on like that sometimes . . ."

Cliff said it was all right. He bought a drink; they

sat wedged in a corner of the bar. Mona couldn't make him out—he looked so sober and controlled, and at the same time so lost, somehow, and kiddish. She knew why the fellows had ribbed him during the act—big, raw-boned, gangling guy that he was, standing there holding her black gloves, skirt and brassiere in his bony flippers. He'd tried to be such a sport and kid the guys right back, and all the time there was that powerful yet lost and helpless look about him.

Where did a fellow like that come from? Where did he fit in? What had happened to him to give him that look, the goddam big goof? He had a swell build, but he didn't seem to know it: he was perfectly happy—or seemed so—just sitting in the smoke and clatter of the bar, drinking his beer, content because she'd told him he was helpful in the act.

Mona knew about men's bodies and about their faces: this one had a fighter's face and a dreamer's at the same time, the bones in his cheeks and forehead made heavy for protection, his mouth so sensitive, his eyes lost and quiet.

But where was the fight in him?

Mona had thought of asking Cliff to take her home, but now she changed her mind. In matters of this kind she always gave her instincts free rein. For her to sleep with a man, he had to be complete. No matter how many times they were together, each time had to be complete just as the man was. In the morning, any morning, both had to be able to get up and go about their business. This one, she felt, could do that. But could she, once they'd been together? Any woman with him would be playing mother, sister, sweetheart, wife, and all the other women that he'd never had.

Mona thought about it but she put the idea aside. In

the change of a juke-box melody she finished her glass and got up, thanking Cliff prettily for buying her the beer.

❧ CHAPTER 38 ❧

IN THE POUND OF THE PLANT, THE ALTERNATION OF THE shifts, the quick succession of days and nights, it was hard to know what it was all about. Voices were talking on the radio; head-lines every night, every morning yelled about something.

There was no inflation, but no bargains either: stocks were up, food was up, skirts were up, hopes were down. At Horizon rumors flew down the assembly line.

It was hard to stick to an idea when the bombs were falling, the radios blaring, and the little newsboys dodged between cars at the stop-lights, peddling the papers with the blurred front pages telling of a nation and a world at war. Officer runs amok, kills five. Tots drown in pool. Nelson in. Nelson out. Knocks Hull. Hull, Knox. Pants to match your coat and vest. Dads drafted. Dads deferred. Shoo, shoo, Baby. When I get home we'll live a life of ease.

Sometimes in Motor Assembly, smoke rose from the big automatics and the hot music of hydraulic hammers, air-hoses, welders, clicking fan-belts, merged into a song of terror.

What next? What now? Something—pass it on. It's hot. Straight from the feed-box—

BOMBED

YOUR PAPA'S OFF TO THE SEVEN SEAS

The talk was bad sometimes, but the breastless bird-shape of the fighting planes in dobs of green and mottled brown and chocolate paint flowed out of the block-long doors of B-Plant on to the testing field, their guns already installed and their tanks filled, ready to go.

Your head got spinning, and the days and nights ran together, camouflaged to look the same. Especially if you spent much time in Swing Shift Row as Cliff was now doing. If you had a girl there was not much sense going to Swing Shift Row, but as yet Cliff didn't have one. Didn't want one.

You could make friends easily in the Row. All sorts of people came in there. Not all of them connected with Horizon. One night there, early in December, Cliff ran into some one he had not expected to see just then—or, in fact, ever. Some one who, as far as he was concerned, was dead and buried.

He had been shooting crap and had won forty dollars. He was in Happy Landings, sitting at a table with Gunny and Roy Connors, counting the dough: later he even remembered the time—two A.M.—which was the hour that "slumming" parties generally chose to hit the Row. Cliff had just made his winnings into neat stacks of bills and silver on the table when the door opened and Pat Tracy walked in—or rather, the girl who had been Pat Tracy and was now Mrs. Klim. There were three other people with her, a girl and two flying cadets.

Pat looked fine. She had on a small hat with a feather

215

that curved around it and a silky dark suit with a short skirt and naked legs the way most of the girls had since they couldn't get silk stockings. Her full, red lips were slightly parted and her eyes were shining with the pleasure of being on a party. As soon as the waiter gave her crowd a table she put down her handbag to reserve the place and went right out to dance with one of the cadets.

She hadn't seen Cliff.

The other cadet and the other girl weren't dancing but were sitting at the table talking, their heads close together. When Cliff came over and took one of the empty seats they looked at him confusedly, as if trying to remember who he was. They seemed to take for granted that it was all right for him to be there. The cadet nodded and Cliff nodded in return; after this the couple paid no further attention to him, concentrating feverishly on their inaudible conversation.

Thinking about it afterward, Cliff could not tell what made him go to the table. In a way, it was a hell of a thing to do. He wasn't on the party, and he had no business butting in. You couldn't jam your way into a foursome date in Happy Landings without starting something.

Gunny, schooled in emergencies, dropped a couple of salt cellars into a napkin and twisted the slack of the cloth around his hand.

By this time Pat had seen Cliff. She left her partner at once and went up to him and took his hands. Pleasure spilled into her eyes and voice as she looked at him, saying the hellos. Back of her, taking somewhat less joy in the meeting, was the cadet who had brought her. Pat finally remembered him and turned around.

"I want you to meet an old friend of mine—"

She never got the name out because the cadet interrupted.

"I can do without that," he said.

"Dick!—Please!" Pat said anxiously. She gave a worried glance at Cliff.

The other couples were standing now, looking from Cliff to the cadet.

"Let's sit down," the cadet said, pulling out Pat's chair.

"Cliff Harper—Miss Spangard and Cadet Hall," Pat said, introducing Cliff to the other couple.

The cadet with Miss Spangard said nothing. He was apparently taking his cues from the fellow who had been dancing with Pat. The latter stood with his hand on Pat's chair. His chin was sticking out like a tank-turret. He was a stocky, broad-shouldered fellow with a brick-red face.

"Okay, buddy," he said to Cliff. "It's been nice to meet you."

"Dick," Pat said angrily, "this man is a friend of mine."

"Fine!" the cadet said. "Only, if he wants to join this party, let him get himself another suit."

"Sit down, Cliff," Pat said quietly.

Cliff pulled out one of the extra chairs and sat down. Every one was sitting now, though the red-faced cadet had his chair pulled out from the table so he could get up quickly if need arose. From the other table, Gunny was looking over interestedly.

Pat said, "Why haven't you called me?"

"Let him get himself a uniform," the red-faced cadet said.

"I'm staying out of this," Miss Spangard said. She got up and went quickly into the ladies' room.

"Please, please, Dick," Pat said.

"I work at Horizon," Cliff said to the cadet. "But there we don't wear uniforms. We make the planes. We don't fly them."

He spoke quietly, not in the least angry. It was funny, that was all, this shanty Irish son-of-a-bitch sounding off about a uniform. He'd probably had fourteen hours in the air and he thought he was Rickenbacker.

"All I know is I don't like civilians horning in on my dates."

"Oh, my God," Pat said with utter disgust.

Rage exploded like a grenade at the base of Cliff's skull. For a fraction of a second he sat weak and helpless, leaning on the table. His anger had taken away his power to act. Then, all of a sudden, he was strong again. He stood up, having decided to kill the cadet. The guy stood up, waiting, and Pat seized his arm, trying to drag him away from the table. The cadet shook her off. Gunny was coming across the dance-floor, and the manager of the establishment, a Greek, reached back of the bar for his black-jack.

Cliff came around the table fast, pulling back his right to loop it at the cadet. The punch never landed; the other student officer had tripped him. The red-faced cadet laughed as Cliff went sprawling, rolling away from the table and covering his head with his elbows to keep from being kicked. He wound up against a wall and scrambled to his feet, rushing at the cadet with his head lowered, trying to tackle him, but the cadet raised his knee, smearing Cliff's face and knocking him down again. Gunny was beating hell out of the smaller cadet who had tripped Cliff, and the shill who ran the crap-game in the back room pushed back the curtain of the passageway and stuck out his mournful yellow face, believing the joint was raided.

218

"Holy Christ," he muttered. He stepped round the curtain and went to the telephone, dropping a nickel into the pay-box.

Gunny slammed his belly against the Greek, holding him off. A waiter tried to dodge past and get in the mêlée but Gunny clipped him with the club he had made of the salt cellars and napkin and the waiter went down.

"Let the boys fight it out," he said. "Let them settle it between them."

Cliff rose awkwardly, rubbing his hands over his eyes to clear them. He was bleeding at the mouth and nose, but now his head was steady. He came in crouching, covering his chin and dragging his right foot behind his left, studying the cadet who waited with his hands up and a bemused look on his face, evidently taken aback by the discovery that Cliff was able to go on fighting.

The cadet stuck out his left like a man who knew some boxing. Cliff, however, wasn't in a boxing mood: he pulled back and slammed his heel into the cadet's groin. As the cadet's head jerked forward Cliff caught him on the chin with the heel of his hand—a tactic he had learned in Raider Training. Then Gunny grabbed his arm, pulling him toward the door. All three piled into the car, turning into San Fernando Boulevard just as the Squad car came round the corner with four cops in it and the siren wide open.

CHAPTER 39

"LADY WANTS TO SEE YOU—"

The cop at the gate had called Cliff over as he came off shift; he jerked his thumb at a small coupé parked across the street.

"Thanks."

The cop glanced at his face and whistled. "Brother! Where'd you get the black eye?"

"Forgot to duck," Cliff said, using a classic phrase.

"That's what you get for fooling around dames," the cop said, but Cliff wasn't paying attention.

He'd started toward the car, walking slowly because his legs seemed a long way from his head. He knew who was in the car even before he saw Pat, sitting with her hands on the wheel and her head bent as if she had been waiting quite a while. Without saying anything Cliff went around to the right side and got in, and Pat started the engine.

"Better drive around the corner," he said. "The buses will be pulling in line in a minute."

Pat looked quickly at his eye and the long gash along his jaw. Then she paid attention to her driving.

"Is this all right?"

They were in a quiet street in front of a vacant lot. Cliff nodded, and she parked the car and turned toward him.

"Cliff, I had to come. I just had to tell you how horrible I felt about last night."

"Forget it."

"I can't, Cliff. I haven't been able to think of anything else. I was so ashamed. Dick is so stupid when he's drunk. Calling you a civilian—"

"I am a civilian."

"Don't, Cliff."

"Don't what?"

"Make fun of me."

"I'm not making fun of you. I'm just stating a fact."

"Please, Cliff, Dick didn't know who he was talking to. He felt like an awful fool later."

Cliff looked seriously at Pat. Then, in spite of himself, he grinned.

"He didn't look so smart, either."

Pat didn't smile.

"It was dreadful. The police came in, but I'd rather not talk about it. I just wanted to say I'm sorry."

"Well, you said it."

"Yes, Cliff."

"Now do you mind taking me back to the bus-stop? I've got to go home and get cleaned up."

"Whatever you say."

Pat's small teeth pressed against her lower lip. Her cheek-bones looked too big for her face, as they always did when she was mad.

"I guess I've got it coming to me," she said, "but I thought—well, I was hoping, anyway, we'd have a talk. It's been a long time."

She was the same Pat, the same face, hair, and the same white hard skin that always looked as if she had just been in swimming in cold water. The low, quiet voice was hers, yet it was not the same Pat. She was sharper, thinner—more grown up, better-looking, colder.

You couldn't imagine her, now, cooking for a bunch

of kid brothers or rubbing out a fellow's Charley-horse.

You could imagine her, in this tailored suit, working in an office full of chromium gadgets. You could imagine her married to an officer.

Cliff looked at the wings pinned over her left pocket.

"Tell your husband it was my fault," Cliff said. "I'm sorry I horned in on his party. And thanks for apologizing. Now let's go on back."

Pat took her fingers off the starting button.

"I guess you've got things mixed up, Cliff," she said. "Dick isn't my husband. He's just a fellow I was out with."

Cliff stared. "Pardon me," he said. "I didn't know."

"I don't know why I should expect you to," Pat said, "only Arch Winston said he'd talked to you, and I thought—"

"Maybe Arch cut down his report a little. But I should have known, all right. Knowing you, I should naturally know that with your husband overseas you'd be running around with some other fellow."

"My husband is dead, Cliff. He was wounded in a bombing mission in Italy," Pat said. "The plane got back, and he went to base hospital. We got word he was getting better, but he didn't. He died. I suppose I shouldn't go out, but I get the mimies sitting home— it's been almost a year—"

"I'm sorry, Pat."

"I'll take you back to the bus-stop. Or I could take you where you live," she said after another pause.

"The bus will be all right."

Pat started the engine but let it idle while she fluffed out her hair and made up her lips in the wind-shield mirror.

"I guess you're working awfully hard," she said, sitting back.

"I am, sort of—"

"Because if you got an evening off, there's so much—well, I wanted to explain about some things. One thing specially . . ."

"I'll call you sometime."

"Will you do that?"

"Sure."

"I don't believe you will. You haven't even got my number."

"I can get it from Arch."

"I could give it to you now. Would you remember it?"

"I could try, I guess," Cliff said.

He had half hoped he would forget the number. He had no intention of calling Pat. Yet 'phone numbers were tricky. Try to remember one and you forget it. But try to forget one and there it was in your brain forever, big and bright.

The number challenged him. There was an invitation and a question in it, like the look Pat had given him the first summer he fell for her. That day her halter came off and she went on swimming without it. Why would he remember an idiotic, kiddish thing like that? Maybe because it was easier to connect Pat, as she was now, with that day and mood, with that look, than with the different, warmer, easier Pat he had known and loved later, and left behind when he went to war.

He was still a long way from her. He was far enough to see more of her than he ever had of any other woman —far enough so he could tell what a peculiar girl she was. A hell of a funny girl. Little red-head double-crosser, beating his time with another guy. Getting married to the guy and then, when he was laid away, running round with jerks like that flying cadet.

Little whore. Probably she was sleeping with the jerk. It made Cliff's blood boil to think of it. If there was one guy he was sorry for now it was that husband of hers sleeping his last sleep overseas. Brother, what that guy had got himself into.

And out of. . . .

Were all women like that underneath, comrades and betrayers, home-makers and whores at the same time? . . . To hell with it. She wasn't worth worrying about.

They had missed the boat, that was all. A smooth wonderful tune had started playing for them and somebody had busted in with a station announcement and the tune had gone off the air. So forget it. The tune hadn't included Swing Shift Row. It had been about something else—love, for instance. Not about two messy guys chin-fighting in a café and the cops coming. Not about a girl and a fellow in a parked car, talking mean to each other.

Cliff had intended going home for Christmas. But on Christmas Eve he got a note from Mary Ellen Winston asking him to come out to a party the next night. "Just an old-fashioned family dinner. Arch and I would be so pleased if you could come. And if there's any one you'd care to bring with you, just let us know." It didn't take a genius to figure out that was some more of Pat's doing. Maybe she thought he'd bring a girl. Maybe it was that kind of challenge, an ultimatum issued because he hadn't called her. He had intended 'phoning Mrs. Winston to tell her he couldn't come, but an idea came to him. Gunny, he knew, had drifted more and more away from his own family. The old Sarge, it seemed, expected to spend Christmas alone in his room at the Rodds'. It would have been lousy to let him do that, and the food would probably be good out at Arch's.

So at the last minute Cliff called Arch's wife and asked if he could come and bring the well-known former Gunnery Sergeant, Earl W. Watrous.

CHAPTER 40

A BIG DROP-LIGHT HUNG ABOVE THE DINING-ROOM TABLE, and the sides of the table were crowded with chairs, every one jammed together so close it was hard to work an elbow free. On the table was a great array of dishes and the Winstons' servant, a neat, glistening colored girl, hurried in and out of the kitchen bringing more all the time: roast turkey, already carved, with plenty of dressing and giblet gravy; and chopped red cabbage for a vegetable. At each place was a side dish of cole slaw with mayonnaise, and a smaller dish containing nuts and raisins: there were olives and celery to be passed, and baker's rolls, sliced bread, and home-made beaten biscuits, and there were wine-glasses at each place and the guests had their choice of light or dark wine. Although it was not cold outside, the window misted with the warmth of all the people eating, drinking, laughing, talking, crowded close together.

Cliff's brain, like the windows, had a film over it; he was rosy in the face and somewhat dizzy from the heat, the chatter of voices, and the three glasses of punch he had drunk before dinner.

Gunny, sitting straight across the table from him, was going great guns; Cliff hadn't seen the Sarge in such form since their San Francisco outing. Pat Tracy was next to Gunny between the Sarge and Arch, who had carved the turkey. On Cliff's left was a girl named Judy Toreno who had come with Norman Budd, a test pilot at the plant. Norman was a very famous flier and had been with Arch's outfit in Africa, Sicily and Italy. He was exceedingly courteous to all present except Miss Toreno, whom he ignored. Once, however, when she reached across him for the coffee cream, he bit her affectionately on the arm.

In addition to this couple there was A. R. Crowell, head of the plant detectives—a clerkish man in a dark suit, with a tough, tired face. A widow who lived in the neighborhood, Mrs. Matilda Steece, had been invited to balance the table. She was a motherly woman who called Mary Ellen "dearie" and was flattering about all the food except the turkey dressing. "Tastes dry to me," she said under her breath.

Mrs. Steece thought Gunny was wonderful. She laughed loudly at all his jokes, keeping right along with him no matter what he said.

"You're quite some Christmas package, Mrs. Steece," Gunny said, winking at Cliff over his shoulder. He helped himself to some red wine.

"Okay, okay, Sarge," Cliff warned in an undertone. "Tie a can on it."

"When I was a younger man," the Sarge went on,

ignoring Cliff, "I was always hoping I would find something like you in my stocking."

"What's the matter with my own stocking?" Mrs. Steece demanded wittily.

The Sarge roared.

"I bet you come with built-in mistletoe," he said.

Pat smiled at Cliff and he shrugged, grinning: no use trying to tone down the Sarge when he was in a mood like this.

Everybody stuffed themselves on the good things to eat, and after dinner Mary Ellen sat down at the piano and played carols—"God Rest You, Merry Gentlemen," "Jingle Bells," and "Good King Wenceslas."

"Sing, everybody," Arch cried, waving his arms.

Watching Arch, Cliff would never have known him for the bored and restless man whom he had seen in his office, locked up with a pack of cards. There was great power for leadership in him, at present employed in making his guests enjoy themselves. He was so anxious for every one to sing the carols that it became absolutely the right thing to do. When they were all warmed up and the punch was circulating once more, Mary Ellen fussed with cords a little and finally began to play, "O Come, All Ye Faithful."

Cliff pulled his collar to loosen it. So far he had not sung a note, but he knew this one. Even Miss Toreno was singing now, sharing a word-sheet with Mrs. Steece. From Gunny came a low base jarring like a church-organ with a loose pipe.

Pat was looking at the fire, forming the words in a firm sweet voice that was not quite singing, but almost.

". . . Joyful and triumphant. . . ."

As Pat sang she put her arm through Cliff's. He was making noises in his throat intended to be musical. She pressed slightly against him, singing with her eyes half-closed. It seemed as if a panel of time had slid back on roller bearings, taking them with it into the recollection of vanished Christmases.

Often the Tracys and the Harpers had spent their holidays together and old man Tracy had brought down from the attic a music-box which had played the Christmas songs they were now singing.

Maybe this segment of lost time to which they were transposed was the real place in which both he and Pat still lived their lives. Anyway, Pat had tried to talk to him. She tried to tell him something and he had refused to listen.

"Sing, you sissy," she whispered.

"Don't know the words."

"Yes, you do. Don't give me that stuff."

She egged him on with small complimentary squeezes of his arm.

When the singing was over, Arch got out a bottle of bourbon. The serious phase of the festivities was now beginning.

"I got this for you, Sergeant. Been saving it all year. You and me are gonna have a special drink."

"Man, oh, man," Gunny said, "you forget I've got to go to work to-night."

Every one was stunned and horrified. Work—on Christmas night! But Gunny explained that the plant holiday was only twenty-four hours.

There was a war on. The planes had to be made.

Gunny was looking at the bus schedule when Pat said she would drive him to the plant. She insisted on it —her car was right outside. It wasn't out of her way in the least, as she was going back to Beverly. She could take Cliff, too, she said, looking at him over her shoulder, her lips smiling but her eyes steady with a question that had been there long ago, in the lost age to which the shift in time had moved them. Or that had been there always.

"Work is the curse of the drinking classes," Arch said solemnly. "At least, it was when there *were* drinking classes."

"Or when that joke was new," Mary Ellen said. At Arch's side, she turned to Cliff and Pat. "I'm so sorry you two have to go."

"My heckler," Arch said, putting his arm around his wife. "How about it, Sarge? Just a short horn before you go?"

"If it's a real short one, Captain," Gunny said. When the whisky was poured he faced the room, raising his glass with a formal, unexpected gesture.

"Here's to all you folks. Best wishes to you through the coming year."

Wind stirred the little palms along the residential streets; on the boulevards the street-lamps in their concrete standards stamped desolate halos on the darkness. Pat, who had asked Cliff to drive, sat between him and Gunny, whose head began to nod as soon as he was in the car. Outside the plant gates, under the flood-lights, the graveyard shift waited to work off their Christmas hangovers on the assembly line. The Sarge was now snoring peacefully, his head against Pat's shoulder.

"Couldn't we take him home? I can't bear waking him."

"We'll have to," Cliff said. "He's never missed a shift. He says absentees should be shot—like deserters."

"But he's not fit to work."

At this point Gunny, with a rare sense of timing, raised

229

his head. "I'm alrigh', sweetheart. Never felt better'n my life."

Cliff hadn't realized the booze had hit the Sarge so hard. He was about to take Pat's side of the argument when Gunny got the door open and climbed out.

"Goin' to my job," he said. "Good night, all. . . ."

Head down, his eyes blinking in the harsh metallic light, the Sarge stumbled toward the gates, which were just opening.

"I'm worried," Pat said. "Is his job dangerous?"

"Plenty. But they say he can't hurt himself. He's got a safety harness."

"I don't care. I don't like it."

Pat looked at the stocky figure around which the crowd was closing. She put her hand on the door as if to run after the Sarge, bring him back. But it was too late. Cliff slipped the car in gear and they drove away.

The sense of a reversion in time, induced by the songs, by the Christmas feeling of the party, and above all, by being with Pat, was still strong in Cliff. Being with her at the party and now this ride together—both were so much like the old days, the lost innocent time, that it was as if nothing had happened to either of them, as if they could make a date to meet after school—and so on the next day, and the next. For the first time in months he felt happy, and his happiness made him relax the stern decision he had taken in regard to her.

Pat was, at the moment, not in the least like a ghost. She was quite obviously warm, fresh, human, and desirable, a girl of exciting tints and overtones instead of a shade exorcised from the mortal earth. She had not moved from the position she had taken while the Sarge was in the car; she was sitting close to Cliff, her thigh and shoulder against him, her nearness thickening his blood like the

230

allurement of a magic island, the enticements of love and sleep blown from a secret shore to one at sea.

Ruthlessly, he battled the spell which was enmeshing him. It was no good. He now admitted to himself that he would like to make up with her; he would like to if it could be done. But he would not yield without proper conditions. He was no sap. If she wanted to talk to him, as she'd once said—if she thought she could explain why she had crossed him up and married the lieutenant—this was her chance.

"Gee, you look serious," Pat said.

"Do I?"

"Uh-huh. What are you thinking about?"

"Nothing."

"Yes, you were."

"Maybe."

"I was thinking about us, about its being like old times."

"I was thinking it could be like old times, only it wasn't."

"Don't think," Pat begged. "Anyway, not now. Just be with me, like we are."

"Why? Because it's Christmas, and we sang those songs?"

Pat's head was bent.

"No. Because it hasn't changed."

"That's what you think."

"It hasn't," Pat said. "We still feel the same way. It's true, Cliff. You know it is."

Thinking of a way to answer this, he stopped the car at an intersection. No, it was no good. Pat was too clever. She would never explain. She would deceive him, use her power over him. If he gave in to her he was done for.

Such were his thoughts as he sat at the wheel of the

car, staring gloomily ahead. With a jolt his attention was directed to what was happening in the road.

There was a sound of sirens, coming nearer fast. Headlights tossed long parallel knives at the intersection, and a squad of motorcycle cops swept past at seventy miles an hour. One of the cops throttled down, turned, and came back to block the intersection. He sat straddling his motorcycle, one foot on the ground, while the transport trucks came in sight. There were perhaps a hundred trucks, all crowded with men sitting under the canvas tops in full combat equipment. The faces of the men inside showed in the open rear of each truck as it passed, whitened and thrown into sharp relief by the lights of the truck following. Woosh, Vroom, Whee, they went, a standard fifty yards between them and a G.I. guard riding beside each driver; the air was full of the roar of the big truck motors and the nasal tire scream which is made by the tires of U.S.A. transport trucks and by no other vehicle on earth.

WHOOSH WHEE VROOM WHOOSH WHEE VROOM

The fellows in the trucks were going to the harbor. When the big trucks traveled like that and as many as that it was because a boat was waiting for their loads.

Pat, like most residents of the city, was familiar with the atmosphere of troop movements at night, but the sight never failed to fascinate and frighten her. Long before the hundred trucks had passed she turned to look at Cliff.

He was shaking. Though he was gripping the wheel his arms and shoulders trembled, and the tremors were taken up by his whole body. Toward Pat, in the glare of the passing truck-lights, he turned a face constricted with agony.

CHAPTER 41

DURING THE DAY AND EVENING, TIME HAD PLAYED TRICKS with Pat as well as Cliff. She too had remembered the music-box. In the old days, when the box had been brought down from the attic to deliver its redoubtable, straggly airs, Pat had tried to seal into herself the tingling sensations of Christmas goodness, of the expectation of gifts and the piny smell of the tree—sensations so powerful that, as they coursed under her skin, she felt that they could easily lift her up to the ceiling.

She had sealed in the lost Christmases, and the feeling was still there. She had it now, sitting in the car at the dark intersection. She felt anxious about Cliff, yet it was clear to her that this fearful trembling was not new with him: that it was a recurrent affliction of some kind, connected with the war. The panic in his face she ascribed to his dread of the disease and not—as the truth was—to his dread of being repulsive to her, his helpless shame that she should see him this way; nevertheless, she chose instinctively the proper means to help him. She reassured him with consoling words; when he tried to explain what was wrong with him, she would not let him talk but, instead, put her arms around him, trying to quiet the palsy of his nerves. Since he was clearly incapable of driving, she made him move over.

It was she who stopped and looked up at her own window, wondering whether her room-mate, another OPA employee, was at home, or whether she had gone to Pendleton to see her boy-friend. In a moment Pat decided that she didn't care. She now had an idea, reasonable enough though possibly mistaken from a medical viewpoint, that to make him stop shivering she had to make him warm. She had him lie on the bed; she made coffee for him.

She covered him with a quilt. To keep the light out of his eyes she turned off the wall switch, leaving only the bed-light. After a time she lay down beside him, first outside the quilt but later inside. She felt sure if she could really warm him with the heat of her own body the last of the shaking would subside.

They lay close together for several minutes and it was just as she planned, the shaking finally stopped. Pat must have dozed off for a while; she thought that Cliff had, too. When she woke she kissed him once or twice, lightly and timidly, and he moved and held her closer. These kisses were nothing, merely a seal on the warmth and the Christmas feeling, but by degrees their character changed. Pat's mouth became ardent and her breathing slightly audible. It seemed wrong and incongruous now to have clothes on; underneath the quilt Pat made small, purposefull movements of disrobing. She tossed certain garments out of the bed and then she sat up and pulled something over her head and when she slipped into Cliff's arms again her body was as naked as her breath.

"See Watrous?"

The time-clock guard looked after the square-set figure reeling toward Metal Process.

The plant cop nodded. "Kind of high."

"You want to report him?"

The plant cop's practised eye studied the roll of Gunny's gait, the set of his shoulders.

234

"He kin make it, I guess. Half of them's stiff to-night anyhow. If we report all of 'em the plant would have to close down."

In the locker, Gunny shed his coat, put on his coveralls. Already he was hating the machine. Every time he buttoned the last button of his work clothes he started hating it but by the time the shift was over the hate would be flattened out of him by the smash of the ram and the rhythmic assertions of the harness until there was no fight left in him.

To-night it was different. As he strapped himself into his harness he felt that to-night would be a showdown. He laid a metal section on the plate, and pressed the starting-button. The ram slid down and the harness pulled Gunny's arms out of harm's way. The ram climbed up again, and Gunny took the punched section off the dye and tossed it in the basket, flicking the scrap onto the floor. He reached in the feed-basket for another section.

He worked mechanically, easily. He didn't have to think. The machine was his brain. Yet to-night he did not give in to it. He kept on hating. Liquor had given him confidence, had crystallized an idea. He had never really pitted his strength against the harness. He had been letting it bluff him.

A man had invented the harness, had given it power. Maybe another man, himself, could break that power. Maybe then he would be free.

Gunny didn't act on the idea at once. It was too good. Better to coast along a while, let the machine think it was still boss. Let the ram come down on the plate, feel the deep thud of it in your guts. Put your hands out, make the discard, flip on a new section, press the button, feel the jerk, feel the Big Brain being kind to you, the harness saving your hands.

Forward and back. Up and down. To-night the punch-press seemed to be working like a locomotive piston, going faster and faster till you couldn't stand it. Gunny's eyes rolled. His breath tore his chest, and his ribs strained against the harness-straps. In. Out. Process. Discard. Process. The pound of the machines around him made a roaring in his ears. He had to fight or get away. He couldn't do either. He couldn't stand there helpless till the booze and the fine hate were lost and he was whipped again.

"You okay, Watrous?"

"Sure! Sure, I'm okay."

Wait till the straw boss with his yellow check-slip moved farther up the shed. Okay, well, he was stronger than he'd ever been in his life. To-night it was a show-down and he was going to win.

NOW.

Gunny tensed his muscles; with a lunge which swung him off the floor, he threw his weight against the harness, trying to break it. A scream tore out of his throat, he hung on, fighting the Machine Brain with all his strength, swearing like a lunatic. His punch-press stopped, the ram halfway down; the straw boss whirled around, ran toward Gunny, many workers leaving their presses to crowd around. Faces greenish in the neon light were bunched like grapes, mouths sagging open like ink-blots.

"What happened? What'd he do?"

"Damned if I know—Jesus, look—"

The straw boss was cutting Gunny out of the harness, unhurt but hysterical with rage, begging to be let alone, to be allowed to wreck the harness.

"All right, folks. Nothing's happened. Break it up. Get back on your jobs."

Three plant cops pushed through the group around Gunny's punch-press; the straw boss knew one of them by name.

"Take him over to the Chief's office, Joe. He's stinking drunk."

Workers still at their stations stared as Gunny was led away.

"What was it? A fight?"

The girl who ran the next hydro had an angle. "It was a fight and how! The guy was fighting the machine. . . ."

CHAPTER 42

THE PERSONNEL DIRECTOR SAID IT WAS A BREAK FOR Gunny that he had a decent record. Otherwise he'd have been fired; he'd have been out of defense work for good. As it was, he would be put in Salvage, given an old guy's job. Ninety cents an hour instead of a buck, two bits. And no more easy six-and-a-half hour graveyard. From now on he would work day shift.

In a way Cliff was glad it had happened. At least now he saw something of the Sarge. They got up at the same time, got off work together; they could wash up and eat supper together and chew the fat even on the nights when Cliff was riding out to Beverly to see his girl.

The rains were over early that spring, and the dry land turned green: the small deserted farms near the Horizon Plant stirred with unused fecundity. Planes took their test flights in skies piled with golden light, and a few weeks later the same planes were covering landings on Pacific Islands and dropping bombs on Hitler's European fortress.

Pat and Cliff, as the weather grew warmer, found pleasant things to do. There was time now for pleasures recently almost forgotten: movies, dancing, love-making. . . . Just eating dinner, just talking. The dialogue was back, their special dialogue which had started so long ago, once more exerting its gentle pull, swirling their lives together.

On Pat's side there was the quality of anxiousness, of seeking an assurance she had somehow lost. On Cliff's side, strangely, there was a quality of strength and hope. Their positions had reversed from the relationship of the first night, when Pat had taken him into her bed to heal him of his hurts. Temporarily, at least, he was the stronger of the two.

Having a girl made a tremendous difference. He had never quite realized how much difference it could make, yet it took something away, too. Centering his life on Pat had altered his status as a member of the Group.

When first mustered out he had felt there was no proper place for him in the world except his old place in the Group. The Group itself had been home, had been what he lived by. Hence his sense of defeat when he felt the Group was threatened with extinction—his desire to keep it together at all costs; hence his indigna-

238

tion, and successful counter-action, when Five-by-Five had been in danger of going to the Domiciliary; his shock at the degradation of Bill Tabeshaw, his sympathy with Gunny's loneliness and confusion and Perry's helpless invalidism.

Once, the Group had come first. Now it didn't. Spending so much time with Pat, Cliff saw the fellows very little.

It had been several weeks since he had attended one of the Sunday get-togethers in Perry's shack.

To all appearances, the session of smoke and talk differed little from many previous Sundays. Perry lay in his high bed, propped on many pillows, sometimes lifting his huge right arm to grip the bar above him and so shift his remnant of a body to a more comfortable position. His eyes, glistening in his seamed black face, moved from one speaker to another; without talking much himself he followed every word with great attention, relishing the presence of his friends. In a corner of the room his mother rocked and nodded; her body, mountainously emerging from a gingham house dress, blended with the shadows cast into the corner by the reading light beside the bed. Mrs. Kincheloe did not seem to be composed of flesh at all but of some smooth and everlasting black material, of great value and malleability. She was glad of the visit of the white men, since they gave pleasure to her son, but she was careful not to intrude herself upon them. After a while, according to her custom, she went into the kitchen, cooked a hot meal: while she cooked, an ancient song, composed of resignation, longing, and the inexorable hopes and sorrows of her race, swelled in her chest and issued from her in a subdued humming like steam coming out of a big kettle. The smells of the cooking and the rhythm of the humming, votive and reassuring, filled the small shack with a sense of Sunday peace.

Outwardly, it was a day like many other days, but now the undercurrents were different. For one thing, Billy Tabeshaw was present; though the others had welcomed him in their old-time fashion, any one of them would have admitted that it was no longer pleasant to be with the Indian. Bill had changed; he had fallen on bad ways. Any man might have his ups and downs, but what had happened to Tabeshaw was not so good. Living out in the warrens of Hoovertown had reduced him physically: he had the thin yet flabby look of a muscular man who has been favoring booze over food. He was having trouble with his eyes; the booze again.... Once Bill's eyes had been like binoculars, able to detect the enemy when no one else could see him, to follow a difficult trail, read the weather, translate the secrets of the jungle. The safety of many men had once depended on the eyes of Bill Tabeshaw. Now, red as fire, Bill's eyes blinked rheumily in little caves under his skull. His hands, so recently skilled in the use of many weapons (and themselves weapons of a deadly sort), shook as he rolled and lighted his perpetual smokes. Worst of all, a sneaking yet murderous meanness had replaced his former effortless daring. Bill had turned into a complainer. His stories were all of one type—of how some one, generally some person for whom he had done odd jobs, or from whom he had sought a job, had maligned, opposed, evaded, or defrauded him, and of what Bill had done or planned to do in retaliation.

Billy Tabeshaw, the Raider Scout, had become a connoisseur of grudges. His most recent quarrel involved Matt Klein. Matt had failed to show up at Perry's: Mrs. Kincheloe, who traded at Matt's market, had heard he was keeping open Sundays due to press of business, but since Matt had never previously failed to show up, all decided that the real cause of this defalcation was this trouble with the Indian.

"That Jew!" Bill said, spitting the words out. "Lousy, smart-aleck kike. Wait till I tell you what he done—"

Gunny and Cliff exchanged looks of amazement. For any member of the Group to attack another was surprising enough; the form of the attack was even more so. Neither in training nor in combat had a man's race been held a subject for comment; whether Slav, Hawaiian, Indian or Filipino, his status had been determined by his personal qualities. To hear "Jew" used this way by a Marine was as cockeyed as if Bill's voice had turned to falsetto.

"What do you mean, you red-skin bastard?" Gunny said. "Since when is a white man a kike to you? Is he sore at you for being a ruttin' Indian?"

"No, wait till I tell you," Bill Tabeshaw insisted.

His story was ludicrous, pitiable—yet it had a nightmare horror. It seemed that Bill, ragged and derelict, had called on Matt at his market and been given a handout of groceries. This had occurred during the previous winter, probably about the time the Indian had started coming to Horizon for charity from Gunny. Unable to get a decent job, disgusted after making the rounds of defense plants (where he was either turned away or hired and then let out as soon as the nature of his discharge became known), Bill kept sponging on Matt until one day Matt told him he could quit coming round. Bill, full of red-eye, goddamned Matt in the presence of cash customers and Matt ran him out of the market.

"How do you like that? Is that a way to treat a pal? Smart-aleck kike!"

"He fed you, didn't he?" Gunny said.

"Why wouldn't he hand a lousy basket of eats out, the rich bastard. He ain't the same guy we knew, Sarge. I'm tellin' you. He's gone high-hat since he got rich."

"What makes you think he's rich?"

"I seen him standin' there all day, raking in the dough. Can't hear nothing in that place, only the cash register ringing it up. He's got all the dough and a swell-looking blonde dame standing there playin' the register like it was a whorehouse piano. A store cram full of eats, an' he won't give a pal a lousy hand-out."

"Why did you hang around there drunk and make him sore?"

"I went back oncet when I was sober. He was just haspin' them big doors down. When he seen me comin' he locked them quick and stepped inside. I had a piece of lead-pipe in my pocket and I guess he knew it. Yelled through the door if I don't scram, he'll put the cops on me. How do you like that—put the cops on his wartime buddy?"

Gunny's brain, unused to complexities, could not unravel this, but he could sense its evil. Cliff, too, was silent and nervous, wishing he had not come. Perry's cropped head tossed on his pillow: his arm swelled as he gripped the bar.

"Lawd," he muttered, "that's bad—never thought to hear a thing like that. Have to ask old Matt about it. Sure as certain," he said, addressing Bill, "certain as I lie here, he didn't never mean that like you took it. Maybe you got him riled, is all. You don't have to ask him fer no hand-out vittles, Bill. We got plenty right here. You just come here if you want it. Ain't that right, Ma? Can't my buddy here set down to table any time he's got a wish to?"

Mrs. Kincheloe, bringing in his tray, nodded confirmation.

"We got plenty, any time a friend sits down," she said, looking at the Indian with a polite face though it was clear from the set of her broad back and the purse of her lips that she had no use for him. Perry—a wisp of life suspended from a supernatural arm—pulled himself up in bed, and Mrs. Kincheloe slipped more pillows behind him. She set the tray on his truncated thighs.

"Yo supper's ready in the kitchen, gentlemen."

To-night there was no zest in the good meal. Only Tabeshaw did full justice to it; he ate like an animal, stuffing big hunks of bread and meat into his mouth, and the heat of the room and the food brought a shine of sweat into his saddle-colored face. When he was full he rose to go at once.

Gunny followed him out, and for some time the two stood talking, just beyond the open door: the Sarge took something out of his pocket and passed it to Tabeshaw.

"Did you give that guy more dough?" Cliff asked on the way home.

"I gave him a key."

"A key to what, Sarge?"

"To our room, out at Rodds'."

Cliff was startled.

"Holy Christ, Sarge, we can't have the Indian living with us."

"Why not?"

"You know why not. He's made a rummy out of himself."

"He's done that," the Sarge said, "but that's only half of it. He's gone bad, and when an Indian goes bad he's poison. Take it from me. I know."

"And you want him out at Rodds'?"

"He's not coming out there. Not to live, anyhow. I give him the key so he'd have a place to hole up when he's got no other place."

"He's got Hoovertown."

"When he's so far gone even Hoovertown won't be no good to him."

"You figure he'll get that far?"

"He's damn near a cinch to. When he does, he'll need a place."

"I don't want us to be it."

Gunny rubbed his hand over his chin the way he'd done in combat, when he wore his full beard.

"You're it," he said, "whether you like it or not. He's not a well man. Son," he said, using the term which came to his lips with Cliff only in moments of the most solemn communication, "son, I don't like what's happened to him any more than you do. And I don't blame Matt, no, nor nobody else for resenting him. I resent him myself. He's about as useful as a shedding rattlesnake."

Cliff looked at the Sarge in wonder. Here was Gunny, himself gray and aging, still strong enough to feel responsible for the Group. The Group was still the center of Gunny's life just as it was for Perry, lying there in bed, depending on the Sunday get-togethers for renewal of the old-time feeling. Matt, of course, had the store: he was making a place for himself. And Cliff knew that he, too, now had a place outside the Group. Even he, little by little, might forget, might become an outsider— but at this thought he scowled and clenched his fists. It must never happen. He more than any of them must remain true to his ideal, he who had seen from the first the necessity for all of them to preserve the Group. Gunny was right about the Indian. He was glad the Sarge had given him that key. No matter what happened, Bill could still come back to the Group as a fellow could to his own family. No matter how low he sank he would have that much left and nothing could take it away.

CHAPTER 43

IT WAS A HOT JUNE NIGHT, SOLEMN AND WINDLESS, WITH long drifts of stars angling across the sky. Cliff and Pat had driven down to the beach in Pat's car and taken a swim just as the sun was going down. Pat was cold then, and as they put on their clothes in the car, Cliff rubbed her back with a rough towel to warm her. They built a driftwood fire, and Pat cooked weiners and roasted potatoes while Cliff fished, standing in the edge of the surf and casting with live bait and three-ounce sinkers. All the way down the beach, as far as Malibu, the fires of other fishermen were winking, the faraway ones no bigger than glow-worms. In the darkness the sea was quiet and slick and the surf at the edge of the firelight broke sharply white. Sometimes a crest crackled with an electric unexpected power, and then there would be silence again, the snap of little waves and the sizzle of the driftwood logs over which Pat was cooking.

When Pat called him to eat, Cliff made one more cast

and left his line. He put the drag on the reel and propped the thick surf-rod on a forked stick in such a way that if a fish struck he could get to it in time. He had meant to go on casting after supper, but instead he got a blanket from the car and spread it down, and they lay close together, breathing the lovely rank cold smell which rose out of the sea.

This was the time. Cliff said, "What about us getting married?" and then took a long breath and lay still.

Pat did not say anything. She didn't move or even seem to breathe: it was as if for that moment she had stopped living. This could mean either one thing or another, and Cliff thought it meant the first thing. Then the pause lasted just too long: he felt Pat's tension under his arm, and with a stupid emptiness he knew it was the second thing.

Pat sat up. She stared at the fire and then at the ocean and she shivered. She started to get up, but Cliff took her by the arm and kept her where she was.

"What's the matter, Pat. Didn't you like what I said?"

"I'm cold, darling."

"You weren't cold a minute ago."

"I am now," Pat said. "Would you mind very much if we stopped fishing?"

"Not at all," Cliff said, but did not move. "You haven't answered my question."

"Please don't, Cliff," Pat said in a hurried, tired voice. Her legs were pulled up under her; once more she tried to get up.

Cliff kept one hand on her shoulder to prevent this. With the other hand he pulled the blanket up and wrapped it all around her. Now only her head was visible, her hair blowing and her face averted in the firelight.

"Now," he said, "you're not cold any more and you can answer me."

The empty feeling in his chest had gone, replaced by a mute, pointless anger. He wanted to break her apart and force an answer from her. Yet this fury was matched by a corresponding desire for her.

"Go ahead," he said. "What's the matter? Are you mad or something? Did I say something wrong?"

Pat began to cry.

"Please, sweetheart, don't. I asked you not to. Please, please don't."

"Do you figure we ought to bust up?"

"You know I don't. I love you more than anything in the world, but there is something wrong with me, and this is it. I can't marry you, darling. I just can't, that's all. It wouldn't be any good."

There was a silence. The fishline's long curve into the surf twitched as the undertow pulled the bait; far out, a crest broke with a sound like tearing silk.

"I suppose you've got reasons," Cliff said. He looked at Pat, but she made no reply. "I may be dumb, but I can't figure what they are."

"I haven't got reasons. Only *one* reason."

"I've got a reason, too," Cliff said.

"Yours is better," Pat said. "Only it's no good for you and me."

"How do you know?"

"Because I know what it is. You want to be sure of things."

"Don't you?"

"I found out you can't. I was always sure of everything. I grew up that way, and when you and I were in love I was sure of that, too. Then you went to the war and I wasn't sure of anything. I didn't know I wanted

247

to get married, but I did. I didn't even want to go out with another man, but all the girls were going out with service men and I went out."

"I never asked you anything about that, Pat," Cliff said.

"I know you didn't, sweetheart, and I've always loved you for it. For that more than anything. I thought you didn't want me to talk about it, so I shut up."

"You were right."

"I know, but I'm going to tell you about it now." Cliff stared at the fire, the veering shadows of which marched across his face. "Please darling, listen to me," Pat said.

"Go ahead."

"All of a sudden I was in love with him. He was a swell guy. He was older, and I thought that was what I wanted. I was impatient and crazy, and I thought if I didn't get married I never would. The only thing that was bad was how to explain to you: that was terrible, I just didn't know—I put it off and put it off, and then—"

"The guy was killed," Cliff said in a slow wondering way, trying to bring this fellow into his mind. It was hard to think of anybody but himself in relation to Pat.

Pat's voice was very controlled.

"You and I weren't ready when you went away. You know that. If they'd only given us more time, just a little more time. . . ." Her voice trailed off.

Who was this "they" she was talking about?

"I wonder if you have to be with just one person," she said, almost childishly. "I mean, for marriage?"

When she did not clarify this, Cliff said, "I guess I don't know what you mean—"

". . . Because," Pat said, following her own train of thought, "there *never* was enough time. Not for you and

248

me. Or for him, either." Her hand tightened on his wrist. "Why wasn't there enough time?" she said. "Why? I wanted to be a wife so much. I wanted to have those things. I would have been such a fine wife, you don't know, if there had been enough time."

"I see what you mean about two people, but that guy was killed. I don't figure I'm going to be. Not now."

"You're going to live till you're a hundred and ten, pray God," Pat said.

"Well?"

"Only I'm not. I've lost whatever it is that makes girls live a long time. That lets them have things. Am I talking crazy?"

"No. But we've got *now*—"

"Yes, yes. We have, and it's wonderful. It's ours and it's forever, only there's a condition. That's how I feel about it. We can have it but we can't poke at it or ask questions about it. We can't organize it."

"Organize, you mean, like having a family?"

The line wagged in the sea and a wave broke. Pat didn't answer, but the answer was "Yes."

"People used to organize it," Cliff said. "What's the matter with us doing it?"

"Because we're not set up for it. Nobody is. The world isn't set up for it any more, or anybody in it."

Pat said this rapidly, in a dry, hot voice, as if reciting from a paper. Like everything else she said, this was clearly nothing she had just made up. She had thought about it. She had it all laid out in her mind.

"You want love to be a bedroom, a yard, and a kitchen," she said as if speaking to herself. "I just want it to be love. You want it to be a house with a chimney."

"What's the matter with a chimney?"

"Nothing. I like them. Only not for you and me."

"You wanted all that stuff with that other guy," Cliff said, jealousy hot under his numbness.

"I wanted it so much I lost my chance for it," Pat said. She put her arms around him, but her face was turned away. "If I had a chimney now I'd want to knock myself against it till I hated everything. Till I broke into a thousand pieces . . . you can't understand that, I suppose."

"No, I can't," Cliff said.

Neither spoke for a while. Then he said, "All I did was ask about us getting married. I didn't mean to get into a fight about a goddam chimney."

Pat fumbled on the blanket for her handbag. She took a comb out of it and, in the fire-light, combed the beach sand out of her hair. She had a bobby-pin in her mouth, and through or around this obstacle she said, "If you can't understand about that, you can't understand about anything."

"I'll be goddamned if I can."

"I don't think there's any use our talking, then," Pat said ruefully but definitely.

"You and me both," Cliff said.

Pat was brushing sand off her thin woolen skirt, under which the curves of her legs showed in the firelight.

"Why don't we go then?"

Pat felt sick at her stomach and her knees were weak. However, she folded up the blanket and picked up the paper carry-all with the supper things. Her voice was firm as she said, "I'll wait in the car."

Alone on the beach, Cliff slowly reeled in the line. The bait was gone and so was one of the hooks. He detached the remaining hook and slipped it into a cork; he put the cork and the heavy sinker in his pocket. Then he put out the fire by kicking sand over it.

CHAPTER 44

NEITHER ONE SAID ANYTHING ALL THE WAY HOME, AND when Cliff said good night he was sure he was never going to see her again. Next day, driving the Goose, he got a fit of the shakes but covered up by going to the men's toilet and staying there for half an hour.

The next week-end Pat 'phoned, and after a struggle with his pride Cliff called her back—not to make up but just to find out what the hell she wanted. It turned out that she wanted him to come over for dinner. Both were very guarded at first, but it was an evening when Pat's room-mate had gone to Pendleton and after dinner they became more normal. They washed and dried the dishes and then they made up their quarrel.

Things went on just as they had before the evening on the beach, except that marriage was now a subject that was never mentioned. Their views on this topic hardened into an invisible but potent barrier like the surveyors' line at which two nations, meeting in a wilderness, divide.

Though Pat made so little sense about marriage, her opinions on many other affairs were quite sensible. When she and Cliff talked things over, her insight was often the clearest and her opinion the guiding one.

The production speed-up of the past months had created new problems at Horizon. Pounding day and night, charged with a sultry energy, the plant was itself a kind of battle-front: the people who worked in it had developed their own kind of civilization, which was constantly changing. It was a civilization which had its special fears and questions, most of them related to Time: Time-on-the-job, the days and nights sliced into segments by the work shifts, and the relentless pressure of the work, the wordless law of the pace-making clocks and rheostats, the faces of the checkers hurrying along the line with their yellow check-sheets, the pressure, the compulsion. And in addition there was the suspicion of Time's treachery, the fear of the sudden end of the war, the peace—so much desired, so ardently prayed and worked for—which also had in it the horror of joblessness and uncertainty.

Where to go? What to do? Save your money, brother. You won't be getting it long. Spend it, brother, you won't be getting it long. Hang on to it. You're going to need it. See what you can get out of it; they'll soak it out of your hide anyway before they're through.

All the men and women in Horizon, from the feeblest swamper taken from relief rolls to the natty executives behind their glass-topped desks in the Administration Buildings, faced this betrayal by Time: each must rush under a gantlet, lashed by a million clock-hands, toward the victory which would bring life to the outside world and destruction to his own.

Victory meant Invasion, and Invasion meant planes. A plane an hour, a plane every half-hour: more planes than the world had ever seen or men believed it possible to build. And to build the planes workers were needed and always more workers: there were never quite enough. As Invasion Day drew nearer, all accepted methods of obtaining applicants had failed and a crisis was at hand.

252

Horizon had always employed Negroes on an equality with whites. This step in itself was almost a social revolution—yet, though functioning with success, it remained a source of tensions.

Old-line factory men talked against it.

"White folks and niggers don't mix. It's agin human nature. . . ."

"Half of them have syphilis. They got diseased blood. If they cut a finger and their blood runs out on the machine, you ketch it too. . . ."

"We got to teach them our trades, so they can grab our jobs after the war. . . ."

"What boss don't want niggers? They'll work for a chaw of tobacco and a corn pone. . . ."

"If they want to work, okay. But let 'em have their own assembly lines. . . ."

"Maybe we need them now but when the war's over where'll we be? Standin' in the bread lines watching niggers grab our lunch pails? . . ."

Beyond much talk was the perpetual crop of rumors, mostly discounted even by the most prejudiced yet still pervasive and disturbing. There was going to be an uprising, timed while the white soldiers were still fighting and the Negro soldiers had returned. Negroes were planning to break down sex barriers and start having white women. The white men in the army knew the date of the uprising and were saving ammunition for an "open season on niggers."

"What about Mrs. Roosevelt, that Eleanor?" This was a question which frequently came up, accompanied by sardonic disapproval.

"Ain't she fraternizin' with them all the time, tellin' them they should have equal rights? Brother, that's goin' too far. Someday there's goin' to be trouble. . . ."

253

Early in July, an incident took place which brought spoken fears out in the open. Desperate for more workers, Horizon asked Washington for help and got it. By arrangement with the War Department, nearby Army Bases issued calls for volunteers to go to work on the assembly line. Soldiers who volunteered had to have mechanical or factory training. If accepted, they would be restored temporarily to civilian status and receive civilian pay. However, they would not be permitted to leave their new jobs except to go back to the Army.

Nearly a thousand soldiers volunteered, a fourth of their number Negroes.

Cliff was just getting to work when the first truckloads of volunteers rolled through Gate No. 7.

On the second floor gallery of the Administration Building stood the company executives, clerks, and stenographers, also watching—the dumpy figure of President Walt Humphries in the center, like some sort of billiken god. Company cops armed with black-jacks and guns circulated through the yard, vainly trying to get line-workers, staring at the trucks, to break it up and go back to their jobs.

Before the swing shift came on, the plant had made its decision. The white volunteers could stay, but the Negroes would have to go. No goddam shines were going to be drafted and brought in to take a white man's bread and butter. Certain ring-leaders, notably one Charlie Mace, a fiery talker, devised the plan of operations.

The Negroes were to be waylaid each day as they came off work. They were to be loaded into trucks and driven to the railroad station. Then they were to be shipped back where they came from. There was to be no rough stuff, but no kidding around either. Those shines would have to go.

CHAPTER 45

"YOUR NAME MORTON VAUGHAN?"

"That's me."

The little Negro with the brand-new lunch box looked startled. He rolled a questioning eye at the white man who had moved up beside him as he passed through Plant Gate No. 10.

The white man had a list in his hand. He put it back in his pocket.

"Walk across the street and get in that truck."

The little Negro hesitated.

"I'm through workin', Captain. Bus waitin' right now for to take me home."

A hand slipped under Vaughan's arm. The Negro's head jerked nervously. From somewhere behind him another white worker had come up. Wedged between the two, Vaughan was hustled across the street. The white men on each side of him were big fellows; they almost swung him off the ground. He scrambled on to the truck, already half-full of colored workers.

Half a block down the street, outside a small café, Cliff stood with a watching group. The men with him hid their nervousness behind irrelevant talk and jumpy, unaccustomed movements. They lit cigarettes, then tramped them out on the sidewalk. They fussed with their hats and scraped their feet and spat; they nudged each other and their eyes swung from the stream of day-shift workers passing out of the gate to the brown rental truck with its rapidly increasing cargo. The white men who were intercepting the Negroes worked in squads of two, and sometimes three. Only black men who had come in with the Army volunteers were intercepted. Each time they stopped a man there would be a moment of brief talk, then a little eddy in the home-going crowd as the Negro was convoyed away from the gate. Other workers, black or white, would turn their heads, look for a second at the thing that was happening, and then quickly look away again. They moved a little faster toward the buses lined along the street.

Better not look at what was happening. Better just forget you'd seen it. Just keep on looking the other way.

Those who watched from in front of the café were hardier souls; they had the courage which belongs to eavesdroppers. It was impossible to tell whether they approved or disapproved of the proceedings, but at all events they wanted to be there, they wanted to see.

Cliff could not have told why he was there. Until a day or two before he had no strongly formed opinion of the issue at stake. Guys in Salvage weren't supposed to know much that went on in the skilled departments. They had not partaken in the secret councils at which the eviction of the Negroes had been decided. Nevertheless, since the whole plant buzzed with rumors, Salvage, too, had picked them up. So vehement had been the talk against the shines, Cliff had felt at first there might be some sense in it. Maybe it really was a plot by the higher-ups to scab white labor. . . .

The men who said so were old factory hands, they were supposed to know. . . .

Cliff had repeated some of their opinions to Pat—not as his own, but just by way of conversation. He had meant to entertain her with the excitement that was seething in the plant, not foreseeing the passion of her reaction.

"They can't do it. They can't be allowed to do it. We've got to stop them somehow."

Cliff blinked. At the plant no one had talked like that. If any one had felt like that he'd kept his feelings to himself.

"Stop them? Gee, Pat, there's no way to do that."

"There has to be. It's the filthiest thing I ever heard of!"

Pat's voice was squeezed with rage.

"Somebody ought to tell the police."

Cliff felt the need to defend himself against some unnamed charge.

"It's lousy, sure enough. But I don't know who can stop it now. Too many guys are in on it. If they got the cops or troops, there'd be a riot. Hell,, the plant might even shut down."

"Don't you ever let me hear you had anything to do with it. If you do, Cliff Harper, I'll never speak to you again. No, I won't, as long as I live."

"I didn't aim to have anything to do with it."

"Well, you'd better not."

"Honest, Pat, you talk like I want them to get rid of the shines. I just told you they were doing it."

"Well, you're not doing anything to stop it as far as I can see. Nor Gunny either. He ought to have more sense."

"Gunny isn't in on it."

Pat, who was drying supper dishes, let a handful of tableware fall in the sink.

"If those men are ready to fight for their country I guess they've got a right to work for it—and keep on working for it, whether they're black or not."

Company policemen were massed in unusual numbers around the gates. If their presence indicated knowledge by Horizon that unusual events were stirring, nobody would have known it. When a Negro was persuaded to enter the truck, the policemen, like the white workers coming off shift, looked the other way.

Before long, the driver of the truck started his motor and gunned it; a man standing alone near the gate jerked his head by way of signal, and the driver threw the truck in gear and rolled up Estrelita Boulevard.

The scene which Cliff had watched was reënacted in half a dozen plant gates during the evening.

Once or twice Negroes resisted invitations to enter waiting trucks. At Gate 17 they put their backs against the wall and fought with heavy stones taken out of a half-finished road. Two white men got skull fractures and another was injured internally. Freed for the moment, the Negroes ran along the street toward the car line, but the driver of the truck made a U turn and started after them. White men were hanging all over the truck end; some of them lost their hold and fell into the road.

The fugitives were almost at the car stop when the truck bounced across the curb to head them off. The white men rushed at the cornered Negroes and beat them unconscious.

Next morning there was not much talk at the plant. If you knew anything it was healthier to keep your mouth shut.

None of the Negro volunteers had reported for work that day.

During the week, five thousand Negro workers at the plant, most of them old-line employees, left their jobs; for a month there was a thirty per cent lag in production. To dispel unpleasant rumors, President Humphries issued a statement covering the situation. All reports of any racial friction at the plant were a lot of nonsense, probably circulated by enemy agents. Horizon's policy of equal opportunity to black and white was well known in the past, and it would be continued in the future. Humphries urged all plant employees to buy extra bonds in celebration of the coming Fourth of July, anniversary of the nation's independence.

⋟ **CHAPTER 46** ⋞

PLANES CIRCLED IN THE BRIGHT SKY; SNATCHES OF MILI-tary band music were heard in the streets. Barefooted kids sold popcorn and candy to the waiting crowd, sometimes tossing up their wares to the spectators hanging out of second floor windows; cops standing along roped-off areas kidded with the girls behind the ropes.

Pat Tracy got up early. She had a date to call for Cliff and Gunny and drive them downtown to watch the parade. She was happy because she did not have to work and because she was going to spend twelve hours of daylight with her lover; it was different and special, somehow, being with a fellow on a week-day when you usually saw him only evenings or on Sunday. She made her breakfast and brought in the paper which she read as she drank her coffee.

She put the dishes in the sink, not washing them because it was a holiday; she felt quite pleased about not washing them. She manicured her nails, then put on a bathing cap, tucking her hair in carefully because it had just been waved and curled, and took a long hot shower, and a long cold one. She dressed with care, putting on a new red-and-white print dress and big straw hat, also new, with a red ribbon around it. She put on her last pair of nylon stockings and her party shoes—patent leather pumps with four-inch heels. She hoped the Sarge would think that she looked nice. This was the first time since Christmas that the old guy had consented to be cast as what he called a "third leg" on one of Cliff's dates with her. She suspected the Sarge knew that there had been some trouble between her and Cliff, and she wanted him to know that things were all right now.

In the yard of a frame house on South Hoover Street, Mr. Clifford Harper, Senior, was washing his car. The water from the hose left a fine mist of bubbles on the painted metal which was heating in the sun. That was all right. If the water had run off, it would have meant the old jaloppy needed a new wax job. In the old days Cliff had always been the car washer. Still, washing the car wasn't the toughest thing a man could do. Mr. Harper really didn't mind. It was funny, though, for him to be doing it just the way he had while Cliff was out there. He had always thought that after the boy once got home he would live at home and make himself a little handy. He had been proud of Cliff as a Marine, but for some reason this was different; he had never quite got used to the idea of Cliff working in a factory, punching a time clock—a boy with brains like that who could have had an engineer's diploma if he'd only stayed in college. . . .

At that hour, in the Watrous house, Emmy and Dorothy, dressed in their best, were sitting in the parlor. They had been trying without much success to explain to Sonny that he couldn't go outside and play, he had to keep himself clean so he would look nice to see the soldiers march. Uncle Harry was going to drive them all uptown . . . and from the bathroom, as if in confirmation of this, came the sounds that Uncle Harry made while enjoying his luke-warm bath.

Mike Petrillo, weeding his garden a few blocks away, had been told by his wife for the third time to come in and dress. Underscoring her words, the clock in Bellcal Hall (its tower visible back of Mike's acacia bushes) was striking the half-hour.

To its strokes Dean Walters smoothed a silk topper with a brush, wondering whether the damn hat was really too shabby to wear and wishing that he, with other faculty members, hadn't been given places in the mayor's box. He would much rather have played golf.

But of all the holiday preparations carried on that morning, by all odds the most exciting were enacted in the shack where Mrs. Kincheloe lived with her son Perry. Mrs. Kincheloe had long since set the place to rights for the day. She had fed and washed herself and Perry and had cleaned the stove and hung her pots on their proper nails above it and watered their yard. There was no grass in the yard, but Mrs. Kincheloe felt it looked more respectable when watered down.

Now she was ready for an act she had long anticipated. Going to a certain closet she took out an apprentice seaman's uniform, formerly kept in a camphored, moth-proof bag. For several days Mrs. Kincheloe had hung it on the line; she held it against her nose to see if it still smelled of camphor and was gratified to find it didn't. Carrying the uniform she went into the bedroom where her son lay on his pile of pillows, waiting for her. He had put on his underclothes. He liked to do this for himself. He looked somberly at what she was bringing him.

"Figger it'll fit, Mom?"

"We'll find ways to make it fit, son," Mrs. Kincheloe replied.

Taking the bell-bottom trousers from the hanger, Mrs. Kincheloe gave them a quick snap to open them up. She reached down into the trouser legs and pulled the bottom of the legs up toward the seat, thus folding them in half from within. She slipped the pants up around Perry's waist, and while he belted them, she put on his blouse, with one arm pulled down inside and buttoned there so it wouldn't flap. These operations tired Perry, and he let go of his iron bar and slipped back on the pillows, lying with his eyes closed while his mother, black and enormous and indestructible, looked down at him with love and pride.

At last it had come to pass, this triumph she had always longed for. At last she had seen her son in his fighting clothes.

CHAPTER 47

IRMA WINTERSTEEN TOOK A CAREFUL, POSED LOOK AT HERself in the mirror and felt satisfied with what she saw. A well-preserved woman of forty-two, she was endowed with quantities of blonde, moist-looking flesh, a downy mustache, and a sleek pyramid of upswept blonde hair. When she first went to work as checker and cashier in Klein's Supermarket her hair, though plentiful, had been neither upswept nor blonde, but Irma Wintersteen was a shrewd woman as well as a sensible one, and in the back of her mind had been the thought of marrying.

A woman, particularly a widow, was bound to have such thoughts. Irma had them even while Sol Wintersteen was still alive, suffering from gall-stones so bad she knew, yes, knew in her heart he wasn't long for this world. One thing she had learned from him was the delicatessen business and another was how to run a cashdesk. After the store was sold and the plot and casket paid for she took a three months' vacation at Soboba Hot Springs. Irma was not one to worry about the future; she never looked at a classified till the last week at Soboba. She had picked out the Klein ad right away.

It wasn't bad. Old man Klein was cranky, but the young guy was okay. Irma decided to change her hair because she noticed that he'd leave the meat-counter to help one or two favored females get what they wanted from the grocery shelves—and all these customers were blondes. The day she'd walked in with the upsweep she had nearly died. The look on Matt's face! He'd been cutting a rump-roast, and Irma was afraid he'd slice his hand off. Still, he wasn't forward. Not a bit. He hadn't asked her out until, as they were shutting up before the holiday, he told her about his colored boy, his wartime buddy, and asked her if she would mind if they gave the boy and his mother a ride downtown, to the parade.

She didn't mind. And if that was his way of asking to escort a lady it was all right, too. Most of them got forward enough, quick enough, once they felt they were acquainted. "It would be a pleasure, Matt," she said, shooting him a warm look from her fine dark eyes. It was, too, sincerely a pleasure, meeting a gentleman once in a while after the riff-raff that used to try to feel her up in the delicatessen, any second Sol's back was turned. Irma had gone uptown that night and bought a yellow print dress and a new foundation so she wouldn't slop around. She bent to brush a little more mascara on her lashes; then she looked at her hands. On a sudden impulse she took off Sol's wedding ring, the worn gold band which he had given her so long ago in Buffalo, New York. She held it to the light to read again the word *Glück* engraved inside it. She should have taken it off long ago; its pressure through the years had made a cal-loused, reddened circle on her finger. For a moment, with a slight scowl, she rubbed this blemish to make it go away; then, hearing the sounds of a vehicle outside, she dropped the ring into her handbag and ran rapidly downstairs.

There was a rattle and groan outside the Kincheloe shack, followed by a metallic cough as an old engine severed contact with its ignition. Matt, freshly shaved and prismatically dressed, climbed out of the small truck blazoned in hand-painted letters,

KLEIN'S SUPERMARKET
FINE GROCERIES   FANCY MEATS

Matt crossed the newly-moistened yard at two bounds: the screen door slammed behind him. He stood in the little bedroom, beaming with holiday face at Perry and his mother.

"Boy, oh, boy. Look at the guy in his salt-water suit."

"Sure looks good, don't he, Matt?"

Mrs. Kincheloe's pride still seemed too big for her face to control.

"Sure does."

Perry inquired worriedly, "Ain't you going to march?"

Matt shook his head.

"I'm leaving that to you guys. Got a lady with me."

"Gunny and Cliff and Bill—they goin' to?"

"I ain't heard they are," Matt said. "We wasn't invited, I guess. Only a few service units got elected this year. But we're gonna be there watchin'. What about you?" he said intently, as another consideration came to him. "You sure they got arrangements made for you —to see that you go along all right?"

"The plans are ready, Matt," Perry said. "This is the day that I been waitin' for. Time we was gettin' started, ain't it, boy?"

"Here we go," Matt said. He turned to Mrs. Kincheloe. "Remember how we brought him in, Ma?"

"I remember," Mrs. Kincheloe said.

The day they had brought Perry from the hospital, Matt had taught Mrs. Kincheloe the first-aid "basket

265

carry." Now, gripping his bar, Perry swung his body clear of the bed by one colossal effort, letting himself down into the seat which Mrs. Kincheloe and Matt made with their interlocked hands and wrists. They carried him with ease, setting him in the back of the truck. Mrs. Kincheloe, after having been presented to Irma Wintersteen, climbed in beside her son, and they began to drive downtown, through the hazy golden sunshine.

During the drive Perry labored under a mounting excitement. His breathing was rapid. His lips moved with the thoughts passing through his mind, his eyes stared straight ahead as if fixed on some objective none but he could see. Observing these signs, feeling the tension of the bone-thin body, weakened by months of lying in bed, Mrs. Kincheloe felt afraid. She spoke into her son's ear, making her voice low because she knew it would embarrass him if Matt got knowledge of her vacillation.

"Perry. You feel all right, son?" And when he shook his head, brushing her inquiry aside, she became more urgent. "Hear me, son. You don't have to do it. Maybe better if you don't. Think on it, Perry."

"I thought on it, Ma."

"You don't have to, boy. No one got a right to ask it, you a veteran like you are."

"That's why I got the chance to do it, Ma. Because I'm a veteran."

"You think it's best, boy?"

"Ain't no other way, Ma. Hush yo'self, now."

Downtown, near the block designated as formation rendezvous, the truck was stopped by traffic. The jam seemed hopeless; horns blew futilely. From near-by cars, passengers were getting out to walk, many of them Negroes. Some of the cars bore lettering of the Sawtelle Veterans' Home.

Perry's nervousness increased. Had they forgotten about him? He was not one of those who could jostle his way through the sidewalk throng to the roped barrier beyond which was the glint of bayonets and the shape of tin hats.

"Kin you carry me up there, Matt? Get me there on time?"

"Why, sure, pal," Matt said somewhat uncomfortably. "Only hold your horses. We'll get there."

"I don't want the boys to go without me," Perry said.

Once more he bent forward to look out of the truck window, and now he saw the Marine corpsman pushing a wheel-chair toward the truck.

Just beyond the barrier, a Negro captain was accosted by a white man in a high silk hat, wearing a badge which designated him a member of the Parade Committee.

"Look here, Captain. These men can't march."

"I didn't understand you, sir."

"They can't march, that's all. The permit doesn't call for what you've got here."

"These men are veterans, sir," the captain said, quietly.

"They're *casualties*. Look at that man," the committeeman said, pointing to the wheel-chair containing Perry. "Do you consider him in proper condition to be seen in a parade?"

"I was not required to pass on the men's condition," the captain said.

The committeeman glared.

"Well, they can't march, that's all."

The Negro captain did not answer immediately. He looked past the committeeman toward the second unit of his part of the parade—one which consisted of two companies of able-bodied colored Marines, marching in formal parade equipment. The gentle sun struck angles of fire from the bright bayonets.

"I figure they're most likely going to march," the captain said.

The committeeman followed the direction of the captain's glance. He looked at the captain's face as if about to reply, but instead compressed his lips and turned away. He could 'phone Committee Headquarters and say what he had seen and let them handle it. The drummers of the Negro band, ahead, were beating small anticipatory tattoos; the committeeman's brain reacted to the sounds unpleasantly.

"There'll be trouble," he said to himself. With this thought came another: might as well, while he was about it, 'phone police headquarters too. Then his responsibility would be over, no matter what happened. Elbowing through the crowd which was now packed solidly along both curbs, he passed close to an enormous Negro woman and a red-headed, hatless white man, both of whom, standing close together, were waving to the casualty in the wheel-chair. No doubt, the committeeman reflected, the whole thing had been organized through civilian contacts—the plans must have been brewing secretly for weeks.

Out of breath and harassed by large worries, the committeeman entered a drug-store, dropped a nickel in the nearest pay 'phone.

Farther uptown, the advance portions of the parade were already in motion. Civil War veterans rode in an open car, following modern tanks and half-tracks: as the first band passed the reviewing stand its selection was overlapped by the band behind, an argument in brasses like two students in a classroom reciting simultaneously.

Applause rose from the line of march as the State Guard passed, a straggly unit made up of juveniles, 4-F's, and over-age athletic instructors; there was cheering for a unit from a battleship led by a fine Naval band. After this there was a pause; the formation dallied, sweating in the warm street.

"What's happening?" Pat asked.

The Sarge chuckled. "Ever know a parade that went through without a hitch?"

The men had begun to march again, but the units now approaching the stand caused the spectators to behave in a new manner. Clearly, whatever type of exhibit was now passing the downtown spectator stands was unexpected. There was no music; the formations marched to a drum-corps. Nor did their passage occasion any applause. Instead, from the ranks of watchers rose a strange sound, an intake of breath, deep, like a groan or a sigh, a lamentation or an obeisance. Now the unseen marchers were abreast of the reviewing stand; they were saluting the colors, and the officers in the stand were at attention and the civilians were taking off their hats. To the fateful and penetrating strump of its drums the formation moved past the place occupied by Cliff, Pat and Gunny. The old man stared, his heavy brows drawn together in a scowl of recognition and bewilderment. Cliff felt a tremor begin in his wrists and back. He bit his lips, clenched his fists to keep the shaking down. The girl at his side stood with her shoulders and head thrown back, tears streaming down her face as she stared at the marchers.

CHAPTER 48

THERE AIN'T NO JIM CROW BULLETS

FAIR PLAY FOR HORIZON'S COLORED WORKERS

END DISCRIMINATION

THE NEGRO VETERANS CARRYING THE SIGNS WERE MOSTLY able-bodied men; in spite of their burdens they moved along spryly, frequently turning to see how those behind were doing.

A detachment of big, sleek dogs came into sight, magnificent animals, padding quietly along on leashes. Theirs was the effortless hauteur of actors arriving at a première. These dogs ignored the stupid yapping of pets which, held at the curb, hailed them as brothers or, occasionally breaking free, trotted out to sniff them. The paraders were conscious of their superiority. Only by looking carefully did one perceive that it was not the dogs who were on exhibition, but the men to whom they were leashed.

The blind Negro veterans led along by the dogs fell roughly into two categories—the wise blind of World War I and the bewildered blind of World War II. These two types were easily distinguished, nor did the observer need to fall back on secondary characteristics such as age—which would, indeed, have been misleading, since for these veterans age was not reflected in the same terms as for ordinary men—gray hair, for instance, being almost as common among the young as the old.

The difference between the two types was a matter of bearing: the young blind colored men had not gained that knowledge of the dark which comes to men who have been blind a long time. Their steps, gestures, movements were at once more fearful and more eager and unsure; if there was a noise in the crowd near them they would involuntarily turn their faces in that direction. Many of these newly blind had the big, healthy muscles of men used to hard work, not yet reduced to docility. Some of them had pushed aside bandages or flaps which covered their eyes as if impatient of such interferences with their vision. In their minds lived the memories of shapes and colors, the angles and shadows, the blaze of noon. Some had eyes, dead craters, behind pulled-down lids; others had only small red creases where the eyes had been, and still others, bare sightless eyes like extinct planets staring at nowhere, jerked by the weak flux of dreams. Each, with his measured or uncertain steps, behind the splendid dogs, moved slowly through the night which enclosed him like a private continent.

Behind the blind came a group of Negro casualties who had eyes and little else—men with jaws, noses, and whole faces shot away, sometimes refeatured by the skill of plastic surgeons into something that resembled a face, sometimes left in the form of a blotched, bulbous scar, pitted with holes. Living eyes, brown and black, the minds of men behind them, seemed in such surroundings like those small homes which one may come upon in a waste land, modern and complete, equipped with windows, chimneys, lawns, and electric wiring, while all

271

round them, only a few yards distant, incalculable desolation stretches out to the horizon.

After these came legless Negroes in wheel-chairs and on crutches; a few with their amputations covered with pads which resembled elephant's feet, pushing themselves along on trestles. "Section Eight" cases were led by corpsmen, some of them with healthy bodies but minds which repeated by rote some phase of combat, youth, or childhood; others shook and quaked perpetually just as Cliff did when he had an attack.

Last of all came three basket cases pushed along on special hand carts. The baskets were covered with canvas tops out of which the black faces of the men, one still bandaged, reared like seals.

The marchers, of necessity, moved more slowly than the other sections of the parade; the result was that the preceding formations got too far ahead and the infantrymen behind were held up. Nor did any of the various categories of hurt, amputated, crazed, blind, or maimed colored fighters move at a uniform pace: the placard-bearers kept going too fast for the less able-bodied. There were intervals when a general pause for realignment and rest had to take place; at many such stopping-places white and colored men and women left the sidewalk and joined the marchers. Cops tried to stop this recruiting process and scuffles ensued, leading to several arrests. Meanwhile, among the casualties, canteens were passed around and words of encouragement spoken. At length, to the measure of their drums, they straggled forward again. And always along the line rose the long breath, the indescribable deep sound of mourning, or protest, or sympathy, or maybe a combination of these emotions.

Cliff was shaking, unable to talk. Gunny, feeling the

parade of Negro casualties was something not fit for eyes to see or mind to grasp (though he himself had in time seen many such, at close quarters), kept asking Pat to leave, and she always replied, "I want to stay, Sarge. I want to stay." She would not leave till the rear-guard of colored infantry had passed, followed by an Ambulance Unit which finished the parade.

As the three friends drove silently toward Hilldale in Pat's car, they could hear, back of them, the interlacing arcs of police sirens.

"You saw him plain?"

"As plain as I'm seein' you now."

"And he was a big guy?"

"Not big, but broad, sort of. And like I said, he was dark-complexioned. Looked like a Mex or something."

The cop made notes.

"You saw him fooling around the rear of the store, and you thought he was a customer?"

"It's the God's truth. My husband was still sleeping —he works nights—and I was settin' on the porch. So I seen this feller tryin' to git in the store, and I said to myself he's short of groceries and he don't know this is a holiday. I figured I would call to him and tell him Mr. Klein had gone uptown to the parade."

"Holiday!" said a clerkish-looking man near the cop's car. "That's when they always rob a store—holidays and Sundays, if they don't do it at night."

He looked around authoritatively, seeking appreciation for his knowledge of thieves' lore. But nobody paid any attention to him.

". . . Then I knew right away something was wrong." The gnomish woman glared at the clerkish man, hating him for his inept attempt to steal her spotlight. "A raggedy Mex-looking man like that, trying to git in a market which was shut. Then I seen he was trying to *break in,* and he done it, and I hollered but Bert didn't hear me. He's my husband, he's still up there sleepin'. Nothing wakes him when he wants to sleep. I says to him sometimes...."

"Okay, okay," the cop said. "Then this guy come out of the store...."

"... And went back for another load. Oh, he had all kinds of stuff. He was staggering, like he was drunk. He took three loads out, and he had a bottle and was drinkin' out of it. His car was right here where your car is, right beside the..."

"Hot car, I'll lay you ten to one," the clerky man said. "They steal a car to do a job in, then they burn it." Heads nodded at this wisdom, and the cop, annoyed, lifted his head from the notebook.

"Will you shut up?" he said to the clerkish man.

"I just said the car was stole," the clerkish man said. He used a superior tone as if the solution of robberies was for him an everyday affair.

"Sure it was stole," the cop said. "Now do you want to make out this report, or kin I do it?"

The clerkish man picked his nose, looking at the cop disdainfully and shuffling his feet as if incredulous that such an oaf could be entrusted with the business of law enforcement. He did not, however, venture further comment.

"... It was a green car, a sedan, I guess, and it had..."

"Thanks, lady, thanks. We got the description of the car."

"I seen that green car, Mister."

This was a new voice—piping but positive. The cop

solemnly regarded the speaker, an Irish-faced kid of eleven or twelve, clutching a baseball bat.

"He was going north," the clerkish man confirmed. "Looked like he was heading out Figueroa. He was sure smokin'; he was trompin' on the pedal."

"What do you mean, north?" the gnomish woman said. "He turned left. That would be south. I guess I know, I was right here."

The cop wrote, "Made escape in green sedan, direction unknown. . . ."

"Anybody see the license plate?"

Nobody had. In the momentary silence, the officer who had been telephoning stepped into the alley.

"The Board has a record of the car—if it's the same one," he said. "Fella just 'phoned in. It was stole this A.M. from a parking lot out by the stock-yards."

The other cop flipped his notebook shut. "Okay, folks. That's all."

As the patrol backed out of the alley, the metallic voice of the sergeant at the headquarters control board was broadcasting general orders, detailing ten cars to the Central Avenue district on a riot call.

CHAPTER 49

SIRENS WERE SELDOM HEARD IN HILLDALE. THEIR FEVER-
ish howls, an echo of events downtown, were like an
illusion—yet there was little doubt of the reality of the
black-and-white automobile parked now across the end
of the street, blocking it off, or of the two patrol-car
cops holding a conference on the sidewalk near Rodds'
Lodge.

The doors, front and rear, of the Rodds' house were
locked, the owners as well as the paying guests having
gone out for the day. Yet the house was not unoccupied:
from the front-room window, his head hardly visible
above the sash, Billy Tabeshaw watched the cops with
interest. Behind him, scattered on the floor, were sam-
ples of his loot from the market—chiefly bottles, several
of them empty.

Former Private First Class William Tabeshaw was
drunk as a skunk, but his senses were alert. He was
nestled comfortably on the floor on hands and knees, at
times chuckling to himself, at times puffing with relish
on a purloined cigar. He was dressed in ancient and
filthy dungarees. From his unwashed and unregenerate
body came a raw, animal smell which filled the Rodds'
sedate little parlor.

Behind the house, one fender and part of its radiator

badly crushed, the stolen green sedan was parked against a tree, one door dangling open.

Billy Tabeshaw's breath came in long slow wheezes; every nerve in him burned with a sharpness of feeling and awareness unknown since combat days. He was enjoying himself. In a low voice, inaudible from more than a foot away, he was talking to the cops, saying what he would have said if they had been able to hear him. Though Billy Tabeshaw at that moment was apparently cornered—an unpleasant predicament for a man who had just committed grand theft—and although he apparently did not possess a weapon of any kind, he was speaking sweetly to the cops in order to lure them toward him, just as in combat he had spoken to the Japs and in hunting had secretly addressed the animals he was pursuing. "Come on in," he was saying. "Come on, you sons-of-bitches. Come on in and get me. . . ."

Both officers were looking at the house, apparently debating a plan of attack. While they were conferring, a small coupé with three people in it pulled up near the radio car. Leaving Pat in the car, Gunny and Cliff got out and walked over to the officers.

"You got trouble, Sergeant?" Gunny put the question quietly to the policeman with the rockers on his sleeve. It went against his stomach somehow to name his own former rank, speaking to this copper.

"You live in that house?"

"Board there."

"What about you?"

The cop looked at Cliff. He had a long narrow head and a face like a gray stone.

"I board there, too."

"Either of you ever see that car before?"

The motorcycle cop's thumb indicated the sedan.

Cliff and Gunny looked. No, they hadn't seen the car before.

"It's a hot job," the motorcycle cop said. "Fellow that took it is in there now. Robbed a grocery down to Central and Cantura."

The cops, having secured the audience so dear to men of their cloth, now ignored it.

"I'll go in the front, Al," the motorcycle cop said bravely. "When I tell him to come out, you make the back. He's liable to pull a fast one."

"Okay," the stone-faced cop said.

"You guys are wasting your time here."

Both cops turned to Gunny.

"I know the guy in there," Gunny said. "I can get him for you. I don't want him hurt."

"What do you mean, you know him?"

"He's an old buddy of mine."

The stone-faced cop stepped up to Gunny. "Look, Dad. We're busy. Screw, will you?"

"Ask him who the guy is," said the motorcycle cop.

"All right," said Stoneface. "Who is the guy?"

"I told you. A buddy of mine. I don't want him to be hurt."

"How do you know who it is?"

"I'm just guessing," Gunny said. "The same as you. But if it's the guy I think, I can save you trouble."

"Come on, Al," the motorcycle cop said, "don't waste time on him."

Stoneface looked at the house.

"Go on in there," Gunny said. "Only I'm warning you, if this is the guy, he's a little trigger-happy."

Neither cop answered. The motorcycle cop, spruce as a doorman in his boots and breeches, walked toward

278

the Rodds' porch. His companion was cutting across the lot next door, trying to circle to the rear of the house. His manner was that of a politician making his way toward a speaking platform. Suddenly from the house came a sharp report. The cop jumped. There was another report and the cop flopped on his belly. Above his head a jimpson weed, deflowered by the bullet, vibrated like a wire.

The motorcycle cop swung around toward Gunny and Cliff. He was filled with fury at these bystanders, as if they instead of the fugitive had fired the shots.

"Stand back! There's a killer in there!"

He ducked behind a small tree at the curbing. Crouched there, he drew his own revolver. Neither Cliff nor Gunny had moved.

"Be yourself," Gunny said. "He's only playing." Raising his voice to boot-camp pitch, he roared at the house. "Cut it out, Bill. You goddam fool!"

Inside, the Indian grinned. He had moved into the bedroom and was now sitting on the bed, reloading Gunny's service revolver. He closed the gun and took a swig of beer. Then he ran back into the front room, resuming his position at the window.

The cop at whom he had fired was now running up the street. His fat behind wagged as he ran; his uniform, spotless a few minutes earlier, was streaked with dust and pin-cushioned with seed-burrs from his crawl across the vacant lot. At the end of the street the tenants of a couple of adjacent two-family homes were standing in their yards, staring with scared faces in the direction from which the shooting had come.

The cop rushed into one of the houses. In a moment he came out again.

"They ain't got no 'phone here," he yelled to his comrade.

There was, apparently, one in the other house. When the cop emerged he seemed calmer. He went to the radio car, returning with a tin case.

"They're sending enough men to make a cordon, Chief. And a tommy-gun."

Stoneface, who had not moved from behind the tree, was opening the case. He removed a pair of small dark-metal cylinders, weighing them in his palm. "I'd sure like to smoke him out before they git here."

"If you go after him with that tear-gas," Gunny remarked, "that boy'll just think you're playing bingo. It takes a lot to make him cry."

"Stand out of the line of fire, Dad," Stoneface said resolutely.

He passed one of the tear-gas bombs to the motor-cycle cop. Both stepped courageously out of the shelter of the little tree. "This is your last chance, In There," Stoneface shouted. "Put down that gat and surrender...."

He waited a moment. There was a stir behind the curtains of the front room; the largest window was then raised about half an inch. Bill Tabeshaw, putting his lips against the crack, made a prolonged rude noise. Then the window was closed. Stoneface threw a tear-bomb at the window but missed; he tried again, this time breaking the window. Meanwhile, the wind blew the tear-gas from the first bomb back into the street, causing both officers to retreat to safer positions. A few yards behind Stoneface, Cliff caught sight of Pat. She had left the coupé and was coming toward them. He motioned her to go back.

280

"That jerk 'phoned for a squad-car," Gunny said. The gas, thin as it was, made his eyes water, but he did not seem aware of it.

"What are we going to do, Sarge?"

"Got to get him out before they come. Otherwise they'll put a tommy-gun against that wall and make him look like a salt-sieve. They'll say he's a homicidal maniac —he shot at an officer."

"If we go after him, he'll figure we're on their side."

"Can't help that."

"I'm comin' with you, Sarge."

"You go on back to Pat. She's gettin' worried."

"I said I'm comin' with you."

Gunny made no reply. He started toward the house, his face serious, his shaggy gray head bare in the sun. Cliff walked a few feet behind him, watching the back door of the house. He wondered if Bill would try to make a break for it.

As Gunny went toward the path to the porch, a strange voice yelled from the house, "Stay away from here, Sarge."

It was the Indian, yelling through the mail-slot. The angle of the slot or the way he held his mouth to it gave his voice an eerie tone. He sounded as if he were out of his head.

"You stay away from here. You and them coppers both. I ain't takin' orders from you."

"I'm comin in, Bill," the Sarge said. He spoke as quietly as if he had been in the same room with the Indian, sitting across a table from him.

"You ought to know better," he said in mild, fatherly admonishment, "cuttin' up that way. I'm surprised at you."

Neither hurrying nor slowing his pace, Gunny

281

mounted the porch. He opened the door and went into the house. Cliff, waiting in the sun, looked into the front room through the open door. Bill Tabeshaw was sitting on the floor beside the door; he had the gun on one side of him and a bottle of beer on the other.

"Hello, Sarge," he said meekly.

"You ant-eatin' son-of-a-bitch. I got a good mind to kick the oats out of you."

"You wouldn't hit a pal, would you, pal?" Bill demanded.

"The hell I wouldn't."

"You gonna let them pinch me?"

"If I don't, they'll fill you full of lead. Come on, now." Gunny picked up the gun. Bill kept the bottle.

"I got even with that Matt, anyways," he said, getting up.

"You got yourself in a beautiful rank, that's all. Step on it, now. Don't make no more trouble for me."

Outside, men were piling out of two police cars. One had a tommy-gun and two had sawed-off shotguns; the rest were armed with six-shooters and black-jacks. A police captain in charge of the detail addressed the stone-faced cop.

"Anybody hurt?"

"No, sir."

"Where's the hide-out?"

"Ain't no hide-out," Stoneface said, his jaw sagging. "There's the prisoner, Captain."

His thumb indicated the stocky, ragged man walking toward them up the peaceful street, a bottle of beer in his hand.

The motorcycle cop stepped forward briskly.

"I'll take that," he said, reaching for the revolver.

The Sarge pulled back his hand.

"Sorry, friend. This is my property."

"It is evidence. It was found on the prisoner."

"If you're speaking of this man," Gunny said, "he ain't a prisoner till he's been arrested—and he's unarmed. Frisk him yourself."

"He used that gun. He fired at an officer."

"This here is a service weapon," Gunny said. "It's registered to me, and I'm keepin' it. If you think you can prove different, go ahead and do it...."

CHAPTER 50

THE CITY QUIETED AFTER ITS STORMY HOLIDAY. NEWS-papers referred briefly to the "extraordinary demonstration by the colored veterans in a Fourth of July Day parade." More space was devoted to an item headed:

MARINE VETERAN RUNS AMOK

William Tabeshaw, twenty-nine, disgruntled at being out of work, held up and robbed a grocery store of his former comrade-in-arms Matt T. Klein at Central and Cantura Street yesterday afternoon....

The news-writer attempted an O. Henry style, colorfully describing the flight in the stolen sedan to the Hilldale boarding house. It was indicated that Tabeshaw had been captured after a running battle with police.

Using the technique perfected by the F.B.I. a cordon was thrown around the bungalow in the quiet residential neighborhood ... It has been established that Tabeshaw left the service with a bad conduct discharge. ...

Readers with a sense of the dramatic were amply diverted by the picture of the sullen, dangerous criminal armed to the teeth, falling into the dragnet set by the police at the risk of their lives.

Bill's big, dirty hands picked nervously at his face; his eyes probed at Cliff standing behind the steel mesh of the jail visiting-room. What was cooking? Were they stalling him? When was the case coming up for trial?

Doubts tripped up the hopes tossed to him through the screen.

"That lawyer's busy, Bill. He's working for you."

"Why don't he do something, then?"

"He will. He's pounding it."

"He better."

Cliff always felt bad after he had been to see Bill. Long ago, when his father had handled a construction job down south, he had gone to the San Diego Exposition. He had seen the animals penned in cages, each cage fixed up with details meant to suggest the environment from which its occupant had come: a clump of grass for those which had run on plains to the horizon, a rock or two for those which had climbed peaks twelve thousand feet high. Some animals had sore patches on their bodies and they aggravated the sores, trying to die. They had given up. Yet these were somehow less to be pitied than those which were still looking for the peaks or the tapering plain. The eyes of these were sick, yet charged with terrible anxiety. They looked through the bars much as Bill looked through the jail screen.

"They got to get me out of here. You tell that lawyer."

"We're going to talk to him again Sunday."

The lawyer's name was Chris Flugleman. He was a dingy, saturnine man whose shingle was displayed in a building which he shared with a bail-bondsman and a detective service. Gunny had been to see him, arranging the Sunday meeting at Perry's.

"Best we can do," the lawyer said, "is plead him guilty and present extenuating circumstances—him being a vet and so forth."

Flugleman was dour but not uninterested; with his finger-nail he scratched a food-stain on his tie. The people in the little room listened to him heavily—the old one, the kid, and the man whose body was an arm. Flugleman couldn't quite figure them out, but, in his own phrase, he "never looked at the inside of a retainer." And the coon's old lady was a good cook ...

Matt, most unexpectedly, had also come to the meeting. He hadn't been to a get-together at the shack for over six weeks; the rattle of his truck outside had not been enough warning. Everybody except Flugleman had a guilty air when he walked in.

Matt knew right away that this was more than one of the old-time meet-ups. He himself brought up the subject of Bill, making his own position clear. "Sure, I was sore as a brindle bitch. Why wouldn't I be? But then I got the insurance dough, and Jeest—he was all gassed up over something. Maybe I shouldn't never of booted him out of the store that day. I'll do whatever you guys say...."

Flugleman's face tilted up and down about an inch. They didn't put away a guy for life for stealing groceries. But shooting at a cop—for that they threw the book

285

at you. Judge de Tole, himself a veteran of the first war, would be on the bench. It would be up to Judge de Tole.

All were in court the day the case came up. Flugleman got them a place down in front, against the rail, and as the clerk was calling, "The State of California versus William Tabeshaw," Mrs. Kincheloe pushed Perry's wheel-chair down the aisle.

Flugleman made quite a speech to the judge after the plea had been entered. He stressed the loyalty which had brought the prisoner's war comrades into court to intercede for him. Flugleman moved aside, pointing them out to the judge by way of proof that Bill was not a common malefactor.

"A man who can inspire such friendship, Your Honor, must have decency in him. And decency is the basis of good citizenship ... the man admits his fault ... is no disrespector of the country's institutions ... he risked his life in battle to preserve them."

The judge chewed the ear-piece of his spectacles. He looked at Flugleman, then at the prisoner, and inquired in a small dry voice, "Are we sitting to decide whether this man served in the United States Marines, or robbed a market and shot at a police officer?"

Flugleman said, "This man makes no denial of his guilt. He throws himself upon your clemency."

Judge de Tole's pug-dog face, which had been sharply attentive, went blank. For a fraction of a second his eyes rolled upward, showing nothing but their whites.

"The Court," he said in a beneficent tone, "recognizes the defendant's past service to his country."

He cleared his throat, looking affectionately at Tabeshaw. For some reason Judge de Tole experienced a feeling of warmth for any culprit at the moment when he was sentencing him.

"But if, on the one hand, the nation owes him respect for having borne arms in the past, it has not, on the other, given him license to employ them against its officers. Nor do previous patriotic services entitle him to run around breaking in wherever he feels like and grabbing whatever he wants ...

"William Tabeshaw," he concluded, still with a look of friendliness, almost sweetness, on his small, wrinkled face, "I sentence you in the first count to serve from two to five years in the State Penitentiary at San Quentin, and on the second count to the same term. Since leniency has been asked in view of the special circumstances, I rule that these two sentences may run concurrently."

The moment he had finished, Judge de Tole's mild expression changed to one of spite: he shot a quick glance, hot with hate, at the Indian, the perspiring Flugleman, and the tense listeners in the front row. Then he hitched up his robe and, nodding to the clerk, walked rapidly out of the courtroom.

CHAPTER 51

"CLIFF!"

The voice behind him was timid, shaky. Cliff, just outside the courtroom door, turned: for a moment he could not identify the little woman in the old-fashioned straw hat, the clothes which looked as if they had come out of a costume show.

"I'm Mrs. Watrous, Gunny's missus."

"Why, sure. I guess I remember you, Mrs. Watrous. How are you?"

"Just fine, Cliff."

She took a deep breath.

"Earl—my husband—he don't come home much any more, Cliff. I guess you know that."

Cliff was ill-at-ease.

"You know how it is, Mrs. Watrous. He's been busy. We all have."

"I know, Cliff. Only, to-day—I had to see him, that's all. I read in the paper that it was to be to-day.... I saw Earl in court, only he went out the other door...."

"He just went down with Bill Tabeshaw. Guess he's going to try to cheer him up. He'll be back any time. If you just wait right here...."

"Thanks, Cliff."

He looked at her curiously. She looked smaller and more shrunken somehow than the few times he had seen her out at Gunny's. The Sarge seldom talked about his missus lately. Cliff could not have told whether the old guy missed her or not. Funny how two people could live all their lives together and then drift apart in their old age.

Opposite the courtroom door an elevator light flashed on, the door slid open. The elevator was crowded with courthouse workers, pasty-faced clerks, secretaries and file workers going out to get their lunch. Cliff took a couple of steps for momentum as he jammed his way inside.

The granite shadow of the City Hall lay across the street; Gunny and Mrs. Watrous crossed with the light, her arm tucked into his. It seemed that they were strangers, yet the press of the years back of them was like a river on the legs of persons wading.

"Do you have to go right back to work, Earl?"

The Sarge shook his head.

"Not right away, Ma. I'm workin' days now."

"You never did like night work," she said dubiously, still not sure of her ground.

They had come abreast of a small lunch-bar and Gunny halted, a pleasant inspiration coming to him.

"Would you care for a cup of coffee, Mother?"

Mrs. Watrous looked almost childishly pleased.

"I'd like it real well, Earl."

"Come on, then. Not that I'm promisin' how it will taste." The Sarge risked a gallant jest. " 'Tain't as if you'd made it, Ma."

"Now, Earl Watrous. You stop making fun of me."

"No, I mean it. And the stuff we get out at the plant— they *call* it coffee. Say, I wouldn't give it to a hog!"

They seated themselves in the varnished-oak booth and the boy took their orders.

"Is the other food all right, Earl? And where you board—do you eat good there?"

"Pretty fair."

With a long gaze, her eyes built around his face the remembered lineaments of a younger, stouter Gunny. "You look sick," she would have said—would have, except for knowing that it annoyed him to be told such things. (In the old days in China when he was on duty night after night, shaking with malaria, and she said, "Earl, you're sick," he would reply, "Now, Mother, you

289

know I'm never sick," and that would end it.)

"Cakes and sandwiches and stuff like that don't fill you up much," he amended. "That's what makes you hit the bottom of a lunch-box quicker than you look for—"

A lunch-box! That was no way, Emmy thought, for a man like the Sarge to be eating.

"Sonny was asking for you."

This was a planned speech and it had its planned effect.

"Boy, I'll bet he's big now."

"He looks just wonderful. You know, Earl," Emmy went on quickly, tripping over the words to get them out before she lost her chance, "Dot thinks he looks like Bob, but I know better. He's the image of his Granddad, that boy is. Even his little body, Earl, it looks like yours, he's better built than Bob. . . ."

"Bob is built fine," Gunny said loyally. "Nothing wrong with that boy."

"I know, Earl. But Sonny is broader in proportion. And he takes after you, too. Know what happened? One day he ran away. He was gone two hours, just toddled off down the street. We couldn't find him. Harry and Dot at work—I was so frightened, I was half-crazy. And where do you think he was?"

"Hadn't gone to the poolroom, had he?" Gunny asked jocosely.

Emmy looked dumbfounded. "Earl Watrous! However did you guess?"

"Honest! Was he there?"

"He surely was. We never even knew that you'd been taking him there. Lo and behold—sitting up in a chair and watching the game. Posty, that boy that runs the place, finally called up the house."

"The little son of a gun!"

Emmy looked at the lunchroom sugar-bowl, clotted where wet spoons had dipped in.

"Earl," Emmy said, "would you come home for awhile?"

Silence came down on the table like a big hand. More than a century of time was sitting there, if you added the two lives together.

"I don't know, Mother—I don't know. . . ."

"Just for a little while. . . ."

"I guess not, Emmy," Gunny said with weary decisiveness. "We're working pretty hard out to the plant—"

"I know. But Earl—"

"Maybe later on. Maybe. . . ."

"Dot said to ask you, too. We're going to be all by ourselves, like." With the nonchalance of a master strategist Emmy tossed in the clincher. "Harry's leaving."

"Harry? Leaving?"

"I was going to write you, Earl. Then I thought no, I'd find you and tell you."

"Why's he leaving?"

"Getting married."

Gunny burst into a laugh that bounced against the ceiling.

"So Bopeep finally named the day! Well, dog my cats. . . ."

"I'm glad she did, Earl. He's out at her folks in Azuza to-day, making arrangements."

"Going to be soon?"

"Next week."

"Well, I'll be damned."

"I'm glad, Earl. Yes." Rebellion shone in Emmy's quiet eyes. She quickly tempered it. "I mean it's right for Harry. It's time he married, about time he had a home of his own."

Gunny was chuckling softly. "You'll be going around like a mother-dog that's lost her pup."

"Now, you stop. Earl—"

"You'll be going over to his house, running it for him. Telling Bopeep how to cook his eggs and wash his shirts..."

"I will not. Not ever. Besides—there are other things I could do." She made another reckless plunge. "*We* could do things, you and me. The way you wanted to. We could go to shows and—I could cook for you. It's not so hard to get meat any more...."

Suddenly she began to cry, the large tears seeming too big for her eyes that shed them on the lined cheeks. "I was wrong not to go to Hilldale with you when you asked me. I've thought of it over and over. It was my fault..."

"Take it easy, Mother."

Gunny spoke gruffly, afraid he too would show emotion: this, in a man, always seemed shameful to him. He spoke to the counter-boy.

"Two more coffees...."

"I'm sorry, Earl."

Gunny was fussing with his pipe.

"I can't stay, Mother, but—well, I would like to see the place. And Dot and Sonny. You say Harry's in Azuza?"

"He'll be there all day. If you could come out just for a little while..."

"Mebbe, mebbe. Judas, this is lousy coffee."

Cliff was shaving when Gunny walked in next morning. The Sarge still had on his best clothes; there was an air of mystery about him which invited comment.

"Had a talk with the missus. I'm going home," he said.

Cliff put down the razor. He carefully rinsed and wiped his face. "If you're not kidding, that's the smartest thing you've ever done."

"Why would I be kidding? I'm getting old, going to lay up for a spell. I ate me some good cooking yesterday. I sort of aim to eat some more of it."

Cliff stood blinking at the Sarge with a foolish, happy expression. The sense of failure which had weighed on him so heavily since Bill's trial was wonderfully lightened. At least Gunny would not share the Group's defeat: he would be out of it—he would be taking an old soldier's ease among the comforts he had dreamed of long ago.

"That's swell, Sarge. Jesus, that's great. Honest!"

"It will kind of ruin this set-up of ours. I could pay my half of the room until. . . ."

"The hell you could. It ought to be worth the difference, getting rid of a crabby bastard like you. I'll rent your half to a pin-up gal."

"I felt kind of lousy about quittin', with the plant short-handed and all."

"You've done enough about winning this war, Sarge."

"That's what I just about decided."

"Only one thing, Sarge. There's liable to be a ladies' wear shortage this year, 'specially in the fur department."

"I don't get you, Cliff."

"What about all that hunting and trapping you were going to do, and that mink-breeding?"

Gunny scowled. He never took personal kidding any too well.

"Rain on that!"

"We were going to make a million bucks! And live like kings."

"We could of, Cliff. Only I just found something out —I'm gettin' old. I swear, I feel it."

"Think of all those ever-lovin' minks, breeding like rabbits."

"They breed better than rabbits. But it's cold up in that country, Cliff. I'd freeze to death up there, at my age."

"What about all the stuff you bought for us to take up there?"

"I'll sell it to a swap shop."

"Sell it to me."

Gunny looked at Cliff to see if he was still kidding. But his face was serious.

"You aim to start the mink-farm by yourself?"

"No, but I can use the stuff—anyway, the pup-tent and the blankets." Though it was clear that if he stayed longer he would be late to work, Cliff sat down at the table.

"I've had an itch to move out of here, Sarge. There's new shipyards being started up north. They pay good money but there ain't much housing up there. Lots of guys are camping. If I had that stuff, I could just flop wherever I felt like it. Or else I could just move along. I'd have my home right with me."

"Hitch-hiking, I suppose."

"Sure. Why not?"

"Only one reason—that's no family sleeping-bag. It would be awful close sleeping for you and Pat—"

"Go ahead, Gunny."

"A pup-tent ain't no place to bring up a baby. Now

I've said my say, and I don't care if you're mad at me or not."

Cliff said nothing for quite a while; he sat there fiddling with objects on the table.

"I asked her, Sarge. She turned me down."

"Then you didn't ask her right."

"I asked her the best I knew how."

"She's your gal, Cliff. I've seen her looking at you."

"All I know is, she said no."

"Ask her again."

"I don't know if I could, Sarge—that is, and mean it. We just missed the boat."

"I'm selling that stuff to a swap shop, Cliff. You won't be needing it."

"You better save it for me."

CHAPTER 52

THEY REACHED A COMPROMISE WHICH WAS HALF A JOKE, half a serious wager: Gunny would leave the tent and blankets in the Rodds' garage. If his guess about Cliff and Pat was right, the equipment was to be sold and Cliff, as trustee, was to give him an accounting. But if Cliff stuck to his decision to go away, then Gunny would make him a present of the things.

The two shook hands on this arrangement; they were quite solemn as they moved the tent and blankets out to the garage.

That night Cliff helped Gunny pack the rest of his belongings. Their good-by was casual, Cliff promising to drop over Saturday and have a game of pool. However, when Saturday came, he 'phoned the Sarge to say he couldn't make it. Getting off work a little early, he cleaned up in one of the plant washrooms and got Roy to give him a lift into Beverly Hills. Pat had not been expecting him; when she opened the door he saw her for a second wearing an expression unlike any he was used to—not the usual look she wore for him, but the questioning blank look that went with opening the door to any one at all. Then in a second it was just as if another girl was standing there.

"Why, Cliff! You so-and-so—why didn't you call me?"

"Just took a chance."

Why did her joy give him a guilty feeling? Had he decided something? He didn't know—wouldn't know till the moment came.

"Don't look at me. I was fixing to wash my hair..."

"And I was fixing to take you out to dinner."

"If you work at it, maybe you can persuade me."

"What do I have to do?"

"Tell me how beautiful I am."

"Gee, you're beautiful."

"Gee, you're a liar. Maybe you'd better tell me what we'll have for dinner. Can you wait while I 'phone Mother? I told her I'd be over."

He had always loved watching her dress, but to-night for some reason he didn't want to look at her. He sat smoking, trying to feel as usual and to make their talk as usual—the special dialogue so long familiar to both—but he knew miserably that he was making a bad job of it. Pat, anxious to please him, hurried into her clothes: she talked gaily, her voice coming to him sometimes from the depths of the little closet, sometimes from the bathroom, over the splash of the shower. Magically, she was ready, except for the stern ten seconds while she put on her lipstick.

Pat snapped out the light over the dressing-table and turned around to face him.

"Is something the matter, Cliff?"

"No."

"You sure?"

"Uh-huh."

"Shall we go then?"

"All right."

At dinner a semblance of their normal time was re-established. They talked about Bill's trial and Gunny's decision to go back to his wife. Pat, like Cliff, was glad of this for the Sarge's sake, but she was wondering how it would affect Cliff. Was he going to keep his room at the Rodds'? Had he thought of changing jobs? He didn't know, he said—he wasn't sure.

Later they were in the car, driving slowly toward Hilldale much the way they had driven on the night Pat first took him home with her. Suddenly Pat said,

"Cliff, when are you going away?"

Startled, he jerked his head around.

"Didn't say I was going anywhere."

"You are, though. You wanted to tell me. Why don't you do it? Then I can stop worrying."

"I'd thought I might go up north."

"Right away?"

"Sort of."

"I knew it," she said softly. "I was afraid—" She broke off. "Will you answer one question, darling?"

"Sure, Pat."

"It's not on account of us that you're going? Of me?"

"No."

"I didn't think it was."

A car was coming toward them—its lights pin-points, then blinding, then past. Traveling fast, a big car heading north. Maybe farther along that car would pick up riders. . . .

"I don't know how to say it," he began. "It's—well, a lot of things that happened—"

"When you asked me to marry you, I was afraid. Not of you, just of us. I know I hurt you then—I hurt myself, too, but I couldn't help it."

"You were right, Pat," Cliff said.

"It was my fault, dearest. I wasn't ready. I knew I loved you, but maybe not enough. I'm still not ready, I don't think, but I know I love you enough."

"I love you, too."

"If you want me to marry you now, Cliff, I will."

"Even if what you said is true?"

"About us not being ready?" Getting her answer from his face she said, "Even if that's true—if you want it, I will."

"I want it," he said. "But I know now you were right. We could have had it if things had worked out different. It would have been swell."

"It would have been wonderful, Cliff," Pat said. "It would have been the best thing that ever happened in the world." Pat's voice did not sound as if she was crying, but she was. "What happened to us?" she said.

"What went wrong? Sometimes I think and think about it."

"You named it just now. We missed the boat, that's all. Everything got moving too fast and we couldn't catch up."

He took her hand, but there was no response in it. "You can say that," she said. "In a way it's what I said to you. But it's different for a girl. I thought I was right then. . . ."

"You were right."

"I don't know. I don't know. I'm all mixed up. I could bear this then, but I can't now."

"Not getting married?"

"No, darling. You going away. I feel like saying to hell with what I know, to hell with my smart little brain. I'd marry you now, just to keep you from going away. That's what a dope I am."

"You're a swell girl, Pat."

"I'm the biggest dope in the world," Pat said. Furiously she dabbed at her eyes, still trying to steer the car.

"You'd better pull over," Cliff said as a passing car swerved around them perilously.

Pat drove to the curb and shut off the motor.

"Don't go, sweetheart. I'll make you happy. I swear I will."

He put his arm around her, wishing to comfort her but unable to do it without lying.

"I'll be back."

"No, you won't. I don't know how I'll stand it. I guess I love you too much, that's all."

"You can't love any one too much. I love you that much."

"Do you really?"

"Sure. Don't you know it?"

"I guess so," she said, trying to search his face. "I guess you do. But I wish you didn't have to go."

"It won't be for long."

"It will be forever."

"I'll just go up there for a while and get me a good job. Not running a Goose, but something good. I'll get myself set. Then I can come back here and get you, or you can come up there...."

"Up where?"

"Wherever I end up. Frisco. Or maybe Portland or Seattle."

Pat wasn't listening. "Why did I have to be right? Why did I have to be so smart? Scared of getting hurt . . . that's how smart I was...."

"It's not like saying good-by," Cliff said. "We'll be seeing each other, plenty. I'll be writing to you, and . . ."

"I'd rather say it the other way."

"What way?"

"Good-by, darling. I love you."

"Good-by, Pat."

"Take care of yourself."

"You, too."

"You can write to me, too, you know. It's not that kind of good-by—we don't hate each other."

Cliff worked to keep his voice steady.

"We're only about a block from Rodds'," he said. "I guess I'll get out here. I can walk over in five minutes."

"All right. Only—wait a minute. Lend me your handkerchief."

She turned toward him on the seat of the car, and by the dashlight studied his face as if to memorize its features. Then she smiled, and in a matter-of-fact voice said, "Now I know what you look like. I told you, I'm the biggest dope in the world...."

MAGISTRATE: LICENSES DAY OR NIGHT
Rooms for Honeymoon Couples

The sign, flood-lighted, hung outside a dingy building, ninety feet across the Arizona line. Through the window, the glare reflected from the flood-lights knifed down on the stout man facing the two people in an office which was part hotel-desk, part wedding-chapel.

"Have you got a ring?"

Matt Klein looked blank. But the lady beside him spoke up bravely.

"I have one, mister."

Opening her handbag, she produced a plain gold band which looked as if it had been worn before.

"Very good. Now repeat after me. . . . I, Matt, take thee, Irma. . . ."

With great care, as if dealing with materials very breakable, Matt placed the ring on the chubby finger presented to him.

". . . Got some nice, clean modern rooms vacant, if you folks care to stay all night. . . ."

Matt shuffled his feet.

"Well, we were sort of heading south. . . ."

A hand pulled at his sleeve; Irma's voice, the first intimation of wifely control, was tender with decision.

"It looks real nice here, honey. Unless you were figuring on some other place."

"Come to think of it," Matt said, addressing the magistrate-hotel clerk, "we're tired at that. Might see what you got here. . . ."

"Now you're talking, friend. I guess you won't be wanting twin beds." The magistrate-clerk's dewlaps fluttered as he savored his own wit, plainly part of his stock-in-trade. "Tell you the truth, there ain't a twin bed in the place."

Taking a key from the rack, he led the way back to one of the courts. There was a gas radiator, a Petty calendar, a fumed-oak bedroom set scarred with cigarette burns. The magistrate withdrew, but Matt did not embrace his wife. Instead, he sat down on the end of the bed.

"Come here," he said sternly.

His bride retreated. With a nervous hand she smoothed her upswept hair.

"Don't you yell at me, Matt Klein. Don't you lift your voice to me, the first minute we're married."

"I want to know something. How come you had that ring all ready? Did you figure I'd forget to bring one?"

The fear ebbed out of Irma's handsome eyes, replaced by a feline sureness of her power.

"Don't you yell at me," she repeated. With small steps, seeming to move her hips rather than her feet, she approached the bed.

"How come you had that ring?"

Irma Wintersteen Klein seized her husband by the hair and pushed his head back.

"That was Sol's ring," she said. "My husband's. I wore that ring for twenty-two years. Now, because I marry a putz who forgets rings, I got it on again."

Matt's jaw sagged; he shoved Irma away from him.

"Sol's ring, huh?"

Jealousy danced in his small pale eyes which looked like punctuation marks. Suddenly, with a violence almost horrifying, he began to laugh.

"The dead guy's ring! Oho, you got it back.... Oho, Judas.... Sol's ring.... Is that rich...."

"Don't you laugh at me, you putz," Irma screamed, striking him.

"Oho, Judas Priest . . . the second-hand bride. . . ."

"Oh, you dirty putz. . . ."

She was slashing at him with weak-shouldered, womanly blows which he parried, still maintaining his insufferable laughter. Tenants of the adjacent court were pounding on the wall.

A man's voice yelled.

"How about some quiet? Other people in this world are trying to sleep."

The struggle between the newlyweds was halted by mutual consent while they united against this attack.

Matt bawled at the wall, "Go chase yourself," while Irma howled, "We pay our money just the same as you, so if you want to sleep go somewheres else. . . ."

Both listened; the protest behind the wall dwindled to a profane muttering. Suddenly Irma struck at her husband's face, the blow partly parried, falling on his ear; he grabbed at her wrist, and the struggle between them was renewed. Finally securing both her wrists in one broad hand, locking her feet between his ankles so she could not kick him, he pulled her head down to his and kissed her on the mouth. Both were immediately streaked with lipstick, giving them the appearance of having suffered dangerous face-wounds.

"My honey-pie. . . . My baby putz. . . ."

"I'll buy you a brand-new ring, with nineteen jewels. . . ."

"I'm used to this one, baby. You can buy me a dress. . . ."

Irma seated herself on her husband's lap; she moaned as he kissed her a second time.

"Don't, baby."

"What's the matter?"

"Be decent. Let's turn out the light."

"What the hell's the difference? Are we married, or are we married?"

"We're married, baby."

"Give us a kiss, then."

Irma complied.

❧ CHAPTER 53 ❧

To Mr. and Mrs. Matt Klein
  With best wishes from his friends,
  Earl Watrous, Perry Kincheloe, Cliff Harper.

Cliff had been entrusted with the eighteen dollars, six bucks apiece, to buy a suitable donation; he had chosen a bronze standing-lamp with a tasseled shade on which the words "Home, Sweet Home," were stenciled in hand-made letters. He had written the card and had the package sent to the market, since he knew no other address for Mr. and Mrs. Klein.

The purchase of the lamp was the last job he'd attended to before starting north; it was also the last coordinated action of the patrol Group—or what was left of it.

There was no more Group. You couldn't argue with

this fact. The guys were scattered, their former closeness broken, even though Matt and Gunny had security, and though Perry—apparently the most hopelessly defeated of all—had won the somber victory of a protest. Yes, there were victories, but they were individual. The Group was gone: Bill in San Quentin, Gunny back home, Perry doomed forever to a bed with a bar over it. All, Cliff knew, would feel the loss of their unity—although perhaps that unity had been more necessary to him than to the others. The Group had been his family in a way; he had grown up in it and it had given him something he could wholly believe in. It had been a religion in the sense that he had felt a complete brotherhood for the others who were part of it in the sense that, in combat—as he had found the night when he was wounded—the existence of the Group had for a while made his own life or death have no importance.

If there had been any victory for him in the months since his discharge it was perhaps that he no longer would die now without the Group to sustain him. This, of course, was something to be proved, but if it could be proved then it was certainly a victory.

Black as a shark's fin, the ridge behind the road notched the whitening sky: dawn was not far off. Down the road the car's lights were a blur in the weird light: the car seemed to be going right by, then it pulled over and a door swung open.

"Thanks, mister."

The man at the wheel looked carefully at the fellow climbing in. Lanky kid, not bad-looking. Worker's hands. Had some kind of pack on his back. Most of them had packs these days.

A kid like this would be okay to take.

The man looked at the old, patched G.I. shirt the kid was wearing.

Talk went in snatches, broken by periods of silent driving.

"Been in the service?"

"Yes, sir. I was in twenty-two months."

"How long you been out?"

"Little over a year."

Pause.

"You must have got in pretty early."

"Yes, sir. And I got out early, too."

"Wounded?"

"Yes, sir. And I had a psychic disability. That's what they called it."

"You over it now?"

"Yes, sir. Anyways, I guess so."

The man shot a quick look at his passenger.

The car, a Cadillac with a C-sticker on the windshield, ate the gray ribbon of the road. Suddenly the driver stepped on the brakes.

"Uh-huh. Here comes Uncle Sam...."

At the intersection just ahead, blocking further progress, an army transport unit was passing, headed for San Pedro. Vroom ... Hsst ... Vroom ... Hsst. ... The two-and-a-half-ton trucks passed at fifty-yard intervals, their big motors wide open, their tires screaming. The two men in the passenger car sat in silence, staring at the convoy, seeing the men in full equipment, their steel hats on and their rifles in their hands, sitting on the floor of the trucks. Now and then the pattern of sound varied as a lighter vehicle passed in the convoy—a jeep or a staff-car.

The man in the Cad glanced at the fellow he had picked up. The kid had a peculiar expression on his face.

The man leaned over to say something, shouting to be heard: his voice rang out absurdly in the backwash of silence as the last truck passed.

"Guess you know all about that kind of traveling, eh, boy?"

"I know a little about it."

The hitch-hiker still had that odd, held-in expression: the man felt perhaps his question had been foolish. He wanted to make amends.

"Cigarette?"

Cliff helped himself from the proffered pack, and each felt for matches. Cliff found his first. With a steady hand he lit both cigarettes, then flipped the match out of the window.

"How far you going?"

"Oregon."

"Lot of defense work up there."

"So they tell me."

The driver nodded. He had attention now only for his wheel, as the big car, settling into its former gait, ate up the miles again. The kid in the service shirt dozed, leaning back against the seat; behind the shark-fin ridge the sun rose like a bonfire.